IN THE SHADE OF
THE ALMOND TREES

IN THE SHADE OF THE ALMOND TREES

A NOVEL

DOMINIQUE MARNY

publishers square

First published in France as *À l'ombre des Amandiers* by Presses de la Cité, an imprint of Place des Editeurs

Translation by Jean Charbonneau

Copyright © 1997 by Presses de la Cité, an imprint of Place des Editeurs

978-1-5040-0073-4

Publishers Square
12 Avenue d'Italie
75627 Paris Cedex 13
France
www.publishers-square.com

Distributed by Open Road Integrated Media, Inc.
345 Hudson Street
New York, NY 10014
www.openroadmedia.com

For Pierre, who gave me "his" Provence

IN THE SHADE OF
THE ALMOND TREES

1919

1

"THE ALMOND TREES!" JEANNE exclaimed as she opened her bedroom shutters.

They'd blossomed overnight and now, caressed by the March sun, they exhibited their delicate and subtle foliage. The young woman spent a long time admiring them. Was there anything else in the world more beautiful than their lightness, their fragility? Overtaken by emotion, Jeanne shivered. Her beloved Provence revealed itself in all its splendor, and this gift from nature was all the more precious because it was ephemeral. "A shower of flowers"—such an odd image, and yet Jeanne could find no other to describe the silky cloud outside the house. She felt like running through it.

Suddenly, memories flooded her mind. She could see herself hopping beside her father as he filled her tiny hands with still-green almonds. She was five or six then, and her entire world was Restanques, the estate overlooking the village of Cotignac. Four generations of Barthélemys had lived there. Could she ever have imagined then, for even a moment, that her happiness would one day be shattered? But on August 3, 1914, Germany declared war on France, and Robert Barthélemy, like all the other brave men in the region, had kissed his family goodbye and left for the Toulon military base, and then the front.

The church bells rang eight o'clock, bringing Jeanne back to the present. Today was the day that her uncle, aunt, and cousins were coming for lunch, and she'd promised her mother to oversee the meal preparation.

She opened her room's large armoire and chose a plain gray dress appropriate for mourning. Then she headed for the bathroom. Pushing her long, wavy hair out of her face, she looked at herself in the mirror. Her olive complexion, large, golden-brown eyes, and dark eyebrows revealed her southern origins. Her lips, which she found too fleshy, betrayed her sensual, if not excessive nature, an impression that was reinforced when Jeanne took off her nightgown to reveal the soft and full curves of her body.

Once ready, she went downstairs. The air was filled with a mixture of toast, coffee, and beeswax.

"I was going to go up and knock on your door," Apolline said as Jeanne walked into the pantry. Tying her apron, the maid added, "Your Aunt Angélique is worried. Two people showed up at her house without warning yesterday, and she doesn't dare bring them here without . . . "

"She should know that our house is always open to her friends just as it is to her!"

"Maybe she's afraid that your mother won't be happy about it?"

"Mother! Do you think she'll even come down to greet them?"

Since her husband's death at Verdun, Marthe Barthélemy had sunk into a deep depression. Nothing could draw her out—not her children, not the future of Restanques. Locked in her private apartment on the first floor, she spent most of her time sleeping or reading romance novels. Her family and friends, who had initially dismissed it as a phase, began to worry. If not for Barnabé, the old sharecropper, the olives and almonds wouldn't have been harvested the previous year. And who would take Robert Barthélemy's place in the future?

"Laurent is old enough to take over," Marthe said every time her daughter asked her to do something about the estate.

"Laurent is only eighteen!"

"Your father wasn't much older than that when he first started to take care of Restanques."

"That's not true, Mother. . . . He always said he did his military service and took agronomy classes before he inherited everything."

"Well, maybe . . . " Marthe would say, before closing her eyes.

This was the sign that the conversation had gone on long enough, and Jeanne would leave the room with a bitter taste in her mouth.

But this morning, all she cared about was the pleasure she felt as she took a pretty porcelain dinner service used only for special guests from the china cabinet. She set the plates on the immaculate damask tablecloth with the embroidered initials of the Barthélemy and Delestang families. Then she wiped the crystal glasses with a rag and placed them on the table where the sun's rays poured over them through the windows.

In the kitchen, Fanny—whose reputation for cordon bleu was second to none—was making a vegetable flan, which Jeanne tasted. She loved the atmosphere in the room, with its white-and-blue tiled floor and its large copper pots and pans where stews, casseroles, and soups simmered for hours. As a young girl, it was where Jeanne had been introduced to the pleasures of good food.

"Get away from here!" Fanny chided her. "You're going to ruin your appetite. Besides, I haven't put in the herbs yet."

By one o'clock, Jeanne felt out of sorts. She should have gone over the house's finances, but the promise of an enjoyable afternoon made her daydream. And she couldn't help but wonder about the two strangers who would soon arrive.

Lost in her speculations, she was startled by the sound of car doors slamming. Through the window, she saw her uncle Raymond struggling to pull himself from the car, while his wife, Angélique, sitting in the driver's seat, lifted the veil from her hat.

A second automobile entered the courtyard as Jeanne appeared on the front steps. Her cousins Michel and Sylvie climbed out of the car, along with a blonde teenager and a man of about twenty-five.

"Jeanne," said Michel, "let me introduce you to my friend Jérôme Guillaumin. And this is his sister."

As the young man walked up to her, Jeanne took in his curly black hair, his aquiline nose, and his strong chin. After an exchange of pleasantries, the Delestang family headed for the living room, everyone talking over one another as usual.

"Laurent isn't here?" Angélique asked, sitting in a wing-back armchair covered with a floral afghan.

"He had to go to Brignoles, but he should be back soon," Jeanne said, before offering her guests a glass of Muscat.

"What about your mother? Do you think she might join us?" asked Marthe's brother. Raymond Delestang had lost his legendary vitality in the trenches during the war.

"I don't think so," Jeanne answered, glancing at the clock on the stone fireplace.

For Jérôme and Nicole Guillaumin's sake, she explained: "Since my father's death, she's lost the will to live."

"She didn't have much of it in the first place," Raymond said. "She's a fragile flower, and an odd one at that. Mind you, our parents never did anything to keep her connected to reality. They even warned me, when I was a child, to never bother her, let alone make her cry . . . "

Jeanne looked uncomfortable and Raymond's wife came to her rescue.

"Come on, Raymond," she said, "Mr. and Ms. Guillaumin aren't interested in all that."

But the source of Jeanne's discomfort wasn't what her sister-in-law thought. As she'd been chatting with her family, the young woman had felt Jérôme's gaze on her, and it troubled her.

She felt awkward, intimidated even, until her brother's arrival.

"Mr. Guillaumin," Laurent said, walking toward his guest, "what a nice surprise! Michel talks about you so often!"

"My cousin Laurent has a passion for botany."

"Ah, I see," Jérôme replied with a smile.

Throughout the entire meal, he had to answer the boy's questions. When and how had he discovered that he wanted to be a botanist? Where had he studied?

"First in Montpellier," Jérôme said, "and then in Paris."

"Paris! You live there?"

"Yes, but not for long. I'm leaving in two months."

"Where are you going?"

"The other side of the world."

"You're so lucky," Laurent said. "My whole life I've been interested in nature. Uncle Raymond can tell you how good I was at making herbaria when I was a kid. And all the books about plants I bought with my allowance. . . . Just this morning I was in Brignoles looking for monographs on the Amazon rainforest."

Michel stared at his cousin, envying his passion. What he would have given to feel so strongly about something, anything! But nothing really interested him. Even Paris, where he'd lived for a few months, hadn't managed to inspire him, even though there was still so much to be done in rebuilding the country after four years of war.

"The first stop will be Bombay," Jérôme Guillaumin said. "Then I'm going to go to Nepal. Then I'll cross the Himalayas to the Sikkim region."

It was now Sylvie Delestang's turn to be captivated. Just like Jeanne, she'd left the boarding school run by the Ursulines Sisters in Aix-en-Provence at the beginning of the summer, and now she wallowed in romantic dreams.

Taking her cousin aside for a moment at the end of the meal, she whispered, "What an attractive man! If he wasn't planning on going to all those foreign lands, I'd get in line. Wouldn't you?"

"*Shh* . . . His sister is watching us."

Since her arrival, Nicole Guillaumin had merely smiled timidly and offered the shortest of answers when asked a question. Tall and slim, she had an athlete's build that her drab blue dress didn't accentuate. There was a sprinkling of pimples all over her face, which evidently bothered the girl, as her bangs covered her forehead and brows, just above her bright eyes.

Turning down a cup of tea, she went over to Jérôme, deep in conversation with Laurent. They discussed the fauna of a variety of continents and countries, and Jérôme was impressed by the young man's knowledge. The Barthélemy boy had broad and unique interests that he surely hadn't gotten from college alone.

"I've always hated compulsory education," Laurent said when asked about his schooling, "and I don't intend to go much longer. What I'm interested in is action! Like you, I want to travel!"

It was the same kind of talk that Nicole had heard throughout her childhood. Her brother had always said that he'd never be satisfied with a quiet, orderly existence. What he'd wanted was to travel to foreign lands and wide-open spaces. But he never would have imagined he'd find those opportunities in a war!

Always insisting on being different, Jérôme had decided to fight France's enemies from the air. Aviators were trained in Crotoy, in the Somme region. He went there and received intensive instruction for several months. Once he'd been deemed ready, he was sent east to join Squadron 64. He would never forget the bond among pilots, nor the freezing dawns when, in small groups, they took off to conduct reconnaissance flights over the German lines. On board his Morane, his stomach churned with fear at the sight of enemy planes appearing on the horizon. Battles followed, and on many occasions, he felt certain he was going to die. Immediately after a bombing run on a village occupied by the kaiser's soldiers, he was struck on the left shoulder. In spite of the horrible pain, he managed to make it back to the base. His fellow aviators were there, watching the sky with worry that he would not make it, just as he worried when, on the ground, he counted the planes returning, hoping that none would be missing.

During his recovery, he promised himself he'd commit his life to knowledge and research. Pharmacopeia was in full swing then. It was up to him to find new ways of treating his fellow man.

Nicole heard him apologize to their hostess before following Laurent, who wanted to show him parts of his garden.

They went around a pigeon coop, then down the steps that led to the yard's first terrace. Restanques spread down a hill over several acres planted with almond, olive, and fig trees, all on terraces held together by stone walls.

"What a beautiful view," Jérôme said as he gazed down at the village and the steep cliff rising behind it. The cliff's watchtowers were in ruins.

"Yes," Laurent said. "And yet, nothing here satisfies my dreams and ambitions, especially not harvesting olives!"

"But your family's reputation is unmatched when it comes to olives."

"That was before the war. My father is dead. . . . "

"It would be a pity not to continue his work."

"People keep telling me that, but I want more out of life!"

In a secluded spot, Laurent grew medicinal plants: angelica, lemongrass, cilantro, mallow, marshmallow, wild pansy, rosemary. Laurent couldn't resist listing them all and describing their attributes.

Sharing Laurent's enthusiasm, Jérôme expanded on his information until their conversation was interrupted by repeated calls from the porch.

"We're going home," Angélique Delestang said when Jérôme and Laurent arrived back at the house. "But if you'd like, Mr. Guillaumin, you can stay with my nephew and then come back later in your car."

"Yes," Laurent said. "Why don't you stay?"

"I promised Michel we'd play some tennis. Let's see each other again tomorrow, okay?"

Standing a few steps away, Jeanne overheard Jérôme, and though she didn't understand why, she was overwhelmed with apprehension. It was a vague feeling, totally unclear, and yet she was convinced that soon the fate of Restanques would be turned upside down.

2

JEANNE NEVER MISSED MARKET day; she loved its atmosphere and its smells. With a basket in hand, she walked from one stand to another as the farmers showcased their tomatoes, eggplants, and the little violet artichokes that cracked between your teeth. Elated by the colors and aromas, she never tired of watching the locals as they came and went. Nothing exemplified life in a village like this weekly gathering, where everyone offered the fruits of their labors. Jeanne smiled at the sight of heaps of onions and garlic cloves and piles of vegetables of varying sizes and kinds. She took a deep breath, inhaling the air filled with savory, sage, basil, and rosemary.

At the end of an aisle filled with a cheerful crowd, she ran into Élise Rouvel, the notary's wife.

"Hello, dear," Élise said. "I was actually going to visit your mother soon to give her the news. Bel Horizon was sold yesterday. A certain Mr. Verdier bought the property . . . a widower!"

Bel Horizon was the estate next to Restanques. No one had lived there for a dozen years, and no one seemed to care about its future. The vines, which had in the past produced excellent wine, lay in waste. Time after time, people thinking about buying the property had come for a look only to be discouraged by the sorry state of the house and the cellars.

As she continued her shopping, Jeanne wondered about this new neighbor. How would things go? Was Mr. Verdier a good man?

A rack of postcards stole her attention for a few minutes. Then she headed for the fountain at the far end of the market-place, where the dentist who catered to the region's villages had set up shop for the morning. Jeanne watched a patient with a horrified look on his face as the dentist stuck his pliers into the man's mouth. A few feet away children gawked at the sight, forgetting all about their pieces of olive oil–soaked bread. Meanwhile, those playing a game of belote on the café's terrace were not distracted. With cigarettes wedged in the corners of their mouths, they were singularly focused on their morning hobby, a glass of wine set in front of each. Week after week, day after day, Jeanne saw them at the very same spot. But in Cotignac, it was the same play being staged all the time. For decades, the drapes had opened on horses tied to the drinking trough, the laundrywomen carrying their wicker baskets, the sacristan smoking one last cigarette before walking into the church, and the florist shooing away the dogs peeing in front of her store.

It was almost noon when Jeanne tied her groceries to her bicycle rack. Restanques was a bit more than half a mile away, up a hill that always winded her but offered a great view of Mount Verdaille. She'd almost reached the top of the hill when she spotted Jérôme Guillaumin's car coming her way. Laurent, sitting in the passenger seat, waved at her as the car went by. Summoning all her energy, Jeanne covered the remaining distance to the estate. As she took the last turn, she saw a woman's silhouette in front of the doorway.

"Good morning, Ms. Barthélemy," the young woman said. After a brief pause, she added, "You probably don't recognize me. I'm Apolline's niece."

"Rosalie! Goodness! It's been so long . . . "

Both remembered playing hopscotch and dominoes together, dressing up porcelain dolls, having tea parties. Until the age of seven, the two girls had spent all their time together. Then Jeanne left for boarding school, and Rosalie followed her father to Toulon, where he had been hired as an unskilled laborer at the military base.

"Let's go inside," Jeanne said, pushing her bicycle.

They chatted as they walked down the cypress-lined path that led to the house, whose pale green shutters contrasted with the façade's white stones.

"So," Jeanne said, "you're going to be helping Apolline?"

"I was thrilled when she offered me the position."

"Are you sure you're not going to miss Toulon?"

"You only miss good times. In Toulon, we were always broke and my parents fought all the time. In fact, my mother never forgave my father for giving up the job as a stableman here."

As they walked, Jeanne observed Rosalie. Her wild, black hair curled around a triangular cat's face with hazel eyes. Her nose had character, her lips were round and thick, and her voluptuous figure stretched a too-tight red baize dress. "One heck of a catch," men surely said about her.

"Do you have a fiancé?" Jeanne asked.

"A fiancé?" Rosalie said, laughing. "Oh, no. . . . "

"Well, as pretty as you are . . . "

"A few guys have asked me to marry them, sure. But I'll never spend my life with a poor man."

Surprised by the intensity of Rosalie's tone, Jeanne remained silent until they reached the pantry, where they found Apolline. For the past several weeks, rheumatism had been slowing the woman down.

*   *   *

By the end of the afternoon, Jeanne was still busy taking care of bills and answering the mail. Restanques' finances weren't great, and she was the only one trying to find solutions. The olives no longer covered their expenses. That only left the almonds. Instead of selling them to a broker, it would be more lucrative to sort and crush them, and then make quality nougat right at Restanques. But in order to launch such a venture, materials were needed, which meant a large investment. Where would they find the money? Her uncle Raymond Delestang could perhaps help her get a bank loan. But before taking such steps, she'd have to obtain her mother's consent. The idea of having to talk to her about it completely stymied her enthusiasm.

Jeanne heard footsteps in the library next door to the office where she was working. She figured it was Laurent, back from his walk. Before joining him, she decided to write one more letter. Once finished, she put it in an envelope, which she sealed.

"Enough chores for today," she said, opening the library's door. "All I need now is a pocket protector and some big glasses to really look like an old pen-pusher."

"You're never going to look like that, don't worry."

Surprised by the voice, Jeanne turned to the sofa. With a book opened on his knees, Jérôme Guillaumin was watching her with a glimmer of amusement in his eyes.

"I'm so sorry," Jeanne muttered. "I thought it was Laurent in here."

"He went up to his room to change."

Standing there in front of Jérôme, the young woman became aware of her tousled hair, her ink-stained fingers and, above all, the incredibly comfortable but completely frayed slippers she was wearing. She was overwhelmed with embarrassment, but it was too late to think about leaving the room.

"Did you have a pleasant day?" she asked, and then immediately regretted her banal question.

"Excellent! Laurent introduced me to the village of Barjols, and then he took me to meet your shepherd."

"Rémy."

"Yes, Rémy. That man knows as much about plants and their secrets as anyone I know."

"He's known for being able to cure people. Plenty of folks would prefer going to see him instead of a doctor when they're sick. People also say that he can tell the future."

"Has he told you anything about yours?"

"No, and it's not something I want to know about."

"You're not interested in the future?"

"Of course I am, but I don't want to be influenced."

Not wanting to discuss the topic further, Jeanne walked over to Jérôme and, pointing at his book, asked, "What are you reading?"

"Laurent lent it to me. It's a book about gannets. They're seabirds, and every spring many of them go to Bonaventure Island, in the Gulf of St. Lawrence. They breed there, and they look after their young until fall, and then they fly all the way down to South Carolina. It's a long trip that they attempt again six months later but in the opposite direction."

"And they don't go anywhere else?"

"Unlike humans, they never want to explore new territories."

"You're just talking about yourself," Jeanne said. "Who says that everyone wants to leave home?"

"I never said I was leaving for good. I'm talking about going away for a while to discover other countries, different worlds. You never wanted to do that?"

"Yes, when I was a teenager. Back then I was hoping to be an archeologist, but then the war came and . . . "

Jeanne stopped speaking. How could she tell this stranger that any real motivation had left her since her father's death?

"Leaving Restanques would feel like a betrayal," Jérôme said, finishing her thought.

"That's right," she whispered. "I can't help feeling responsible for this place and everyone who works for us."

Jérôme remained silent. The sun was going down, and through the window he could see the lower branches of a lime tree grazing the lawn that lead to the first olive groves. A dog barked in the distance. Jeanne lit a lamp and sat in an upholstered chair. Through a mirror, Jérôme could make out her profile: the small nose and slender neck around which shone a thin gold chain. Without knowing why, he felt a great inner serenity. When was the last time he'd experienced such a sensation of calm, of peace?

Rosalie disrupted their tête-à-tête, walking into the room with a log and kneeling in front of the fireplace to start a fire.

As soon as she'd set foot in the house, the maid had tossed her bindle into the room she'd be sharing with her aunt and, donning an apron, got right to work. As she started polishing copper candlesticks in the dining hall, she remembered the Restanques of her childhood. The house, back then, had looked like a castle to her. In her mind's eye she could see Robert Barthélemy on horseback crisscrossing his property, overseeing the work of the laborers. It was a time of abundance, a time of innocence. Jeanne would call her over to the house to play and for a few hours, Rosalie was pulled into a privileged world. Yet, there was always that moment when she had to abandon the dolls that weren't hers. Back in the maids' quarters, her mother would make her some soup. She would eat it without pleasure before saying her prayers and going to bed in a corner of the family's room. Her father snored every night. As much as she tried plugging her ears, the noise kept her awake. It was during one of those forced bouts of insomnia that she swore she would one day be rich. Just like Jeanne, she would own velvet dresses and tie her hair up in fancy ribbons. Just like Jeanne, she would learn to play the piano, and she would drink from a silver tumbler engraved with her name. A seat would be reserved for her in the front row of the church, where she would wear an expensive mantilla. Ten years in Toulon had not put a damper on her dreams, even though she lived in a smelly apartment with an angry alcoholic father and a crying mother, in a state of poverty that kept getting worse. In spite of it all, Rosalie had always believed in fate. And when Apolline asked her to come back to Cotignac, she felt like her destiny was taking a turn for the better.

The maid blew on the flames and then got up. Jeanne had left the library, and the visitor was flipping through a large book.

She was about to leave when Laurent stepped into the room.

"Did I take too long?" he asked.

Without waiting for Jérôme's response, he gazed at the young woman.

"Mr. Laurent," Rosalie said, not attempting to hide the delight she felt at discovering that the boisterous little boy she'd known had turned into a handsome young man.

How old was he exactly? She figured he was eighteen, but he looked older than that.

"You were too young to be able to remember me," she said.

"You're wrong about that! I hated you for stealing my sister away from me. You two just loved to exclude me from your games."

They both laughed at that memory, and then Rosalie went to the kitchen, where Fanny and Apolline had begun preparing dinner.

"Hurry up and eat," her aunt ordered. "Then you have to make madam's bed for the night."

Marthe Barthélemy was sitting at her dressing table when Rosalie reached the bedroom's threshold. The heat inside the room was unbearable, and the smell of lilies permeated the air.

With hesitant steps, the young maid walked in. Had Mrs. Barthélemy even noticed her presence? With a comb in hand, the woman seemed completely lost in her thoughts. The top of the dressing table was a mess of small perfume bottles, nail buffers, and other items, and the room was strewn with dresses and clothing that had been thrown here and there. On top of the chest of drawers, next to sea shells and other knick-knacks, were photos of Mrs. Barthélemy and her late husband. It was as though time had stopped in the room, with its stifling atmosphere filled with melancholy. Many times Rosalie had heard that Marthe Barthélemy had never gotten used to Restanques. When she'd left Marseille to be with the man of her dreams, she'd imagined a life with her knight in shining armor that would resemble a fairy tale. A harsh first winter and then two closely spaced pregnancies that confined her to bed completely destroyed her illusions. On top of that, Robert hardly interacted with his wife, instead spending all his time and energy administering the estate. Dynamic and enterprising, he expanded his olive groves and took care of the fig trees that his father, when he was still alive, had neglected. For a period of twelve years or so, Restanques' reputation was exemplary. The olives were delicious, the oil that they produced was second to none in the region, and the figs were very much appreciated by the connoisseurs.

The property was made up of a country house that Robert's ancestors had build at the end of the eighteenth century. At the same time, large barns had been erected in the back of the main house, around a rectangular courtyard. The harvest and the hay were stored in there. Next to them were buildings to house the staff: four farm boys, two maids, one horse-keeper, a gardener, and Rémy, the shepherd, when he wasn't out with the herds in the fall. When the harvest came, the laborers slept and ate in a vast barn next to the pigeon coops. As farm foreman, Barnabé enjoyed the privilege of having his own living quarters, which he occupied with his wife.

If anything seemed different today, it was that things weren't getting done as fast as they used to. But Marthe didn't have the energy or the heart to tackle the situation. Who was she living for now anyway? Her own children had always been strangers to her. All Laurent thought about was traveling the world, and Jeanne didn't have the same quixotic personality as Marthe. As for the company of her brother and sister-in-law, it brought her very little comfort. All she had was her solitude, which, day after day, was choking her. How foolish she had been to believe in destiny and eternal love! It was true that Robert had always shown her affection, but his death had left her without protection.

The sight of Rosalie walking into the room startled her.

Marthe put a long black string around her neck before muttering, "Ah, yes. Apolline told me you were going to be here." All this black! How she hated the clothes and accessories that symbolized her widowhood! Looking at herself in the mirror, she once more opined about life's injustice. At nearly forty years old, she thought she was still attractive. Yet, hadn't she joined the ranks of women whom no one ever looked at anymore, old maids that were expected to venerate the memory of their deceased husbands? God, how could she go on living without happiness?

3

HEAVY, SEASONAL WINDS THAT blew for two days straight had dispelled the clouds. Still, Jeanne disliked this strong wind. It frayed her nerves.

She was about to leave for Entrecasteaux to visit the Delestangs when Rosalie informed her that a visitor was asking to see Marthe Barthélemy.

"A certain Mr. Verdier," she added.

Verdier. Jeanne had heard the name, but she couldn't place him.

"Where is he?"

"In the entrance hall."

The man was fifty or so. By the way he was dressed, Jeanne figured he was not a traveling salesman. But she didn't like the way he looked at her, like some sort of predator.

"Please allow me to introduce myself," the man said in a honeyed voice. "René Verdier, your new neighbor."

Jeanne now remembered the conversation she'd had with the notary's wife at the market.

"And so you're going to settle in Bel Horizon," she said, inviting him to follow her to the living room. Once there, she couldn't help adding, "You're a brave man."

"I always dreamed of owning vineyards."

"Sorry to be so blunt, but the ones you bought are not in the best shape."

"Don't you worry," Verdier said. "I'm going to get rid of everything and plant those American vines that everybody seems to like so much."

It was true that since the beginning of the century, many winegrowers ruined by attacks of phylloxera had turned to vines imported from the United States.

"Well," Jeanne said, "you're right to be optimistic. Cotignac is known for its miracles."

"Is that so . . . "

"Nobody told you that Louis the Fourteenth owed his birth to the Virgin Mary? She appeared to Brother Fiacre as he was praying in his convent's chapel and told him that Anne of Austria would soon give birth to a child after thirteen years of sterility. He told the queen the news and then urged her to make three novenas, the first one in the church of Notre-Dame des Graces, right here in Cotignac."

"And you believe that nonsense?"

"Nonsense or not, Louis the Fourteenth was born ten months after the revelation. Later, the queen asked the monk to bring our church a painting of her son kneeling before the Mother of Christ, offering her his scepter and his crown."

"It's a nice story, but I remain skeptical."

"You shouldn't. To get a miracle, you have to believe in them."

As she spoke, Jeanne wondered why she was telling the stranger all this. Her round face, rosy cheeks, and full figure made it obvious that she was more interested in the pleasures of life than spiritual matters.

"What about you?" Verdier asked. "Do you feel secure here at Restanques?"

"Of course," she lied.

"An estate this size can't be easy to administer."

"We manage."

"I would have liked to introduce myself to Mrs. Barthé-lemy as well, but . . . "

"She's indisposed."

"Nothing too serious, I hope?"

"Just a cold."

"Well, hopefully some other time, then," René Verdier said, getting ready to leave.

"When are you planning on settling in Bel Horizon?" Jeanne asked.

"In the fall," Verdier said. Looking at the furniture and objects around him, he added, "But unfortunately, I'm not going to live in an environment as refined as yours."

As they headed for the exit, Verdier stopped in front of a pastel of a smiling Marthe holding a bouquet of flowers.

"Your mother?" he asked.

"Yes."

"You don't look like her."

"That's right. People say that I'm the spitting image of my father."

After a brief moment of silence, Jeanne asked, "Do you have any children?"

"No. My wife never could give me one. She could have used Notre-Dame de Cotignac. May the poor woman rest in peace. . . . "

Those last words were uttered with a mournful tone that didn't fool Jeanne. Everything about that widower was phony, and she wondered what he was up to.

The sight of the almond trees that the wind had emptied of its fruits in just a few hours made her forget about Verdier. A delicate white carpet was now covering the ground, and Jeanne would have to wait an entire year for the almond trees to replenish and regain the beauty that gave her the chills.

*   *   *

The car, driven by the sharecropper, crossed the windswept countryside before entering the village of Entrecasteaux. The houses were grouped around the castle where, years ago, Madame de Sévigné had spent some time. Dominating a garden that was designed by the famous landscape architect André Le Nôtre, the castle's façade, with its beautiful wrought-iron railings, rose to the sky. As she admired it, Jeanne remembered her cousin's reaction when she often dared her to do the unthinkable.

"I think we should sneak into the castle," she'd say.

"Are you crazy?" Sylvie would respond every time.

"No, I'm not. I bet there's treasure in there."

The car pulled up to the Delestangs' house. A long path lined with laurels led to the front door. A large yellow dog rushed down the steps from the double spiral staircase. When it recognized the intruder, the dog stopped barking and went over to Jeanne for some petting.

In the living room, Sylvie and Nicole were playing cards, while Michel read the paper.

"There you are," Michel said, as he got up to greet Jeanne.

"There's no one else here?" she asked.

"Mother and Father went to Draguignan to visit some friends. As for Jérôme, he's in Aix."

"Oh," Jeanne said. "I didn't know he'd left."

Jeanne couldn't help herself. She was overwhelmed with disappointment to learn that Jérôme wasn't there.

"Only for the day," Michel said. "He had business to take care of over there."

Jérôme came back before dinner. Laurent had preceded him by a few minutes, after having spent the day at the college in Brignoles.

"I can't stand that prison!" he said to everyone. "I can't wait to be free!"

"The school year is almost over," Michel said. "Then you'll be on vacation and you can enjoy yourself. You can go to the sea and have some fun."

Michel didn't notice that his cousin seemed to care very little for the idea.

It would have been difficult to find two young men as different as Michel and Laurent. Michel had little ambition, happy to exist in his father's shadow. To enjoy peace and quiet, he did the bare minimum on the farm, which produced decent wine and excellent honey. Laurent, for his part, was always looking for a challenge. His expression betrayed this personality trait when, later in the evening, he proposed a game of poker.

Everyone sat around a table covered with green felt and concentrated on the game—everyone . . . except Jeanne. She kept glancing at Jérôme, studying his features. He also seemed to be competitive, and he won many hands. She liked the sound of his laughter as he collected the losers' chips.

"Jeanne," Jérôme said, "I'm going to have to teach you how to bluff. I didn't have good cards, but I managed to make you think otherwise."

Jeanne concentrated a bit more and, with a bit of luck, won the next hand.

"You're going to turn me into a professional player!" she said.

How long had it been since she'd felt so light? She was actually having fun!

Nicole Guillaumin left the table for the piano. She and Michel had prepared a duet. Sitting next to each other on the piano bench, they began singing popular American standards, and everybody joined in during the choruses. After drinking some cherry liqueur, they all sang cabaret tunes. Only a few embers still burned in the fireplace when Jeanne asked Michel to take her back to Restanques.

"I'll give you a ride," Jérôme said. "Are you coming, Laurent?"

"No, I'm going to sleep here."

Ever since they were kids, the Barthélemy and Delestang cousins had been in the habit of spending the night at each other's houses. Jeanne had stopped doing that, but not her brother.

Neither of them said anything in the car during the first part of the drive. Was it fatigue on Jérôme's part? Shyness in the case of Jeanne?

"That wind is still strong," Jérôme finally said. "In Aix this afternoon, it was blowing stuff all over the place in the streets. And at my parent's house, one of the chimneys fell on the roof."

Jeanne asked him about his home, and Jérôme began telling her about the house with its windows opening on Montagne Saint-Victoire. Forgotten images came back to his mind: the cool air in the large vaulted rooms filled with the smell of lavender, the long naps under mosquito nets, the wisteria-covered arbor, and the afternoons he'd spent chasing butterflies, freeing them as soon as he caught them. For his twelfth birthday, he'd asked to visit Montpellier's botanical gardens. It was a revelation. To serve nature, he decided, he was going to discover its secrets. Once he graduated high school, he went back to Montpellier to begin his studies in natural sciences, and then the war broke out. . . .

When he reached that point, Jérôme stopped talking, and Jeanne didn't push him. They were almost at their destination. Blinded by the car's headlights, a rabbit darted for the side of the road.

The car stopped in front of the house.

"It must be very late," Jeanne said.

"A bit past two," Jérôme said.

"Are you going to be in Entrecasteaux for a while?"

"Until the end of the week."

"Laurent is going to be sad when you leave."

As she uttered the words, Jeanne could not have begun to imagine the confrontation she'd soon have with her brother.

*   *   *

"I need to talk to you," Laurent told her two days later as she was about to meet up with Barnabé, the sharecropper.

"Now?"

"Yes, please."

He seemed anxious, and Jeanne thought maybe he'd been expelled from college.

"Well," Laurent said, "I want to leave Restanques, and you have to help me."

"What are you talking about? What are you saying?"

"You know I always wanted to travel!"

"I know you have to get your degree first."

"Yes, I know. But after . . . "

"We'll see when we get there."

"I want to meet up with Jérôme in Asia."

"Are you out of your mind?"

"Not at all."

"What about him? What does he think about it?"

"He's totally fine with me tagging along with him on his trip."

"A very expensive trip . . . "

"I thought about that. Don't worry. . . . Father put some money in an account for me. I could take out part of it."

"Out of the question," Jeanne said.

Tears welled up in her eyes.

"What did I say that was so bad?" Laurent whispered. He walked over to his sister. "Come on, please don't cry. I didn't want to upset you."

"Well you did. And what am I going to do while you go on your fun trip? Take care of property that nobody cares about?"

"Not for long. A year, maybe . . . "

"I'm supposed to believe that?"

"So you're not going to support me?"

"No, I won't."

"Jeanne, I beg you. You have to understand. I have the opportunity to fulfill a lifelong dream. It's no accident that my path crossed Jérôme's. Look at me, and stop crying. You should be happy for me."

Unable to say anything, Jeanne wept over her future and the solitude she was going to have to endure.

"Here," Laurent said, offering her his handkerchief.

The conversation started again, but in spite of the young man's insistence and the strong bond that they'd enjoyed since their childhood, Laurent wasn't able to gain Jeanne's approval.

"I need to think about all this," Jeanne said after she calmed down a bit.

Her father's death had made her anxious. How could she live with the thought that Laurent might be exposed to danger while on his expedition? An accident could happen. That night, she couldn't sleep as she imagined the worst-case scenario. Jérôme Guillaumin suddenly turned into some kind of evil being in her mind. How she now wished he'd never visited the Delestangs!

And yet, he was also her only hope, so she asked to meet with him as soon as possible.

He was waiting for her in Entrecasteaux, near the castle's terrace. He put out his cigarette as soon as he saw Jeanne coming his way.

"My letter must've surprised you," she said.

"I'm guessing it has to do with Laurent."

"Good guess."

And then, anger rising inside her, she said what she'd come to say.

"My brother is still very young. He doesn't realize the possible dangers of a trip like this, and he knows nothing about our financial situation. He can't leave me . . . "

"But you're not counting on him now."

"That's because he's still in school."

"And you don't think that this trip would be a good educational experience for Laurent?"

"No, I don't."

"I think you're wrong."

"It's none of your business."

"So what are you expecting of me?"

"That you make Laurent change his mind."

"Out of the question."

"Do you realize the harm you're going to cause him?"

"I don't agree with you, and I promise I'm going to look after your brother."

"How can I trust you?"

"My dear Jeanne," Jérôme said, a smug tone in his voice, "I think I've proven that I'm a responsible man. I'm being sent on a mission to bring back specimens of the Himalayan flora. Laurent will be a very apt assistant, and I'll be able to teach him many things about nature."

In a softer voice, he added, "It's funny, but I see myself as a young man when I look at Laurent. At his age, I was also dreaming of traveling the world and discovering foreign lands."

"Stop being so self-centered! This isn't about you; it's about my brother."

"How can you accuse me of being self-centered when all you're thinking about is yourself? You say you love Laurent, and yet you're trying to clip his wings."

If Jeanne's eyes were pistols, Jérôme would have been shot dead on the spot.

"Too few people have passions," he said. "Don't stifle your brother's."

Jeanne remained silent for a moment. How could she respond to that? Next to them, on top of a low wall, a tabby cat was napping in the sun. An old woman called it over, to no avail. Down below in the village, a bell rang. In a few seconds, children would be charging out of the school.

"I think you should reconsider your position," Jérôme said.

"I'm not interested in your advice. And no matter what happens, I'll never forgive you for having jeopardized my relationship with Laurent."

Without waiting for a response, Jeanne turned on her heels and got on her bicycle.

It was almost noon, and the women were coming home from the fields to prepare a lunch that would be followed by a siesta or, in the case of some men, a game of *boules*. The sound of pots and pans clanking and women singing came from opened windows. Indifferent to her environment, Jeanne remembered the uneasiness she'd felt the very first time Jérôme Guillaumin had appeared at Restanques. It hadn't taken long for her to find out why.

4

THE HEAT WEIGHED DOWN on the Var region like a lead cloak. As much as Jeanne fanned herself, her face remained covered in perspiration. Lying on a chaise lounge, she could see the intense light of the early afternoon through the shutters' gaps and didn't feel like getting any work done. The heat, though, didn't deter the cicadas from filling the air with their screeching calls! She would have loved to be able to fall asleep, if only for a short nap, but she had too many worries. In less than a week, Laurent was going to board a ship in Marseille and head for Bombay. To obtain their mother's assent, Jeanne had helped Laurent. What made her change her mind? Affection, the source of all trouble, had eventually made her reconsider. The entire episode had been a huge burden on the household. Even Apolline had gotten involved.

"Poor kid," she said, "he looks out of sorts."

What the maid didn't know was that the desire to leave Restanques wasn't all that occupied Laurent's mind. And it was better that way, for if Apolline had guessed that Rosalie was distracting the boy, she would have sent her niece right back to Toulon.

Attracted to the young maid, Laurent found a reason to

go to his room while Rosalie was cleaning it each day. Did she know where his penknife was? Had she seen the stamp he'd put aside for his collection? And he always managed to walk by her when she was hanging clothes on the line behind the shed.

On the evening of June 23, as Cotignac was getting ready to celebrate Saint John's Eve, he spotted her in the crowd. To the sound of fifes, folk pipes, and tambourines, the mayor walked to the pyre in the middle of the square, and Laurent, accompanied by Michel and Sylvie, was waiting to dance around the bonfire with all the other villagers. The church bells rang, the mayor lit the fire, and everybody cheered and began to dance. Illuminated by the flames, faces emerged from the shadows, and Laurent was upset at the sight of an attractive man holding Rosalie a bit too tightly. Children lit firecrackers, and panicked dogs ran every which way. The dancing slowed when the bonfire began to dwindle, and Laurent took the opportunity to join Rosalie. Grabbing her hand and forgetting about his thirst, he followed Rosalie and the rest of the crowd around and around the fire.

Once the flames died down, people were able to jump over the embers, and many did, mostly teenagers and young adults.

"Careful not to steps in the ash!" someone said. "It's bad luck."

Rosalie lifted her skirt and said, "Okay, let's see if I'm going to get married this year."

And she jumped.

Laurent was right behind her, and the two of them then went over to a water fountain.

The ball was about to start, and couples began to assemble under the lanterns. This celebration of the summer solstice was all the more special, as nobody had felt like reveling during the war years. Life was finally getting back to normal, and now men and women—young and not so young—felt like flirting, and some couples even looked for quiet places to be alone.

Without even saying a word, Laurent and Rosalie walked toward the river, and with the glow from the village lighting their way, they made it to an old washhouse.

Once inside, Laurent timidly pulled Rosalie toward him. It was the first time he'd taken a girl in his arms, and he was afraid of looking clumsy. Why hadn't he agreed when Michel had offered to take him to a brothel? His fingers caressed the nape of Rosalie's neck and then slid down the length of her shoulder. He felt her shiver, and he leaned forward for a kiss. Everything progressed smoothly on that June night. . . .

"Let me . . . " Laurent whispered, and he began unbuttoning the top of Rosalie's dress.

A sweet smell that made his head spin even more wafted from her skin. Because of the darkness, he couldn't make out Rosalie's expression, but her heavy breathing told him that she wanted him to continue. Soon she was naked, and when he entered her, she called out. That is how, in the cool night air of Provence, in the darkness of an old building, with the sound of the Saint John's Eve celebrations in the background, they made love for the first time.

Laurent and Rosalie remained in their hideout until dawn. They could hear people continuing the celebrations in the village, but they didn't pay it any mind. They were too focused on each other, too busy enjoying the pleasure of being together. They fell asleep as the sun was rising.

Laurent woke with a start.

"My God . . . the herbs," he said, gathering his clothes.

According to tradition, people had to pick the Saint John herbs on the morning of the twenty-fourth: garlic, wormwood, goose grass, catnip, mint, thyme, and a slew of others.

"Are you coming?" Laurent asked Rosalie.

She stretched and then began combing her hair before saying, "No, I'm going home. My aunt must be looking all over the place for me, and it's best that people don't see us together."

*   *   *

Over the course of the following weeks, they kept looking for ways to be together. Since he'd first experienced Rosalie's kisses and caresses, Laurent had become insatiable. And for her part, Rosalie was becoming aware of the power she had over this boy.

The arrival of laborers hired to pick up the almonds forced them to be even more careful. But they managed to meet up every day in a cave that very few people knew about. It was high up on a rocky promontory, with a view of the countryside below. As a child, Laurent used to take refuge there to bird-watch.

"I would stay up here for hours," he told Rosalie. "I brought cookies and books. It was like a haven for me. Here I could watch the birds fly in the sky above me, and I could dream up stories in which I was the hero . . . "

Rosalie didn't much care for these excursions into the past, as her hold on him seemed to lessen. People at Restanques often talked about Laurent's enthusiasm for travel, and Rosalie was afraid he might leave soon. Her intuition was right, and when she learned through Apolline and Fanny that he was planning a trip to Asia, she had a hard time holding back her tears. What would become of her in this house, this environment that would no longer be so exciting? Whether she admitted it to herself or not, her relationship with Laurent was not just a fling. Rosalie had never before experienced what she felt for this boy she never should have looked at in the first place, let alone slept with. "Out of sight, out of mind," the saying went. In her anguish, Rosalie prayed that it was true.

As for Laurent, he was busy gathering the scientific equipment he'd need for his expedition. Events had unfolded so rapidly, he felt like a rudderless ship on the ocean. In less than a month, he'd leave his family and his country to travel the world. Euphoria had given way to worry. Had he been right to insist on leaving Restanques? This place, under the July sun, looked like some sort of paradise. At times he was almost mad at his mother for having allowed him to go on the trip.

Marthe had started the discussion as they shared a glass of wine on the lawn, enjoying dusk's cool air.

"Jeanne told me about your project," she told her son. "I can't imagine you're really serious about this. . . . "

Until dinner, she engaged in a sort of emotional blackmail with Laurent. But he wasn't affected by it. Had he ever truly considered her his mother? As far as he could remember, he knew her as a women inhaling smelling salts or calling the maids over to order them to take the children away when they stayed in her room too long.

Apolline was the one who'd given him tenderness and consolation when he was a child. She was the one who'd introduced him to the secrets of nature with stories that stimulated his imagination and walks in the countryside during which they'd pick wild flowers, herbs, and mushrooms.

And so, apart from delivering him into this world, Marthe hadn't been much of a mother to him. Her lamenting about his decision to leave seemed downright offensive to him.

Out of patience, he screamed, "Nobody's going to keep me here! Do you understand?"

"Laurent," Marthe said. "Be reasonable. . . . What will people think?"

"What will people think? . . . That's all you care about. I don't give a damn about that!"

They didn't speak to each other for three days after that, and to avoid another confrontation, Marthe ate in her room, while Laurent spent most of his time at the Delestangs'.

"Jeanne," Apolline kept saying, "you're the only one that can fix this."

As she pleaded on Laurent's behalf, Jeanne realized how

much she loved her brother. Dismissing her own misgivings and worries, she found the arguments that managed to convince Marthe.

"Laurent is spiteful," she said, "you know that. Life around here is going to be impossible with him around if you don't let him go on his trip. Besides, he'd end up complaining about you everywhere he went."

Faced with those notions, Marthe decided to give in, and Laurent was able to start packing.

The day before he left, Laurent needed to be by himself. It was his way of starting a new chapter. After crossing the fields where laborers, poles in hand, were knocking down almonds, he took a path that led him to the top of the hill. It was summertime, harvest time, and all over the fields bales of hay were ready to be picked up.

Under a blazing sun, the village of Cotignac seemed to be snuggling against its cliff. It was siesta, and the shutters of most of the houses were closed. From his observation post, Laurent imagined how, in an hour or so, the villagers would wake up and children would come out of the houses to play marbles and men to play a few games of *boules*, while women would set chairs outside and sit and chat with neighbors and friends. Young women would walk by them, arm in arm, exchanging confidences and laughing.

As his departure approached, Laurent noticed more and more how strong his ties were to this land of contrasts, at once peaceful, mysterious, untamed, and joyful. With this realization came an oath. One day, he would create a garden, a sort of earthly paradise that would contain the planet's most beautiful plants, in Provence. Farfetched? No doubt. But to strive toward beauty, harmony, and peace was his main goal in life. He lay on his back, stretched, and looked at the sky. The sun's rays bathed him, blinding him. He felt like shouting and singing . . . but he had no one to share his joy with.

Jérôme was thousands of miles away, and here people's preoccupations were centered on their daily routines. . . .

Back home, he ran into Rosalie. Her hair was wet.

"I went for a swim during my break," she said, as he guided her toward a thicket.

Her skin was still cool from her swim.

"No," she said, when he tried to pull her toward him.

"What's wrong? Are you mad at me?"

Surprised by her silence, he insisted.

"Talk to me."

"Apolline is waiting for me," said Rosalie.

"Fine, then. . . . "

Offended, he turned around and headed for the house without realizing that Rosalie was crying as she watched him walk away. How could she have admitted to Laurent that she was going to miss him to the point of wanting to die? A gulf would separate them, and with every month, every year, that gulf would get wider and wider, because even if Laurent did come back, he'd want to marry a woman of his own class. She was overwhelmed with worry. Why and for whom was she alive? Did she even have the right to ask herself that question?

5

MICHEL OFFERED TO DRIVE Laurent down to Marseille. It was late morning when he parked his car next to the front steps where the traveler's luggage was piled.

Surprisingly, Marthe had left her bedroom to kiss her son goodbye.

Grabbing his hands, she said, "Don't forget to write often."

"He already promised to do that," Apolline said, so upset that she said the words in her native Provencal.

Upset himself, Laurent decided to rush the goodbyes. At the last moment, he turned to the house, hoping to catch sight of Rosalie. But she remained hidden.

Sitting in the passenger seat, Jeanne pretended to be cheerful during the drive. Then the automobile entered the bustling city.

The atmosphere was unparalleled for all three. They were in France, but people speaking every language in the world were walking the streets. Moroccans in fezzes, turbaned women, military men, traders from every continent zigzagged their way around horse-drawn carriages, trolley cars filled with passengers, and automobiles of all types, from clunkers to luxury models. They came and went along La Canebière,

Marseille's main artery, between the Palais de la Bourse and the Old Port.

On the Rive-Neuve wharf, hatless women filled their baskets and wheelbarrows with fish being unloaded from trawlers and other fishing boats. With their chirpy accents and colorful vocabulary, they teased one another or shouted at the fishermen mending their nets nearby. Scorpion fish, gurnards, and mullets would soon wind up at the market on their way to becoming tasty and fragrant soups.

Michel's car headed for the opposite wharf, but traffic was so heavy that passing city hall was difficult. Bent under the weight of impressive loads, porters made their way among bicycle riders, travelers, children selling newspapers, and a great variety of others.

As the car inched toward Fort Saint-Jean, Laurent admired the countless liners, freighters, schooners, and clippers out on the sea, their flags flapping in the wind. Some were setting sail, others were arriving, and some waited for a place to dock.

Warehouses, built in the middle of the nineteenth century, lined the open basins of Joliette Square. The warehouses were made of stone and brick to prevent fire. At the foot of the holds, the dockers who'd managed to get hired for the day grabbed the bags and bundles brought down by the hoists and carried away the tea, indigo, cotton, corks, and rice that had filled the ship. Those hauling flour had white faces, while the ones dealing with coal were all black. But did anyone really have an identity in this place of transit? How many people arrived here with the hope of a better life and then left for yet another destination?

Taking in the mingled smells of tar, rust, and fish, Laurent looked at the sea gulls hovering above the harbor, their cries responding to the wail of the sirens. Some workers were pulling on hemp cables tied to a liner, while others were repairing the hull of a fishing boat. A bit farther, a large chimp, suspended in the air in a cage, was angrily striking the metal bars.

As Michel found a spot to park his car, they all made their way to the offices of the British company P&O, where Laurent completed the paperwork necessary to board the *Queen Victoria*.

Near the building, Chinese, Spaniards, Egyptians, and Vietnamese boarded liners en route to their own personal El Dorados. Deafened by the toll of the bells, the pounding of hammers, the shouts of sailors, the loud goodbyes of people on the dock waving their handkerchiefs, Jeanne also felt like leaving everything behind. She wished she could occupy a cabin like the one Laurent was about to share with a young missionary. She, too, would have liked to travel the world.

Michel said that he and Jeanne would wait on the dock until it was boarding time, but Laurent said he'd prefer they leave now.

"You're probably right," Jeanne said.

Everything happened very quickly: Laurent's cheek pressing against hers, Michel taking her by the arm, and the taste of salt filling her mouth.

Before walking away from her brother, she said, "Laurent, promise you're going to take care of yourself."

"Of course. Don't worry. I'm going to be under Jérôme's protection."

"Oh, him . . . I wish I'd never met him!"

"Come on. Everything is going to be fine. And I'm not going to be away that long."

"That's what you say now. But so much can happen!"

"The same could be said of you."

"For me, it's going to be the same old routine."

"In that routine, don't forget to take care of my plants."

"How many times are you going to tell me that?"

Next to them, a father and son were hugging, and Jeanne thought of all the separations that took place every minute, every hour at the foot of Notre-Dame de la Garde basilica, but also the many homecomings. In her distress, she thought that a visit to the church might calm her down.

"I won't be long," she told Michel.

"You've got to be kidding me! I'd much rather have some ice cream on La Canebière."

"We'll go after."

Jeanne reached the top of the hill, where the imposing neo-Byzantine church stood. Built less than a century before, it had been dedicated to "the good mother." Standing in the church square, Jeanne admired the city, the sea, and the surrounding countryside. Down below, Marseille rumbled. Jeanne could feel its pulse. How many people were being born, struggling, succeeding, suffering in those high-end streets and those foul-smelling alleys? *Business, exile, asylum*—the words overlapped to define one of the Mediterranean Basin's jewels. From the Frioul Islands to the Château d'If, ships left a trail of foam in the sea as the sun's rays continued to splash the hills of L'Estaque. That was where adventure was to be found and experienced, in that magnificent view.

When Jeanne finally entered the church, the contrast between the exterior light and the semidarkness inside surprised her, but little by little she could make out the countless votives on the wall nearby, each telling the story of someone saved by the Virgin Mary. Convalescents, castaways, survivors of terrible accidents—all had wanted to express their faith and gratitude. Was it the geographic location, or was it the worship dedicated to the Mother of God and, in return, the protection she offered? No matter, Jeanne couldn't remain unmoved in this place. A short distance away from her, a man was praying, head in hands. To avoid disturbing him, she tiptoed over to the deserted crypt. She went downstairs and found a statue of Mater Dolorosa surrounded by countless candles. It was there that Jeanne found her inner peace. Rejecting fear and grievances, she decided to trust destiny. War and its litany of guilt, sacrifices, and grief was over. Nothing prevented Jeanne from listening to her own wishes.

Picking up a candle, she lit it and added it to the others, saying a short prayer for Laurent.

La Canebière! Anyone wanting peace and quiet in Marseille had to avoid this street at all costs. Soldiers on leave, women looking for lovers, middlemen of all sorts, sailors, crooks, and reputable folks all mingled there in a cheerful cacophony.

As soon as Michel and Jeanne sat at the terrace of an ice-cream parlor, a loud mechanical piano started to play, interrupting their conversation. Tired from an emotional day, Jeanne's eyes were getting heavy when her cousin called out to a man wearing an elegant gray tussah suit and a boater hat.

"Régis!" Michel said. "I thought I might see you around here. But let me introduce you to my cousin, Jeanne Barthélemy."

Régis smiled as he looked at the young woman's expressive eyes, the curly hair escaping her wide-brimmed hat, and the small pearl cross on her black percale dress. She hadn't taken off her gloves, which covered what seemed like the hands of a little girl.

"Come sit with us," Michel said.

He explained to Jeanne that Régis Cuvelier was the one who'd introduced him to sailing. They often went out to sea together.

As Jeanne's attention was drawn by a scene at a nearby table, she nodded absentmindedly at what her cousin was saying, which annoyed Régis. What was so interesting about a couple, a prostitute and her pimp, fighting over something while a small dog yapped away at their feet?

"I'm organizing a picnic on Sunday on the coast. Would you like to come?" he asked Michel.

"Sure. Have you invited a lot of people?"

"The usual gang."

Régis leaned toward Jeanne and said, "What about you, Miss Jeanne—would you like to join us?"

"Maybe. I don't know."

"I'll take that as a yes," Régis said.

If those words hadn't been uttered in a cheerful voice, Jeanne would have no doubt put Régis Cuvelier in his place.

He put a hand on her wrist and added, "I would just love to have you with us."

Nobody had ever talked to her this way, and that made her feel special. She looked at him more closely.

He didn't look to be older than twenty-five, but he behaved like a man who was used to giving orders and having people follow them. He wasn't, at first sight, what could be called handsome, but he did possess a certain amount of charm that compensated for a face that was too square, slightly drooping eyes, and a stocky physique. His smile was irresistible, warm with a hint of insolence.

On their way back home, she asked Michel about Régis. Who was he? How long had he known him?

"His family owns an important soap factory in Marseille. He's been running it since his father became sick. Tuberculosis."

"Well, he seems to like having a good time."

A golden light was spreading over the countryside, in the bristling leaves of the cork oaks and the bamboo trees. As they drove, they passed villages high up in the hills, under a sky slowly turning pink. A herd of goats crossing the road forced them to stop. After her anxiety in Marseille, Jeanne was enjoying this return to nature, to pure air, to a calm and harmonious environment.

Arriving at Restanques, she was surprised to see her mother in the company of René Verdier.

Sitting under a cedar, they were both drinking champagne.

"Mr. Verdier is moving into Bel Horizon," Marthe told her daughter after Jeanne greeted the man.

"You're forgetting, Mother, that I told you about this a little while ago."

"Yes, maybe. In any case, I'm happy that such a lovely property will come to life again."

Had Marthe had more to drink than usual? Jeanne had never seen her mother with eyes so bright or that odd, charming smile of hers. It was as though she'd forgotten all about her son's departure, her bitterness toward life, and her financial worries. Could it be that Mr. Verdier, though he was no Prince Charming, had awakened Marthe's inner Sleeping Beauty?

"I'd like your advice on certain renovations I want to make," Verdier said. "Would you come over?"

"With great pleasure," Marthe said without hesitation.

Jeanne said she was exhausted and excused herself. Everything in her room was clean and tidy—the white mosquito net around her cast-iron bed, the manicure tools, and the hairbrushes and perfume bottles lined up neatly along her dressing table. She sighed with relief as she took off her dusty shoes. Then she removed her wrinkled dress and lay down on the bed's quilt. So much had happened today, so many emotions! The knocking on the door snapped Jeanne out of her reverie. It was Rosalie bringing the clothes she'd just ironed.

"So, Mr. Laurent wasn't too sad?"

"Sad? Are you kidding?"

The sound of glass shattering interrupted Jeanne.

"I'm so sorry," Rosalie said, picking up the pieces of the bottle of eau de toilette she'd just dropped. "I'm so clumsy! And I cut myself on top of that."

A drop of blood, then another, fell on her white apron.

6

FOR ROSALIE, LIFE HAD lost its luster. She performed her duties with diligence but remained detached from what was going on around her. Her distress was all the more intense, as she had no one to talk to. Sometimes she walked into the library to look at a world map and try to follow Laurent's travels, but since she couldn't read, the atlas was pretty much incomprehensible to her.

Refusing to shut herself in her room during siesta, she got into the habit of going for a swim. Every afternoon, she made her way to the Cassole River and swam for a while. Then she dried herself by lying under an alder, the sun filtering through the leaves. Her body would then relax, and she'd fall asleep.

On the way back to the house, she sometimes came across laborers heading for the almond fields. As soon as they saw her, they lowered their voices and said things she knew had to do with her.

One of them, Joseph, couldn't stop looking at her when she brought the workers their meals at suppertime. This didn't escape his wife, Augustine, and Rosalie knew she resented it.

Wearing a large straw hat, Augustine worked alongside Joseph, tapping the small branches of the trees with long sticks to make the green almonds fall to the ground. She did that until the end of October and then, with the arrival of winter, turned her attention to the olive groves. Separated from her children, who were cared for by her in-laws, Augustine performed the same tasks day after day to survive. Thankfully, the Barthélemy family treated their employees well. The lodging and food were fine. As for the overall atmosphere, it wouldn't have been bad if it weren't for that maid.

Rosalie had caught Augustine's husband's eye in a big way. But what could she do about his attraction for the young woman, especially in such a close environment?

François, Augustine's brother, also hated Joseph's attitude toward Rosalie, which seemed to suggest she was some sort of conquest. How many times had he been tempted to tell his brother-in-law to shut his mouth after some passing innuendo? But all he'd gain from confronting this vain giant of a man would be a beating and being sent back home, to Briançon, where he'd work the fields and feed the farm animals. If only he didn't have to depend on Joseph! But nothing had ever gone François' way. After the death of their parents several years ago, he'd gone to live with Augustine and her in-laws. They were poor and crude folks. Time passed without any moments of joy until Joseph, back from the front, decided to look for work. Provence needed laborers, and all three headed for Cotignac, where they were hired by the Barthélemys.

François wasn't much older than Laurent, the young boss. He'd watched him leave for college, admiring his presence and his nice clothes, knowing that he'd never had those kinds of opportunities himself. With Rosalie's arrival at Restanques, he discovered jealousy.

He'd fallen in love with the girl as soon as he saw her. Spying on her, he soon found out about her relationship with Laurent Barthélemy. Once, he saw Rosalie's naked body in the sunlight as she and Laurent made love behind a bush. Her skin was

milky white, her breasts round like apples, and the rest . . .
When François thought about it, his senses flared up. Taking
refuge in his pipe dreams, he imagined himself and Rosalie fleeing this place so they could indulge their passion for each other
in some exotic land. But when he ran into her, all he could do
was lower his eyes and mumble "hi" or "good evening."

Ever since her lover left, Rosalie had been in the habit of
spending her evenings in the building where the almonds were
dehusked, to help out. That way, she didn't have to be all by
herself.

Sitting on a high stool, a pail at her feet, a large stone on
her knees, she'd take a shell in her left hand, place it on the
stone, and split it open with a piece of wood. She'd then drop
the almond into the pail. Once it was full, all the almonds
were poured onto a long table. All around her, girls and
women from all over the region performed the same task. The
almonds were eventually put in bags and sent off to a broker,
who would sell them.

Looking at the bags being taken away one day, Jeanne said
to Barnabé, the old sharecropper, that it was a pity they were
depriving themselves of significant income by not producing
nougat.

"It's really too bad," she said.

"I agree, Ms. Jeanne . . . but how could we do that?"

"My father always said that every problem has a solution."

As she uttered those words, Jeanne thought of Régis Cuvelier. Michel admired his business acumen. . . . Maybe he could
give her some advice? It was in that frame of mind that she
headed for the picnic.

Régis, wearing swimming trunks, was starting a fire when
Michel and Jeanne arrived at the foot of the Sormiou cove.
Next to him, in a large pail, were several freshly caught fish.

Scattered along the rocky beach, young men and women were busy emptying wicker baskets, some setting food on large white-and-blue blankets, while others placed bottles into puddles that had formed between rocks, to keep the wine cool.

"Here's more!" Michel said, handing Régis a basket full of bottles of wine made at Restanques.

Jeanne said hello to the host of the picnic, and then, shaking hands with people she was meeting for the first time, heard names that she didn't remember. She was entranced by the sea and couldn't wait to swim in it.

In contrast to the midday heat, the water felt frigid to Jeanne, but little by little she got used to it. Above her the cliff rose toward the sky, inhabited by swifts and blue robins. She felt like she was at the beginning of time. Nothing altered the beauty of a landscape that no man had touched. She turned her face to the sun, shut her eyes, and ran her tongue along her salty lips. Was there anything more pleasant than this sensation of forgetting about everything and simply enjoying the moment? She might have forgotten all about the picnic if Régis hadn't called out from the shore. "Aren't you hungry?"

He was waiting with a terry towel and wrapped it around her. She felt his hands caress her shoulders through the fabric. It was a fleeting gesture, but it made Jeanne uncomfortable. Immediately, he guided her toward the others, who were sitting under pine trees nibbling on olives and anchovies while the fish sizzled on the grill. Intimidated, Jeanne listened to them talk about the exhibitions and receptions they'd gone to. Compared to the young women who were going on about some flower show they'd attended, she felt like a rube.

As everyone chatted and relaxed, Régis took care of the food and made sure the wine was cool, and that all his guests were comfortable and happy. Jeanne had never seen anyone with such energy. When he finally sat down beside her, a certain Henriette gave her an angry look.

"I don't know anything about you," Régis said.

"You can ask Michel. He loves to gossip."

"Nothing is worth more than information taken from the source."

"Well, I live in Cotignac . . . "

The white wine was starting to go to Jeanne's head. She still could taste the octopus and sea urchins she'd eaten, and her nostrils were filled with the smell of the fennel that had been sprinkled on the sea bass. This feeling of contentment lasted into siesta, when she fell asleep to the sound of the cicadas.

When she opened her eyes, she realized that Régis had left. She fixed her hair and went over to Michel, who was playing charades with a few of his friends.

"Would you like some coffee?" one of them asked Jeanne.

"No, thank you," she said, before deciding to take a walk along the cove.

As her feet ached from the rocks on the shore, she took a steep path up the cliff and kept on walking until the sound of people attracted her attention. A few feet from her, in a hollow of the cliff, a couple was making love. Naked, Henriette wrapped her legs around Régis. Neither one saw Jeanne. Blushing, her heart beating fast, she spun on her heels and hurried away. All of a sudden, the day had lost its magic, and the young woman wanted nothing more now than to head back home.

Hours passed, and people swam in the Mediterranean, including Régis.

"Let me teach you the breaststroke," he offered Jeanne.

"Out of the question," she said.

"Are you scared?"

"Absolutely not!"

"So . . . "

The way he challenged her with a smile made her change

her mind. Repressing her exasperation, she followed him until she was waist-deep in the sea.

"Now," he said, "watch and listen."

After showing Jeanne the movements, he forced her to lean forward and then picked her up.

"Don't worry," he said. "I'm holding you. Just imagine that you're a mermaid."

"Easy for you to say!"

Her muscles tight with apprehension, Jeanne tried to synchronize her arms and legs, but she couldn't overcome the fear of looking foolish in the eyes of Régis and the uneasiness of Henriette watching them from the shore.

With one hand under his pupil's chin and the other under her stomach, Régis said, "That's better. Keep going! Left, right, left, right . . . Let's get that ball that Michel just threw in the water."

"That's way too far!"

Régis's silence made it clear that she had no choice. Gathering all her strength, Jeanne struggled toward the direction of the ball, until she sank.

"It's okay," Régis said, as he helped Jeanne to her feet.

As soon as she'd finished coughing and spitting, they both burst out laughing. A complicity between them was established when Jeanne discovered that this swimming lesson had, in fact, been a life lesson. Next to Régis, she once again found the strength that her father had once instilled in her. Listening to him, anything seemed achievable if you wanted it badly enough.

The sun was setting when everyone decided to leave. They all did their part to clean up the beach. Then Jeanne slid her dress down over her salty skin and tied the laces of her canvas shoes. On the horizon, a sailboat could be seen against the pink sky. Unable to detach herself from this picture of serenity, Jeanne was the last one to climb to the top of the cliff, where the cars were parked.

Making her claim clear, Henriette had seated herself in Régis's car. She looked very pretty wearing a small straw hat, though a pretentious smirk made her Madonna face unpleasant.

"Come on, Régis," she said. "Hurry up, or we're going to be late at the Cabriès'."

Her use of the word *we* upset Jeanne. How serious was the relationship between Régis and Henriette? What were his true feelings for her?

One car drove off, then another. Michel sat motionless behind the steering wheel. He and Régis made plans to see each other in two days.

"What time?" asked Michel.

"Why don't you pick me up at the factory at the end of the day?" Régis said. Then, lowering his voice, he added, "Then, we'll go . . . "

7

TWO DAYS LATER, MICHEL parked on a street in the Corderie neighborhood and walked to the Cuvelier Soap Factory.

The plant was about to close, and women in dark shirts were busy stamping the pieces of soap that had just been cut up after drying in a concrete basin.

"You'll find Mr. Régis in shipping," the foreman told Michel.

Michel crossed the rooms where the various phases of soap production were taking place. During the mashing phase, vegetable oil was mixed with sodium and then poured into vapor-heated vats to separate the oils into fatty acids and glycerin. Next, the glycerol fluid was removed prior to the cooking process. Then the pellets were discharged and cleaned with salty water to neutralize the sodium and cleaned again with fresh water to eliminate the surplus salt. After a settling period and a mixing process, the soap, now more liquid, was poured into vats where it hardened. A smell of cleanliness filled the air.

With the help of two workers, Régis was inspecting the batches about to be shipped out.

"I won't be long," he told Michel. "Why don't you wait for me in my office?"

Michel found himself in a room that looked like it had been decorated by a gypsy. All around him, folders, samples, and brochures were piled on tables and desks, while the display cabinets were crammed full of all kinds of objects. Photographs hanging on the walls in dusty frames told the history of the company. In one of them, Régis's grandfather held some of the first soap made in the factory, surrounded by a number of his workers. Next to it hung a variety of certificates guaranteeing the quality of the products.

A bell rang. The workday was over. Michel heard a volley of voices and stomping feet as the workers left the factory all at once. One woman stayed on to finish cleaning a vat. From her posture and her reddened hands, Michel figured she'd been at this hard job for a long time. She probably had nobody to go home to, and that was why she remained.

Régis finally appeared in the office.

"All done," he said. "Let's go!"

Turning to a tarnished mirror, he ran a hand over his black hair and adjusted his tie, and then grabbed his jacket.

They walked over to the other riverbank of the Old Port and then took a series of narrow streets, heading for the Vieille-Charité. Fleeing the stifling heat of their homes, the docks, or their offices, a wide variety of people gathered in this part of town known for its illicit pleasures. On the buildings' façades were signs with the names of bars, cafés, hotels, and tattoo parlors. Amid the sound of street organs, clients paused in front of the establishments, deciding whether or not to walk in, while other thrill seekers strolled by them.

Régis and Michel had to walk around two sailors sitting on the sidewalk. Both drunk, the sailors were singing some obscene song. A bit farther, a girl smelling of musk and sweat offered her services.

"Maybe next time," Régis told her with a chuckle.

Michel noticed how comfortable his friend seemed in this shady environment.

As a teenager, how many times had Michel himself asked questions about this neighborhood after first hearing about it? His parents always refused to answer. As soon as he had the chance, he'd visited with a few friends and, behind the door of a brothel, squandered his savings to become a man. He hadn't stopped coming to Vieille-Charité since, as the surroundings fulfilled his longing to live outside his usual bourgeois conventions. Again, tonight, rubbing elbows with men of all races and faiths, he felt very far away from his home and his ties.

The smell of fried food and sex wafted from various windows. With her elbows against a balcony's railing, a woman wearing nothing but a girdle swore at a man on the street below. He shouted back in a foreign language. Michel raised his head. Clothes hung from lines, forming multicolor spots on the buildings' cracked façades. With the back of his hand, he wiped his sweaty brow.

"Am I ever thirsty," he said.

"Don't worry," Régis said. "We'll take care of that in no time."

They wound up in a square with a fountain and lopsided houses that reminded Michel of an operetta set. A group of noisy kids ran by them, followed by barking dogs. Indifferent to the mayhem, the two men headed for a cul-de-sac and stopped in front of a heavy door. Régis knocked, and soon the spy hole opened. Two dark eyes appeared.

"Well, I'll be . . . " the woman's voice said behind the door. "Hello, strangers!"

Régis hugged their hostess as soon as she let them into the entryway. The walls were covered with violet plush.

"I know," he said. "It's been a while since we've been here." Then he added, "Hmm, you smell good."

"Okay," Miquette said with a smile. "Don't try to flatter me."

Grabbing Michel's arm, the young woman said, "How about you, handsome? Is everything okay? Madam figured you guys were mad at us."

"Why would we be mad at you?"

"That's what we were wondering."

They entered a living room lit by a tawdry chandelier. Women of all ages, shapes, and sizes were waiting for potential clients. Régis, who knew most of them, was hoping to come across someone new when his eyes fell on twins. They were both sitting on some fat man's knees. Their hair was braided, and they wore identical blue blouses. They were barely twenty years old.

Picking up on Régis's expression, Miquette said, "Madam is very proud of having them."

"She should be."

"But it's more expensive, you know. Because they won't leave each other."

Régis turned to Michel.

"What do you think?"

"Knock yourself out," Michel said, without much enthusiasm.

It wasn't the first time their tastes had differed. Usually Régis went for girls, whereas Michel was attracted to women with experience.

Twilight brought the usual heightened activity in the neighborhood's brothels. Sailors and soldiers on leave, embarrassed members of the upper class, bawdy old men, politicians looking for a thrill—they all came to satisfy their sexual urges, to assert their manhood. Over the gramophone music, they drank cheap champagne while eyeing women who pranced around in see-through blouses over girdles or camisoles. Blondes, brunettes, redheads; thin, chubby; slender Vietnamese, wild Poles, Mexicans with warm voices—the sampling was varied. How could it have been any different in a port city visited by people from all over the world? At Madam Lea's, anyone could find what they fantasized about, as long as they had the means to pay for it.

As he smiled at a woman with high cheekbones, Michel walked over to the one who replaced Madam Lea when she wasn't around.

"So, Lilou," he said, "you're ignoring me?"

"Well, you still remember my name?"

"Very funny."

He ran a fingertip along the shoulder strap of her very low-cut dress. Lilou's ample breasts had always been irresistible to Michel. It had been Lilou who'd deflowered him, and he'd often come back to her after that, as she knew best how to please him. How old was she now? Forty? She had circles under her gray eyes, and little wrinkles formed at the corners of her mouth, but she still had the same radiance that Michel had fallen for the first time. Lilou loved her work and performed as though it were her life's goal. With her, you always got your money's worth.

"Are you free?" Michel asked her.

"As soon as I'm done with that one," Lilou whispered, gesturing with her chin toward a large man smoking a cigar at the bar.

Michel went over and, after ordering himself a drink, watched couples and trios head upstairs to the various rooms.

Amid a burst of laughter, Madam emerged from an adjacent boudoir. Through the half-opened door, Michel spotted the police commissioner, a regular. Wrapped in a pistachio-green dress, the owner of the brothel was a larger-than-life character. People said that she'd started on the sidewalks of Toulouse and, after making quite a bit of money in North Africa, settled in Marseille, where she opened her own place, which she ran with an iron fist.

"No one catches bugs in my house," she liked to brag.

She had pimps working for her, men who knew how to spot a newly fired housemaid or a woman who'd been abandoned by her husband or lover. The war had produced no shortage of widows without income who were just starting out in the trade.

Seeing Régis, Madame threw herself into his arms.

"I was told you're getting married," she said. "Is it true?"

"Me? Getting married? It's news to me! Who's the lucky gal?"

"I thought you'd tell me."

"Don't worry, my love. You'll be the first to know when I decide to tie the knot. But for now, your little twins are the only objects of my affection. Very nice."

"I'm not surprised you like them."

From atop its perch, a parrot let out a squawk, but nobody paid attention. Night was falling, and several of the men were about to leave, already trying to come up with the excuse they would give their suspicious wives once they got home. But how many of them really had no clue about their husband's double lives?

"The poor women . . . " Lilou said with a grin. "If they only knew what their men asked us to do, they'd have heart attacks. On the other hand, if they let their husbands touch them once in a while . . . For that we have the Catholic Church to thank, and the priests driving it into women's heads that making love is sinful unless you want to procreate. Without them, we'd be out of work. . . . "

After twenty years in the business, she'd encountered countless men who, in her bed, were fleeing marriages in which having sex was a chore. Disappointed and frustrated, they came to Lilou looking for a bit of solace. Their masks dropped and, with the women they paid, they finally dared to be themselves in the act of lovemaking. Pathetic. Thankfully, there were also young, single men like Michel who'd had their first dalliances with her. While other clients went on and on about their sorry lives, with Michel she simply had to give him pleasure and enjoy it.

The night was nearly over when Régis and Michel headed back. Both tired, they didn't say much. Through the windows of cafés, they spotted those who waited for the moment, most likely at dawn, when their solitude would be less painful. Empty bottles littered the sidewalks, and some partiers still lingered. As Régis and Michel neared the shore, a fight broke out in front of them. A woman with a very colorful vocabulary was giving her boyfriend an earful. The light of a lamppost right above them gave the scene a theatrical aspect, but Régis paid it no mind. Never would he tire of looking at the harbor swept by the beam of its lighthouse, and a bit farther away, Marseille's transporter bridge crossing the body of water he couldn't live without. Breathing in the salty air, he watched the ships docked nearby and listened to their hulls creaking to the movement of the water. With its lantern breaking through the darkness, a single fishing boat headed out to sea. In a short while, sailors and fishermen, their faces still creased from a night's sleep, would crowd the docks, their voices filling the air. A son of this ancient city, Régis had it in his blood. He fed on its stature, its strength, its music. Thinking of it, his eyes welled up. Was it the alcohol, fatigue, or the genuine love he felt for Marseille? He lit a cigarette and sat on a low wall. He felt dirty, morally and physically, but what did such a sensation matter in the face of this wonderful sight that taught him humility?

A few steps away, Michel stood still and silent. Though they'd known each other for a long time, their relationship had never reached the level of close friendship. In fact, they shared little more than their vices, as they'd done tonight. Régis yawned, put out his cigarette, and rose to his feet. The factory was going to open in less than three hours. Sleeping was out of the question, so he decided to go home and drink plenty of coffee.

Michel dropped him off in front of the family house's gates. Built right on the coast, it offered a view of the sea. Régis took off his shoes and tiptoed his way across the vestibule, as the floor there creaked at the faintest touch. He reached his bedroom and looked at his bed but decided to ignore it. Instead, he went to the bathroom. The frigid water he splashed on his face was like a slap. Lifting his head, he saw in the mirror an exhausted face and puffy eyes. He continued to wash up, careful not to make too much noise, his parents being light sleepers. Ever since he'd caught tuberculosis, his father, Bernard Cuvelier, had a hard time lying down without coughing frequently. As for his mother, nights had been torture ever since Colette, Régis's oldest sister, had died of peritonitis three years earlier. Their house, which had been filled with happy activity when Régis was a child, had turned into a sort of sarcophagus. Régis stayed out of it as much as he possibly could.

Drying his hair, he returned to his room, where, on a long oak table, several tennis trophies stood lined up next to a chessboard and the model of a clipper. There was also the picture of a smiling Colette. Was it necessary to continue living with those who were gone? In a bowl of trinkets were lottery tickets and passes for the hippodrome. Régis picked up the day's mail and went through the envelopes without opening them, even the one with Henriette's fancy handwriting. Taking him by surprise, a face came to his mind, that of Jeanne, Michel's cousin. . . .

8

JEANNE AND RÉGIS SAW each other again at the Hyères regatta. He'd invited her for lunch at the villa he'd inherited from his mother's side of the family. Michel joined them, but otherwise they dined alone. Had Henriette been ditched? Jeanne hoped so.

The house had been built fifty years before, in the Moorish style popular back then, with fountains and basins built into the ceramic walls. Régis's presence in such a setting seemed odd to Jeanne. It was easier to imagine him among simple furnishings, as nothing about his personality seemed flashy. He was sure of himself without being pretentious, and therein lay his charm. Adding to that was an exceptional vitality, the impression he gave that nothing could stop him, and his willingness to enjoy the moment. In his presence, worries simply vanished. All that mattered was having a good time!

On the terrace that overlooked the Giens peninsula, Jeanne drank a cup of coffee while watching the ships go by below. A soft wind blew against her face, bringing a scent of pine and roses. Lying in a hammock, Michel smoked a cigarette, feeling like a third wheel. When Régis suggested they go down to the harbor, Michel said he had some errand to run and that he would meet up with them later.

While Régis drove his car through the streets of the "palm tree capital," Jeanne remained quiet. The crowd was so thick on the wharfs that they had to keep to the Pesquiers marshes.

"In a month," Régis said, "the pink flamingoes will be here with their young from the Camargue. Thousands of other migrating birds also come to these marshes: ducks, coots, cormorants. In the spring, it's sandpipers, avocets, and stilts."

As she listened to him, Jeanne remembered Jérôme Guillaumin telling her about gannets and their migration patterns. Why did every man she encountered feel like he had to give her lessons in ornithology?

Régis had slowed down. With the sun's rays caressing her skin, Jeanne felt exhilarated by her surroundings—the sky high above her with its fleeting clouds, the sailboats out on the Mediterranean. They continued driving until they reached the sleepy village of Giens, then headed for Darboussière Beach, where Régis pulled to a stop.

"Are you wearing good shoes?" he asked Jeanne.

She reassured Régis by showing him her flat soles.

"Good!" he said.

A path followed the coastline. Régis took it first. He'd removed his jacket and rolled up his shirtsleeves.

"Everything okay?" he asked, turning to Jeanne.

Out of breath, trying to ignore her vertigo, she stood right behind Régis as they climbed a hill lined with green oaks and pine trees.

"Look how gorgeous it is," he said.

"Yes," she muttered, without looking down.

At the top of the hill, she leaned against a large rock. Régis walked up to her. The ambient smell of mastic and myrtle mixed with Régis's cologne as he leaned toward her. Their mouths connected, timidly, clumsily at first.

"Don't be afraid," Régis said, as he began undressing her.

Thinking he was being much too forward, Jeanne tried to get away from Régis, but he was persistent.

"Someone could see us," she said between kisses.

He unbuttoned her dress and began caressing her breasts. He muttered words she didn't understand.

"Just relax," he finally said.

Embarrassed, Jeanne turned her head to the side. She didn't realize that her timidity was, in fact, turning Régis on more than any loving words she could have told him. Minutes passed, but she'd lost any concept of time. All that mattered was her own pleasure, though she felt guilty about it and knew that it was taking her places she didn't want to be. She felt Régis's body against hers and, suddenly terrified by the precision of his hands, she pushed him off with a force she didn't suspect she had in her.

"What's the matter with you?" Régis demanded.

Already, she was up on her feet, gathering her clothes.

In a much softer voice, Régis added, "You don't like me?"

"That's not the point."

"What is it, then?"

"I don't know."

She was speaking the truth. Everything had happened so fast, too fast. And now that she'd come to her senses, the man standing in front of her seemed like a total stranger.

Silently, they headed back to the car. For Jeanne, the day had turned grim. Indifferent to the seagulls' cry, the beauty of the wild flowers dancing in the wind, she hated herself for having behaved like such a prude, and Régis's frigid attitude only made her feel worse.

Michel was waiting for them at the villa. Jeanne said she had a migraine and wanted to return to Cotignac. Not only did Régis not try to make her change her mind, he barely said goodbye to her.

*   *   *

Over the next few weeks, Jeanne tried to forget about that afternoon, but she couldn't. She still regretted her behavior. How could she turn back the clock? Her preoccupation prevented her from properly taking care of Restanques. The almond harvest was in full swing, and all the pickers, joined by Rosalie, were hard at work in the fields.

Every morning the young maid waited for the mailman to arrive and, after taking a look at the stamps on the envelopes, brought the mail up to Mrs. Barthélemy and Jeanne.

"Any news from your brother?" she asked in a detached tone of voice.

"The sea crossing went fine. He's in India now."

India! Rosalie had never heard of that country, but, in a low voice, she kept saying the word. *India* . . . Trying to find out more, she sometimes eavesdropped on Marthe and Jeanne's conversations. She picked up some information: sunscorched fields, crowds of people in tatters, the Brits controlling the country. Once, Marthe talked about epidemics and famine, and Rosalie felt crushed. What would her life be if Laurent didn't come back?

On Sundays, sitting in the back of the church, near the font, she prayed for his protection. With her savings, she would sometimes buy and light a candle, a small glimmer of hope amid her torment. Then her day off would arrive. What was worse than those hours of rest and painful solitude? Since returning to Cotignac, she hadn't tried to make friends with anyone. Aimlessly, she walked through the countryside. It was during one of her walks that she ran into the neighbor who, twice, had come to introduce himself at Restanques.

He was inspecting the uprooting of his vines when, hearing her steps, he turned around. With her tanned face and arms, Rosalie was a model of youth and health.

"Don't we know each other?" he asked.

"I'm a maid at Restanques."

"That's right." Straightening his small frame, he added, "Tell me why a pretty girl like you is walking around like this all by yourself."

"That's not really any of your business," Rosalie said.

René Verdier gave her a quick head-to-toe and said, "You're going on a date, right? Or you're coming back from one."

"You're wrong."

"Really, now . . . You don't have a boyfriend?"

The sun was making him sweaty, and Rosalie couldn't stand his breath, which reeked of wine, but she didn't let on.

"Are you happy at the Barthélemys?"

"Yes."

"If you ever change your mind, I'll hire you. Your pay will be better. By the way, what's your name?"

"Rosalie."

As she was about to walk away from Verdier, she felt his eyes on her breasts, her waist. Another man who wanted nothing but to take her to bed! Plucking a piece of tall grass, she munched on it until she reached the main house's court-yard. There was something unusual in the air.

François, the young laborer, was there. Rosalie asked him what was going on.

"It's Barnabé," François told her. "He went to take a nap and then . . . "

"Then . . . what?"

"He's dead!"

"Barnabé . . . " Rosalie said. "That can't be! I saw him this morning. He was on his way to the village."

Stunned, she looked all around her. The doctor's car was parked in front of the outbuilding. All the laborers had gathered around it. Some of the men had taken off their caps and clutched them to their chests. A woman was crying on some-one else's shoulder. It was Apolline, who considered Fanny and Barnabé members of her family. Rosalie slowly walked over to the crowd. Through the window of the room where the sharecropper had lived, she saw Jeanne trying to comfort her cook. Rosalie shivered, thinking how you could become attached to someone, live with them, love them, only for all those years of togetherness to disappear just like that. . . .

A few steps away, Jeanne had the same thought, but added to it was the odd sensation of being confronted by her father's death, a death that had never seemed real to her.

One morning, two strangers had shown up at Restanques to inform Marthe that she was a widow. Only in the silence of the night had Jeanne been able to imagine fields devastated by iron and fire, trenches where soldiers waded through the mud among dead bodies. Dead bodies like Robert Barthélemy's.

The cold sensation that had entered her veins and her limbs that night remained abstract, until today. It had taken old Barnabé's passing for her to truly take in her father's death. Lying on his bed, the man she'd always seen as a lingering reminder of her father now had the spectral look of the deceased.

"I don't understand," Fanny kept saying. "He was fine."

Looking lost, she finally let the doctor take her to the adjacent room.

"Mrs. Barthélemy isn't here?" he asked.

"She was told what happened," Jeanne replied, trying to hide her annoyance. "She should be down any minute now."

It had been more than an hour since Barnabé had been found, and Marthe was still avoiding a situation that made her uncomfortable, just like a child. Jeanne was embarrassed and distraught by her mother's attitude. She could never count on her for anything and would probably never be able to in the future either.

People waited for Jeanne outside, so she stepped out of the house. Everyone was silent. She looked at Rosalie and tried to find strength in her eyes. Birds chirped in the trees nearby. It was like any other summer day, except . . .

"Barnabé will live in our hearts," Jeanne heard herself say. "He loved Restanques, and he was always a great worker. In memory of him, take good care of Fanny. She's going to need your support and friendship."

Marthe finally showed up as the doctor was getting ready to leave.

"What's going to become of us?" she whined.

"We'll figure that out later," Jeanne said.

9

IN THE FOLLOWING WEEKS, Jeanne rose every day at dawn to oversee the operation of the estate. After inspecting the farm and the stables, she laid out the workers' schedules for the day. Refusing to deal with brokers, she kept all the almonds that had been picked since the beginning of the harvest. The time for dithering was now past. She bought from her Delestang cousins the honey she'd need and ordered pistachios. Making white and black nougat, she improved the recipe passed down by generations of Barthélemys and promised herself that by Christmas she'd have earned the money that was necessary to keep Restanques afloat financially. She'd also repay a large part of what she'd borrowed from a bank in Draguignan. Without telling anyone, she'd asked to meet the manager, a cold but courteous man. She explained the situation to him and what her plans were, and they came to an agreement.

Jeanne finished setting up her production workshop in the middle of September.

"Fanny, you promised to help me out . . . "

The cook nodded every time Jeanne said that, but she'd lost her enthusiasm. The man's voice that had always been heard at Restanques had vanished. All that was left was a nos-talgic trace of it. At times, Fanny could hear the voice when, lost in her memories, she wandered back to the days of her youth, when she'd fallen in love with Barnabé, who'd come to work in the fields. He'd decided to stay because of Fanny. Forty-three years of loving each other, forty-three years of hard work at Restanques. God, why hadn't she died first? It would have been so much easier that way. . . .

"Fanny, I need you," Jeanne kept telling her. "I won't be able to make it by myself."

They began with black nougat, the real thing according to folks in Provence. In a large copper cauldron, they poured twenty pounds of multiflower honey that they brought to the boiling point. Then they added twenty pounds of almonds. In spite of the pain she felt in her arm, Jeanne kept on stirring the concoction with a wooden spoon.

"It's turning black," Fanny said. "We have to remove it from the fire or it's going to taste bitter."

She removed the cauldron from the fire and stirred the mixture another five minutes while Jeanne fetched wooden boxes with molds lined with wafer paper.

"Are you sure it cooked long enough?" she asked.

"Have you ever tasted bad nougat since I started working here?"

One after the other, the boxes were filled. Fanny placed one last sheet of wafer paper on top of the mix and then a board that she weighed down with a rock. The nougat could now cool.

The following morning, Jeanne was so excited she skipped breakfast. With a knife, she cut a piece of nougat and concen-trated on the flavor that filled her mouth. Fanny was right. It was delicious!

It took many days for Jeanne to come up with the right packaging, a small bag adorned with the Barthélemy label.

She looked at it from all angles and decided it was both pretty and appealing. She prayed that the candy-store owners she'd be reaching out to would agree with her.

With a certain amount of apprehension, Jeanne opened the door to a candy shop known in the town of Brignoles for the quality of its products. She knew the owner, as she often came to buy the violet mints she so adored.

"I'm not here as a customer," she began, before explaining the reason for her visit.

"My husband isn't here," Ms. Vespucci interrupted. "He's the one who makes decisions."

"I'll be back tomorrow, then."

As she walked toward the exit, Jeanne felt as though she hadn't been given the same consideration as usual. She'd gone from customer to solicitor. No matter! She headed for a more modest store struggling to make a name for itself.

With its old counters, tarnished mirrors, and countless glass jars filled with hard candy, caramels, and multicolor lozenges, the place had an old-fashioned charm that pleased Jeanne right away. A couple greeted her. The man was in his forties. The woman was younger and held on her knees a little boy eating a piece of licorice.

After admiring the package and tasting the nougat, Mr. Bénard offered to take twenty bags on deposit.

"Times are hard," he explained.

Jeanne had never imagined such a situation. Was she going to take the risk of having unsold nougat after Christmas? Trusting her intuition, she decided to put her faith in the Bénards and, once the prices were set, she committed to deliver the goods the following day.

"Can we do the same thing with the white nougat if you like it?" she asked.

"Absolutely," Mr. Bénard said.

She had more success in Draguignan. One candy-store owner bought fifteen bags outright. But she still had so much to do, especially with the white nougat. For that, she'd ordered a very expensive mixer that was to be delivered the following week.

In spite of her fatigue, she stopped over at the Delestangs' to tell her uncle and aunt all about her long and eventful day. Who else could she talk to about her worries and hopes if not the two people who remained her only link to the carefree days of her childhood? In the yellowish halo of the lamps, she relived the evenings when, munching on a chestnut, she listened to the local storyteller who, every fall, came to Entrecasteaux. Thanks to him, she was familiar with the folktales of her native Provence. She loved and felt closely linked to the region's rivers, its trees, its scents, its people.

"How are you managing without Barnabé?" her uncle asked.

"It's not easy, but we can't afford to hire a replacement."

"Maybe you should think about selling."

"Selling Restanques? That's out of the question!"

Surprised by the vehemence of her reaction, Jeanne wondered what had triggered it. In fact, the idea of selling their domain wasn't so crazy.

"I have to keep the property for Laurent," Jeanne finally said.

"Are you sure he's not going to want to travel some more after this trip?"

"He promised he'd come back."

"Everybody has the right to change his or her mind," Michel said.

For a short moment, he'd been standing on the living room's threshold. The golf pants he was wearing told Jeanne what he'd been up to that afternoon.

"Guess who I played golf with," he said to his cousin.

"I don't know."

"Régis Cuvelier. He was asking me what you've been up to."

"Is that right?" Jeanne said, turning red.

Régis! She'd thought about him less lately. And yet, just to hear his name made her heart beat faster.

"He's supposed to come over next week to order some wine. We could go over for a visit."

They arrived at the worst moment. Covered by her large apron, Jeanne was in the middle of making white nougat. For the past three days, she'd been experimenting with her new mixer and its large copper double-wall container. First she poured in the lavender honey, and then the egg whites and the simple syrup. As Jeanne did that, Fanny grilled the almonds on low heat. She was working them into Jeanne's mixture when Michel and Régis walked into the sweet-smelling workshop.

"Our timing is excellent," Michel said, walking over to the oven.

"You're going to burn yourself," Fanny said, as Michel prepared to dip a finger into the paste.

For her part, Jeanne could only think about her sweaty face and anything-but-elegant ensemble. Trying not to meet Régis's gaze, she concentrated on her task with the unbearable impression that he was enjoying her embarrassment.

"I'm sorry," she muttered, "but I'm a bit busy at the moment. We have to fill all these boxes."

"We'll help you," Régis said.

"No, I—"

"Tut-tut! If we do it together, the job will be over soon, and then we can enjoy ourselves."

Régis grabbed a spoon, and Fanny told everyone what to do. For the first time since Barnabé's death, she was smiling. She even spoke of how her mother, a wonderful cook, had taught her all about the fine cuisine that the Barthélemys had enjoyed over the previous decades.

Once again, Jeanne was won over by Régis's enthusiasm. She even caught herself laughing at his quips and singing along with him as they finished the job.

"Where should we go?" Régis asked Jeanne as they washed their hands.

"Do you know Sillans-la-Cascade? It's a pretty village."

Caressed by the late fall sun, the countryside was shimmering. Jeanne loved the color of the trees, wavering between gold and red. The smell of moss and wild mushrooms filled the air.

Michel had decided not to join them, so once more she was alone with Régis. He put a hand on hers.

"Are you happy to see me?" he asked.

"Yes."

In Sillans, they walked into an inn, where the owner offered them some Mirabelle-plum pie with orgeat syrup.

"Would you like a glass of white wine with that?" Régis asked.

"It's a bit early for that. Are you trying to get me drunk?"

"Are you ever going to trust me?"

"I was only joking. Mostly. . . . "

Until now, no one had ever managed to make Jeanne lose her composure like Régis did. This man had the power to make her feel wonderful, and then completely annoyed a second later.

"Eat your pie while it's warm," Régis said, "and tell me what's going to happen to that nougat we made so lovingly. Is it going to some orphanage at Christmastime?"

"I wish. . . . "

Suddenly, Jeanne found herself telling him all about the difficult time Restanques was going through, her constant battle against Marthe's apathy, and her worries that Laurent, no matter what he said, would never want to take over the estate. He was a nomad at heart.

"My godmother owns a candy store in Marseille," Régis said. "I'll talk to her about you."

And then he launched into a strategy for her. Hyères, Toulon . . . To hear him tell it, nothing was impossible. There was no reason why she couldn't be successful. Not attempting to hide her interest, Jeanne listened intently. Finally, someone was saying what she had not dared express, and the energy she'd always felt inside her was matched by Régis's.

The sun was setting when he glanced at his watch.

"Six o'clock," he said. "I'll take you home."

As they drove toward Restanques, he continued to ask Jeanne about her plans, and suddenly, she regretted that the conversation wasn't more intimate. Was it that he was no longer attracted to her? In that case, why had he spent so much time with her today? As he dropped her off in front of the house, she hoped for some sort of a gesture from him, anything.

"Have a good evening," he said. "And don't forget to go here with your samples." He scribbled a few words on a piece of paper and gave it to Jeanne. "After you do that, you'll be a part of the inner circle."

He didn't ask me for a date, Jeanne kept saying to herself as she took the path to the house. *As a matter of fact, he's probably laughing at me. . . .* Disappointment took hold of her throat. Why in the world would she let herself be attracted to a man who could basically have any woman he wanted? And the irony was he wasn't even her type! She began to find flaws in Régis's character, but they all vanished when she remembered his charming smile, the smooth tone of his voice, his communicative laugh . . .

"Ms. Marthe will not be dining with us tonight," Rosalie told Jeanne as she walked up the front stairs.

"She went out?"

"An hour ago. With Mr. Verdier. They went to Brignoles."

"My mother and Mr. Verdier!"

At midnight, Marthe still wasn't home, and Jeanne began to worry. But then she heard the rumbling of a car engine and went to her bedroom window. Under the light of the front steps, Mr. Verdier helped Marthe get out of the car and then kissed her hand before leaving.

When Marthe appeared in the hallway, Jeanne stepped out of her room and said, "You didn't tell me you were going out."

"You're not sleeping?" Marthe said. "Well, I must've forgotten to tell you."

"You forgot!"

"It happens."

"Where did you go?"

"We had dinner at a restaurant. Is that a crime?"

"I don't like that man."

"Why not? He's considerate . . . He's very nice."

Had Jeanne ever seen this happy expression on her mother's face before? Behind her veil, her cheeks were rosy, and she was all smiles. Could it be that she'd fallen for this widower? Jeanne didn't trust him one bit. He looked like a con artist to her. . . .

There were more rendezvous between them over the next few days . . . as well as several visits to a dressmaker in the town of Carcès.

"Nothing good can come out of all this," Raymond Delestang said when Jeanne told her about her worries. "As soon as I have a chance, I'll talk to your mother."

Relieved, the young woman turned her attention to making her nougat. Régis's involvement proved a godsend. Ms. Pascale ordered one hundred bags and paid cash for them.

Still, the bills continued to arrive at Restanques. Taxes, repairs to farm equipment, a significant leak in the ceiling, the replacement of gutters . . . Jeanne was counting on the olive harvest at the end of November to correct the estate's precarious situation. There were also worries concerning the staff. A stable boy stepped on a rusty nail. An infection set in, and he almost lost his foot. Then Augustine suffered a miscarriage.

She had been out in the almond fields when blood began running down her legs. Bent in two from the pain in her belly and lower back, she made her way to a bush and, away from prying eyes, wiped herself with handfuls of grass.

Annie, the young woman who had been working near Augustine, realized she'd gone.

"Augustine!" she called out.

She looked for Augustine and found her behind the bush.

"My God! You're sick!"

"Shush! Don't say a word about this to anyone. Especially Joseph!"

Augustine broke down in tears because of her pain, her despair, and her fear of the consequences. Over time, her husband had become harsher and harsher with her, sometimes downright violent.

"You can't stay here," Annie said. "Let's go back to the house. We'll say you have diarrhea."

But soon Augustine's fever worsened, and Annie decided she had to tell Apolline. Right away, Apolline went up to Jeanne's room.

"Have her taken to the room next to yours," Jeanne said. "I'll be right over."

Until the doctor arrived, Jeanne stayed at Augustine's bedside. The sick woman wouldn't answer any of Jeanne's questions.

"What are you afraid of, Augustine? You know I mean you no harm."

Once again, Jeanne felt her helplessness in the face of the chasm that existed between her and the people working for her. In spite of months and sometimes years of cohabitation, the feeling of distrust remained. She did everything she could to change it, but centuries of beliefs and preconceptions prevented the establishment of any sort of genuine dialogue.

"Augustine . . . you have to tell me what's going on."

"It's Joseph," the woman finally said. "He swore to me that if I ever got pregnant again, he'd leave me. You see, Ms. Jeanne, we already have two kids . . . "

"Tell me the truth. . . . You took something?"

"Some plants."

"Who gave them to you?"

Augustine wouldn't answer that question. The short silence that followed was broken by Jeanne.

"You went to the abortionist who lives by the Cassole River, didn't you?"

For two days, Augustine hovered between life and death.

"Unfortunately," the doctor said when he thought she was out of danger, "she's probably going try this again."

If Jeanne didn't know much about love, what she was learning about relationships did nothing to reassure her. Was it possible to so easily lose control over someone else or, even worse, live in fear of your husband? Marthe, Augustine . . . and pretty much all the female characters in the novels she'd read gave Jeanne a decidedly bleak view of love, relationships, and marriage.

"If you only knew how awful Joseph is with Augustine," Apolline told Jeanne one morning.

"Well, we certainly haven't seen much of him at his wife's bedside."

"That's because he only has eyes for Rosalie."

"Rosalie?"

"As soon as he sees her, his face turns red. I don't know what stops me from slapping him upside the head. Thankfully, Rosalie isn't going along with it. As a matter of fact, I was watching them the other day and I thought she was going to gouge his eyes out she was so mad at something he said. But Augustine is doing nothing about it all. Let me tell you, I'm sure glad I never got married!"

10

THE OLIVE HARVEST BEGAN in late November, and, in spite of her fatigue, Augustine took to the fields with the rest of the workers.

The air was cold on the late fall morning, and she enjoyed the heat given off by the brazier she carried from tree to tree. The basket in which she dropped the olives she picked was hanging from her neck.

"I'm getting hungry," Annie shouted at her.

Annie picked olives with dizzying speed.

"Thank God the lunch break is soon," Augustine said.

Each day seemed like the ones before it, but Augustine didn't mind the work. She felt useful out in the fields, and when she received her pay, she forgot momentarily about what she'd done to herself. She was happy to be able to buy her children new clothes.

"I miss them so much," she told Joseph.

Each time, he replied with a shrug.

If he could, would he like to go back home to the Basses-Alpes region? She knew the answer to that question. . . . She often dreamed of family life on a farm they'd own. It was a pipedream she kept believing in, just as she'd never given up when she'd decided she wanted to marry Joseph many years ago. Did she regret having done that now that her destiny was linked to this difficult man? Everyone thought that Joseph was full of himself, unfaithful, and rude, but Augustine continued to think that by being loving and patient with her husband, she would conquer his demons.

Augustine was emptying the contents of her basket into a large bag when Jeanne, on an inspection, showed up. They would have a good crop this year, but that was true of pretty much every year in the region. Cotignac was known throughout Provence for the quality of its olives. The olive, emblem of the Mediterranean world, had been a major crop as far back as the middle of the fifteenth century. It was a gold mine for the locals until the terrible winter of 1709 wiped out all the groves. But in the following years, the olive tree, known for its vigor, began to multiply again, to the point where groves were the size of forests by the end of the eighteenth century. More mills had to be built to extract from the fruits the smooth and aromatic oil that connoisseurs celebrated like great wine. In 1900, fourteen of those mills were operating night and day, as nearly fourteen million pounds of olives were harvested yearly. It was too much! Prices went down and so did profits, and the owners of olive groves decided to form two cooperatives. The first one, called La Défense, was created in January 1905 and the other followed six months later. As it was more left-leaning politically, it was called La Travailleuse—The Worker.

From the beginning, Robert Barthélemy had brought his crop to the La Défense mill. As a child, Jeanne often accompanied her dad there, and things hadn't changed in that place where the olives were thoroughly cleaned with cold water. A granite millstone then crushed them, pits and all. The paste was spread out over a natural-fiber disk, then piled one on top of the other and placed under the press to obtain the juice. Next, a flat spoon was used to gather the oil on the water's surface, and the oil was transferred into glazed earthen jars, which were shut with wooden covers. As her father worked, Jeanne never tired of looking at the color of the precious liquid that went from golden yellow to emerald green. When she dipped a large piece of bread into it, all of Provence was contained in those few drops.

Come nightfall, after a long day in the fields, Jeanne would relax in front of the fireplace. The heat was soothing. Nights were getting colder. Soon she would have to get ready for Christmas, and then January would come, making her feel even more isolated and lonely.

Marthe didn't have the same bleak mindset. In the middle of the afternoon, she left her room to make her way to Bel Horizon and meet René Verdier. He'd invited Jeanne to join them for supper a number of times, but she never accepted, until her mother insisted she change her mind.

"It's important to be on good terms with our neighbors. The way you never accept his invitation is downright rude."

"You compensate by being there all the time."

"What do you mean by that?"

Jeanne sighed and said, "Why won't he leave me alone? I didn't ask anything of him, and I have no interest in going to his house."

But in the hope that her mother would stop harping on the subject, Jeanne finally went to dinner at Verdier's.

"Come in, come in," he said, and showed the two women to the living room. It was filled with hunting trophies, dried flowers in glass vases, and mediocre paintings.

Watching Verdier as he poured Marthe a glass of port, Jeanne noticed that he'd put on some weight. His vest stretched across his stomach, and his shirt collar seemed to strangle him.

"Would you like some grenadine?" Verdier asked Jeanne.

"I'd rather have a glass of port."

As they chatted, Jeanne realized just how well acquainted

their host and Marthe had become. They'd also made plans, including a trip that would take them to Nice, Menton, and Genoa, on the Italian coast. Jeanne felt terribly awkward as she listened to them both, feeling like a voyeur, but she tried to hide her embarrassment. She refused to give René Verdier the satisfaction.

During dinner, Marthe and Verdier talked about how wonderful the region was. It was as though there had been no war, no bereavement, no hardship! But then the conversation turned to Restanques.

"Your mother told me that you're going through difficult times," Verdier said to Jeanne.

"We're going to be fine."

"Fine! What makes you so optimistic in these hard times?"

"I have no other choice, do I?"

"That's what I'm talking about. For a pretty girl like you, there are other options than living here in the boonies."

As she listened to Verdier, Jeanne glanced at the maid, who was clumsily placing a dish that contained garlic mayonnaise in front of Marthe. She looked barely sixteen. Her black, straight hair escaped from the white cap she wore, and her face expressed a false submission.

"You'd be much happier in Toulon or in Nice or—why not—in Paris," René Verdier continued.

"As long as my brother is away, I'm not going anywhere."

"But he could be gone for a very long time! Didn't you tell me, my dear Marthe, that your son is a nomad at heart?"

It took everything for Jeanne to keep from getting up and leaving the house, where everything reeked of vulgarity and deception. Instead, she decided to remain calm and avoid Verdier's trap.

"I even complimented him on his dog," Jeanne told her Uncle Raymond the next day, "and it's a horrible-looking mutt with a broken ear." Sounding worried, she added, "He has his eyes on Restanques. I'm sure of it."

"Aren't you exaggerating a bit? He just spent a fortune to buy Bel Horizon."

"That's not enough for him."

"Well, for him to buy Restanques, you and Laurent would have to put it on the market."

"Uncle Raymond, you're forgetting that mother owns some of the land."

"And you think she'd want to get rid of it?"

"Who knows?"

Neither one of them wanted to make any more assumptions, especially Jeanne, who had a hard time with the idea that her mother might have feelings for a man, whether it was René Verdier or anyone else. How could she have ever loved her husband if she could forget about him so quickly? Images of her past came to Jeanne: her parents taking her on a boat to Port-Cros Island, having picnics on the banks of Besse-sur-Issole Lake, her mother and father chatting and laughing together in the living room, Robert removing a splinter from Marthe's finger and then kissing it to ease her pain, and many more scenes of discreet tenderness between her parents.

Disturbed by the present, Jeanne didn't even want to think about the future. Was she wrong to so desperately want to save an estate that her own mother and brother didn't seem to care much about at all? What about her youth? Why was she wasting it here? Why didn't she do like Sylvie and enjoy the life of a young woman?

In mid-December, she decided to accompany her cousin to Marseille.

"At the same time," she said, "I'll deliver some nougat."

She'd received three orders over the previous two weeks, which exceeded her most optimistic expectations. It was true that her nougat was uniquely delicious. Black or white, it was presented in a pretty bag with a golden ribbon that gave it a festive look.

Before walking into the busy candy store, she gazed through the window at the chocolate, the *calissons*, the frozen chestnuts, and the candied fruit. The smell of vanilla hit her nostrils as she made her way to the counter. There stood Ms. Pascale, the manager, who asked Jeanne to leave the package in the back room.

"You're going to have to bring me some more next week," Ms. Pascale said. "Mostly black. . . . "

The success of her operation made Jeanne feel less weary. Life was getting a bit more joyful, and it was with enthusiasm that she walked with Sylvie down the Allée de Meilhan where, each year, the Santon Christmas Fair took place.

Amid a good-natured atmosphere, people gathered in front of stalls and tables to admire the painted terracotta figurines that made up the nativity scene.

The event was the legacy of a certain Jean-Louis Lagnier, who, at the end of the eighteenth century, created a character he could reproduce endlessly with a mold. Others imitated him, and the makers of those little figurines, known as *santonniers*, set up shop not only in Marseille, but Toulon, Aix, and Aubagne. Soon, their creations, at once realistic and poetic, became part of the region's Christmas tradition, and in people's homes there stood little statues of maids, millers, midwives, and representatives of other professions and trades practiced in Provence.

"Mama asked me to buy a priest," Sylvie said. "The cat broke ours yesterday."

She leaned over a small boy to examine a cluster of figurines on a table.

Captivated by this miniature universe, Jeanne hesitated before selecting a kneeling couple and a spinner holding a distaff. Then she decided to add a cleaning lady carrying a basket filled with clothes, as well as a rural policeman. She was about to pay when the silhouette of a man caught her attention. Régis! Her heart began beating faster, but then the man turned around, and the mirage vanished. She'd never seen the man standing there before.

"Your change, miss," the salesman repeated, handing her a few coins.

"Right . . . " Jeanne said. "Thank you."

She turned to Sylvie, deflated. All she wanted to do now was run to see Régis.

"I just realized I left a package at Ms. Pascale's that wasn't meant for her. I'm going to go get it. Why don't we meet in front of the Palais de la Bourse at five?"

Without thinking about it further, she hurried to board a streetcar that dropped her about a hundred yards from the Cuvelier Soap Factory.

She was greeted there by a worker.

"Mr. Régis just left to go see a customer," said the girl, wiping her hands on her apron. "But you might try the tobacco shop down the road. He often stops there."

On the street corner, Jeanne recognized Régis's car.

Stepping out of the shop, Régis said, "Jeanne! What a nice surprise to see you! What are you doing here?"

"I wanted to thank you," Jeanne said.

"Thank me for what?"

"For helping me out. You've been a blessing, you know. Thanks to you, I've actually started making money."

"That hat looks nice on you," was Régis only reply as he gazed at Jeanne.

"Really?"

"Do you want me to drop you off somewhere?"

"The Old Port."

On their way there, they only talked about superficial

things, and Jeanne chided herself silently for once again hoping for the impossible, until Régis said, "I'm not sure if you should have come by today, but—"

Defensively, Jeanne interrupted him.

"You wish I hadn't?"

"Quite the opposite."

"Then why haven't I seen you for such a long time?"

"You ask too many questions."

If Jeanne had been letting Régis dominate her up to that point, she wasn't anymore. Why should she behave like a little girl with a man who seemed to enjoy embarrassing her? Why was she so afraid of letting him know that she'd miss him? Everything at that moment became clear to her, especially her own desires.

Leaning toward Régis, she said, "Kiss me."

As he hesitated, she added, "What, you're not interested?"

"How can you say that!" he said.

Régis's embrace was devoid of tenderness, but she didn't care. She concentrated on her own sensations as their tongues mingled. How long did they remain like that, in a car that passersby tried to ignore?

"Stay with me," Régis said, as she moved toward the car door.

"I can't. Someone's waiting for me. . . . But let's see each other again soon. . . . Wherever you want."

"Come over to Hyères tomorrow afternoon."

With winter's arrival, the villa had lost its vegetation, particularly its flowers, but Jeanne didn't care about that, just as she didn't care about the cold in the living room. It was there that she found Régis kneeling before the hearth, lighting a fire.

"I'm sorry, it's freezing in here. I just arrived."

Jeanne said nothing. She walked over to him, bent down to lean against his shoulders, wrapped her arms around his body, and kissed the back of his neck. He pressed himself against her, and soon they were rolling on the floor, undressing each other. Shivering under Régis's fingers as they caressed her breasts, she discovered the pleasure of being touched and of touching someone else, as Régis quickly told her what he liked. Naked against him, she was fascinated by the texture of his skin and the pure bliss that the contact with his body brought her. That was until pain overwhelmed her. Régis had suddenly turned into some sort of predator brutally imposing his will. Then he rolled onto his side and, apparently forgetting about Jeanne, tried to get his breath back.

Absentmindedly, Jeanne grabbed her coat off the floor and covered herself with it. Then, eyes fixed on the fireplace, she came to grips with a reality that was vastly different from the idyllic scenario she'd imagined these past few weeks. She slowly turned to Régis. He was sleeping. Jeanne got up to wash away an act that had lost all its luster. Shivering, she went upstairs, where she found the bathroom. Looking at her own pitiful reflection in the mirror, she hated herself for being so naive. How could she have been so stupid to actually expect vows of love from a man who didn't care one bit about her? Back in the living room, she was surprised to see him awake smoking a cigarette.

"Where were you?" Régis asked. Then, opening his arms, he added, "Come over here."

Pressed against his chest, Jeanne's mood softened.

"Are you in such a hurry to leave me?" Régis whispered.

Then, impervious to time and all else, Jeanne abandoned herself to pleasure. The only thing that mattered to her was the ecstasy she was now experiencing with her lover, away from everyone and everything, in this house that had become their secret haven.

11

IN THE NEXT FEW days, Jeanne's mood kept swinging from euphoria to doubt and back—euphoria in the time leading up to seeing Régis and doubt as soon as they were together. What were his true feelings for her, she wondered? So many times she wanted to ask him, but pride and timidity prevented her from doing so.

"You're hiding something from me," Sylvie told her.

"What are you talking about?"

"Don't try to lie to me. I can read you like a book."

Jeanne hesitated to confide in her cousin—not that she didn't trust Sylvie, she just felt like keeping her affair a secret. But, finally, she did discuss the more pleasant aspects of her relationship with Régis.

"You're so lucky to be in love!" Sylvie exclaimed. "If only it could happen to me, too!"

"*Lucky* . . . Is that the right word?"

Sylvie didn't pay any attention to Jeanne's comment. She was already talking about the upcoming engagement, preparing her trousseau, and, even, in veiled terms, the wedding night.

"Of course, you guys have kissed."

"Yes, but . . . "

"Is it the same as in novels?"

How many times since they had been teenagers had they imagined their first kisses? They had talked about it endlessly, with Sylvie being both thrilled and stressed at the very idea of kissing a man. Now, sitting on Jeanne's bed, she shivered vicariously.

"How I'd love to meet a man who'd steal my heart," she said. "There was that botanist who went to Asia with Laurent . . . "

"Don't you talk to me about him!"

In spite of the letters she received from Laurent in which he praised Jérôme Guillaumin's qualities, Jeanne would never forgive him for being the instigator of a trip she considered so dangerous. That opinion had only been reinforced when she learned that her brother had caught malaria in Darjeeling.

Jérôme Guillaumin wrote to Marthe about it: *After a critical phase during which I didn't want to alarm you, I can now promise you that your son is on the road to recovery.*

"We have to force Laurent to come back home as soon as he's well enough to travel," Jeanne had said.

She felt terribly guilty at the thought that while her brother was struggling against death in India, she was in the arms of Régis.

"How are we supposed to do that?" Marthe said in an angry tone. "He never listens." Then she added, "No one listened to me when I opposed his proposal to travel around the world, and now it's too late."

Rosalie was in the living room as the conversation took place, and she almost broke down crying with worry over Laurent. If, after all this time, his absence had stopped being so painful as when he first left, what she'd just heard reopened the wound.

"What's the matter?" her aunt asked later in the day. "You're dragging your feet."

Anger filled Rosalie's heart. Would she have to hide her feelings and continue to serve others for the rest of her life? The sight of Apolline's crooked back and her gnarled hands after all those years devoted to the service of the Barthélemy family reminded Rosalie of what she did not want to become. But how could she escape this trap she was in, this unacceptable fate that seemed to be in store for her? If Laurent didn't want her when he came back, would she have to settle for some laborer who'd never be able to provide for her properly? Augustine, Annie—they, too, were the incarnation of what Rosalie fiercely rejected.

Up before dawn, the two women dipped their pieces of bread in chicory and then, warmly dressed, their heads wrapped in scarves, they made their way to the olive groves that were slowly emerging from the darkness. The harvesting of green olives was over, and it was now time to pick the violet ones. Men set wooden ladders against the trees and, with small rakes, combed the branches to make the olives fall down into nets or large bedsheets spread across the ground. François, Augustine's brother, worked with a speed that was the envy of many. Agile, he went up and down his ladder faster than anyone else and picked over four hundred pounds of olives daily.

"He's going to break his back one of these days," Annie said, warming her hands over the brazier. "And I wonder why he's working so hard. We get paid the same no matter how much we pick. What's he doing with his money anyway? He never goes into town. At his age, that's not normal!"

Nobody knew that François was planning on giving Rosalie a Christmas present.

In total secrecy, he made his way to Brignoles, where he hesitated between a sewing box and a mirror with a handle decorated with white mother-of-pearl. He finally picked what he considered to be a woman's indispensable item, one that would enable Rosalie to gaze at her own beauty.

But as Christmas Eve approached, François grew more and more worried. Would Rosalie laugh at him and his present? Should he give it to Augustine instead? Circumstances helped him make up his mind.

He was coming back from the warehouse in which the olives were stored before being shipped to the cooperative, when he heard someone cursing and the sound of broken glass coming from another storeroom. There he saw his brother-in-law trying to snatch the broken bottle out of Rosalie's hand. Her blouse was torn, leaving no doubt as to what was going on.

"This time," Joseph said, slurring his words, "you're not getting away from me."

"If you come any closer," Rosalie said, "I'm going to kill you!"

"You think I'm scared of you?"

As he spoke, Joseph walked toward his prey. Just then François jumped Joseph and began pounding him with his fists, missing half the time. The two men fell to the floor and rolled around, fighting. If Rosalie hadn't smashed the bottle on Joseph's head, he would have choked François to death.

"He's bleeding," she said, looking at Joseph, lying at her feet.

She turned to François, who was trying to catch his breath.

"What if he's dead?" she said.

"Don't worry," François replied. "It'd take more than that to kill the bastard. You only knocked him out."

"You think?"

As she spoke, Rosalie was trying to cover herself.

"What are we going to do now?"

François thought about it. He loved his sister too much to tell her the truth about her husband. But how was he going to explain the bruises he'd sustained during the fight?

"Don't stay here," he finally told Rosalie. "And don't say anything to anyone about this!"

With weak knees, François went over to the fountain, filled a pail with water, and came back to the storeroom to empty the water on Joseph's head. The man grunted and began moving and then opened his eyes. He seemed totally lost for a moment, and then his memory came back to him. He tried to get to his feet. His head weighed a ton.

"You son of a bitch," he mumbled at the sight of François. Clumsily, he tried to get a hold of the young man. "You're going to pay for what you did," he said.

"No, I won't, Joseph. You leave me alone, or I'm going to tell Augustine everything."

"Oh, yeah? You do that, and we'll see what happens to you after."

As his mind became clearer, Joseph couldn't believe that it was François standing there in front of him. His brother-in-law had always been so mild and restrained.

"What's gotten into you?" he said.

"And don't you touch Rosalie ever again," François said.

"What, you're in love with her or something?" Unable to hide his jealousy and bitterness, Joseph added, "What would she do with a loser like you? You think she'd be interested in an orphan who's got nothing in the world to his name?"

Confused and angry, François walked away from Joseph without a word. Night had fallen, and it was cold out. Still, he didn't want to join the others. Leaning against a wall, his fists balled in his trouser pockets, he looked up at the stars. Nothing since his birth had been easy for him, but he continued believing that one day his efforts would be rewarded. And tonight, he was clinging to that belief. . . .

In the farm workers' quarters, everyone sat around the table, waiting for the soup to be served. Augustine was knitting. Tomorrow, she would leave Restanques to spend three days in the Basses-Alpes region, and the thought of being with her children lessened the sadness Joseph was causing her by being so mean-spirited all the time. She even had the impression that he was avoiding her. Had he ever loved her? A feeling of despair overwhelmed her as she realized she would never enjoy a normal family life. How much longer would they have to live away from home? That afternoon, Jeanne had given her a few items for Christmas: a bar of nougat, some cookies, a block of sheep's cheese, a head of celery, a few figs, and a bottle of wine, everything wrapped in a white towel. Augustine raised her eyes as François walked into the room. He looked sad, and there was a welt on his cheek.

"What happened to you?" she asked.

"Some idiot opened a door right in my face," he grumbled.

The two brothers-in-law didn't say a word to each other throughout the entire evening. Still, no one noticed the tension between them. As she did every night, Rosalie served everyone a meal. Many times, François tried to meet her gaze.

"Rosalie," he called out as the young maid crossed the courtyard on the way to her room.

"What is it?" she said.

"Well, I wanted to ... "

Rosalie was holding an oil lamp, and François could see the irritation on her face.

"I have a present for you," he finally blurted out.

"A present!"

"I hope you like it. But let's go over there. People could see us. . . . "

He showed Rosalie to the laundry room, then handed her the box wrapped in pink paper.

"Why are you giving me this?" Rosalie asked. "We hardly know each other."

François stood back and watched her set her lamp on a table, rip the wrapping paper open, and struggle with the box before taking out the mirror.

"It's pretty," she muttered, raising the mirror to her face.

Not daring to move, François enjoyed Rosalie's presence and took in the details of a scene he'd imagined many times, the two of them together. Unfortunately, a sound coming from outside broke the spell.

"Put out the lamp!" he told Rosalie.

In darkness, he could smell her, a mélange of soap and freshly cut grass.

"Rosalie," François said, "I . . . "

"Phew! They're gone!"

Had she interrupted him on purpose? He fumbled for his lighter, and soon there was light in the room.

"This was very nice of you, François," Rosalie said, holding up the mirror. "You shouldn't have."

Spontaneously, she walked over to him and kissed his cheek like he was an old friend.

"Really, I didn't expect this. Thank you. And thank you for earlier. I don't know what would have happened if not for you."

As soon as she left, François felt more alone, more helpless than ever before in his life. Rosalie obviously had no feelings for him whatsoever.

A bunch of snoring men awaited him when he walked into the large room he shared with other farm workers. Without taking off his clothes, he fell onto his cot and, face buried in his pillow, cried like a child, his dream having been shattered. Rosalie would never be his.

Jeanne was not looking forward to the holiday season. She worried about Laurent's health and Restanques' future. Typically, a tall Christmas tree was set up in the house, but the property remained devoid of decorations. Only the nativity scene served as a reminder of a holiday that the people of Provence celebrated with their families.

Respecting the tradition, Raymond Delestang invited his

sister and niece for supper at Entrecasteaux. This would be followed by midnight mass.

The fireplace was filled with logs that Michel would light in the early evening. In front of the hearth stood beautiful porcelain plates filled with wheat grains and lentils. Sylvie draped everything in cheerful red ribbons.

The nativity scene was the pride of Angélique Delestang. Over the years, she'd collected an entire village of figurines. Next to a miniature river, sheep ate grass while dogs climbed a hill made of cardboard covered with green moss. An elaborate lighting system illuminated the houses, the stables, and all the other buildings. Everyone looking at this work of art felt like a kid again. Jeanne, won over by the magic of the decorations, set her presents at the foot of the Christmas tree, then walked over to admire the table covered by an immaculate cloth. They would enjoy an elaborate meal before heading to the church. Three candles burned in silver candlesticks on the table, and thirteen small myrtle breads had been set between the plates and the carafes in which the house's best wines were waiting to be tasted.

Marthe, wearing a crepe de chine dress with sleeves decorated with velvet knots, sat to the right of her brother, while Jeanne sat to his left. Michel was facing them, flanked by Angélique and Sylvie. At the end of the table, a cover had been set for the poor person who, perhaps, would knock on their door, as Christmas was also a time to give to the less fortunate. The atmosphere was festive. They ate spinach omelets with garlic and parsley, and then fried fish with an eel stew, cabbage au gratin, artichokes with a pepper vinaigrette sauce, and leeks. This was followed by dessert, an assortment of walnuts, almonds, hazelnuts, and dried figs, as well fresh grapes, oranges, dates, and mandarins piled in beautiful bowls and surrounded by flowers. Jeanne brought some nougat, which everybody loved. Even Marthe, who until now hadn't complimented her daughter on her work, said that it was delicious.

"You should be proud of your daughter," Raymond said. And, in a mean way, he added, "She inherited her father's qualities."

"What about my qualities?" Marthe said, insulted.

"Come on!" Angélique said. "You two aren't going to fight this evening, are you?"

"Aunt Marthe," Sylvie said, "would you like a piece of cake?"

She winked at Jeanne, but her cousin's mind was wandering.

How was Laurent doing? She imagined him by himself—weak and almost certainly sad to be away from his family for the holidays. She remembered the Christmas Eves they shared together as children, wrapped in blankets, struggling not to fall asleep so they wouldn't miss any part of the magical evening.

In church, the ceremony helped Jeanne find an inner peace. The priest stood in front of the altar and spoke to the congregation. In the crowd, Jeanne spotted the teacher who'd taught her how to read, the Delestangs' maids, and their sharecropper. All seemed happy and proud to sit on the benches that their forefathers had occupied. Turning around, she saw René Verdier a few rows back, looking prim. At the end of the service, he went over to Marthe and whispered a few words into her ear. She replied with a young woman's smile. Embarrassed, Jeanne mingled with the other worshippers. People came to her, wishing her a Merry Christmas and a Happy New Year. In spite of this, she felt lonely. She had no choice but to admit to herself that she was missing Régis. It had been days since she'd seen him, and the silence, the emptiness, left her hopeless. Accustomed to reaching the goals she set for herself, Jeanne felt completely powerless when it came to her relationship with Régis. Was it even a relationship?

12

JEANNE LOVED WINTER DAYS when the sun shone brightly. She loved them even more when Régis would take her to an inn on the coast, where they would have lunch before heading upstairs to the room he'd rented. The memory of those afternoons would burn inside her until their next rendezvous, which was always arranged at the last minute, forcing her to accomplish great feats to free herself. But nothing could prevent her from seeing her lover! In his presence, the smallest things in life were like a feast: the cry of the seagulls, the smell of fire coming from tall chimneys, the sea breeze, the fruity taste of wine and cassis. She was charmed by Régis's laughter and couldn't resist his words when, as they made love, she sometimes experienced moments of apprehension. Still, she had the feeling that he wasn't taking their relationship seriously. He asked about her work but nothing that was personal. She waited several weeks before talking to him about it.

"Do you have any idea who I really am and what I care about?" she whispered as they drank coffee on the terrace of a café in the village of Lavandou.

Surprised, Régis asked, "What's that all about?" He peered into Jeanne's eyes and added, "Is something the matter?"

"I'm wondering about things. . . . "

"Why don't you just enjoy the moment? Isn't it nice, here, right now, together?"

"Not really."

"Well, we don't have to stay."

He was fishing for some coins to pay for the bill when Jeanne said, "This is much too easy, Régis. I'm mad at myself for accepting the way things are between us. For days and days I don't hear from you, and when you finally feel like seeing me, I just come running."

"No one is forcing you."

Stunned by his words, Jeanne felt like slapping him.

"You're right," she said finally.

"Come on, Jeanne, you're being ridiculous. Calm down and show me that I wasn't wrong in thinking you weren't like the others."

"What do you mean? They're not at your beck and call all the time?"

Régis tried to grab Jeanne's hand, but she didn't let him.

"What am I to you?" she said, wishing she could be more indifferent.

"I thought it was obvious that I like you."

"That's all?"

"What more do you want?"

"Nothing. You're right."

Régis stood up and, in a calm manner that Jeanne envied, dropped a bill on the table.

"I'll take you back now," he said.

Standing next to Régis's car, Jeanne felt distraught, confused. Things had gone downhill so fast.

"Régis," she said, "try to understand where I'm coming from."

"You're too complicated."

"Maybe."

Régis walked over to Jeanne and, putting his arms around her, asked, "Has the storm passed?"

While they kissed, she wondered if things would always be this way. Would she always experience this sense of insecurity, this feeling of frustration?

As they did every time they saw each other, Régis dropped Jeanne off in Brignoles, where she took a bus to Cotignac. As she got out of the car, he hesitated between relief and regrets. Jeanne was asking for something he couldn't give her since he didn't believe in love—only in pleasure. . . . As for marriage, he was incapable of seeing it as anything but a contract sealing a partnership. By bringing feelings and emotion into the institution, the Judeo-Christian culture had altered its original meaning, and the women Régis met were hoping for a miracle. Nothing made him want to run away more than eyes filled with love, or romantic declarations. Though he thought he was very upfront, most of the women Régis dated wanted to marry him. His family pestered him about it as well.

"It's high time you started a family of your own," his mother kept saying.

Once, she even added, "Your father doesn't have long to live. Don't you want to give him the joy of having grandchildren?"

Descendants! Since his sister Colette's death, he was the only one who could grant his parents this wish that bordered on obsession. But how could he do that? What he wanted was to be single and free, an attitude that was considered terribly selfish.

"That way I won't suffer," he said to justify himself.

When his parents had returned from the clinic his sister had been rushed to and told him she had died, Régis's world collapsed. Ravaged by sadness, he kept thinking about Colette, the big sister who had always been so alive and joyful. When she passed, he promised himself he would keep from becoming attached to anyone. And, until he met Jeanne, he'd managed to do so. Why did Jeanne have to remind him of his sister? It was troubling him.

It was early evening when Régis arrived in Aubagne. Henriette was waiting for him at a café. They'd planned on going to the movies and then meeting up with some friends. Maybe they'd go dancing. His relationship with Henriette required little effort on his part other than being nice to her, as their families had known each other for generations. Henriette's grandfather had made a fortune in the marine transport industry, and he'd helped Régis's father when the soap factory went through some difficult times. Régis's father then sold some of the company's shares to Henriette's grandfather.

"She's a great fit for you," Régis's father often said.

Each time, Régis simply shrugged.

If Henriette had any thoughts of getting married, he would've avoided her. But thankfully she, just like him, only cared about having fun.

"We're going to miss the start of the movie," she said as soon as Régis arrived. "Let's go."

Tired, Régis would have preferred to have a drink, but she insisted.

In the car, she spotted a compact at her feet and picked it up.

Before Régis had time to do anything, Henriette read the initials engraved in the metal box.

"*JB* . . . Those aren't you mother's initials!"

"That's right."

"So, someone forgot it."

"Looks like it."

"We're going to have to get it back to its owner."

*   *   *

Jeanne was not thinking about her compact when she got home. Her mother, sitting in the living room, greeted her with an enthusiasm that was unusual.

"I was waiting for you to have some tea. Where were you?"

Jeanne didn't answer. She sat in an armchair as Marthe poured the tea.

"I have some news," Marthe said, concentrating on her task. "I hope you're not going to be too displeased . . . "

Jeanne remained silent, which didn't make things any easier for Marthe.

"You know how lonesome I am . . . "

"Yes . . . "

"Well, I've had an offer to get married again . . . to Mr. Verdier."

"Verdier?" Jeanne said. "Are you out of your mind?"

"Not at all. He cares for me, and I enjoy his company."

"Have you looked at him? He's a vile, vulgar man!"

"How can you say that?"

"Ask anyone. Uncle Raymond, for example. . . . "

"I certainly won't. He never takes my side."

"What about Laurent? Have you considered how he's going to react to this?"

"Why would I bother with that when he only cares about himself?"

Absentmindedly, Jeanne took the cup Marthe was handing her. She was suddenly very cold. Her mother was forgetting all about her dead husband to be with a man they knew nothing about, except for the fact that he clearly had his sights set on Restanques. She turned to the window and, seeing the branches of an olive tree dancing in the wind, memories flooded her. She could hear her father's voice. She could imagine him walking the groves. Was it possible that Marthe had already forgotten about him—his elegance, his big heart, his wonderful spirit, his kindness—to enter a shoddy relationship?

"So he asked you to marry him?" Jeanne asked.

"Yes."

"And you said yes?"

"That's right."

"Well, there's not much to add, is there?"

Marthe simply nodded.

"Where are you going to live?" Jeanne asked.

"Bel Horizon."

"I thought you hated that place."

"I never said that. Besides, we're going to travel a lot. He promised to take me to Paris soon."

"He's that well-off?"

"He inherited from his wife."

"Nice, and now you get to enjoy that money."

"Jeanne, your tone is unacceptable!"

"My tone is unacceptable? What about your behavior! Have you even imagined the shame we're going to feel having Mr. Verdier as our stepfather? As for the rest, I hesitate to bring it up."

"Say what you have to say."

"What kind of marriage contract are you going to sign?"

"That's none of your business!"

"Everything that has to do with Restanques is my business since I'm responsible for it."

"If it will make you feel any better, you won't have to take care of the olive groves that I own."

And so, what Jeanne had feared was happening. René Verdier was taking over Restanques and, ironically, he hadn't had to spend a cent on it. All he'd had to do was pretend to be in love with a woman who craved romance. The olive groves that Marthe owned were among the estate's most prolific and profitable. Made up of centuries-old trees, they always produced a great amount of high-quality fruit.

"It's going to be impossible to keep this house if we can't count on that revenue," Jeanne said.

"Well, you and your brother can sell it."

"What about all the work Father put into it?"

Jeanne wiped away the tears streaming down her cheek.

"Well, someone else will be able to make the estate even better and more profitable with the kind of money we don't have."

Glaring at this woman who'd given birth to her, whom she loathed more and more, Jeanne could feel her world crumbling around her. Why had she bothered respecting the past and traditions? What had been the point of putting so much work into Restanques all these months?

As she went up to her room, Jeanne imagined René Verdier moving into the house where generations of Barthélemys had lived. Walking by the linen room filled with her ancestors' trousseaus, she stopped and opened the door. Inside the large wardrobes lining the walls, bed sheets, tablecloths, and quilts told, in a way, the story of a family who, from one marriage to another through the ages, had never betrayed Provence. Spindles of lavender wrapped with white ribbons made everything smell wonderful, including the underskirts and camisoles that had belonged to Eglantine, Jeanne's maternal grandmother. She'd died when Jeanne was nine years old. Tonight, Jeanne remembered how, without ever raising her voice, the old lady ran the house with an iron fist. Velvet netting had held up her hair, and she always had a gold cross with white pearls pinned to her dress. Never hiding her preference for Jeanne, Eglantine had passed on to her granddaughter her love for the estate that she and her husband had, throughout the years, cared for with a passion. How many times had they both walked around Restanques hand in hand? At that very moment, Jeanne could feel the fingers of the small woman who'd taught her the love of the wind and the birds, how to appreciate good food, how to act properly, how to choose her words when it was time to speak. Eglantine also passed on to Jeanne her inner strength and her love for life. That, at the present time, was what prevented Jeanne from capitulating even though she felt all alone in the world. Who could she count on from now on? Her lover and her brother, the two men she felt closest to, were both only interested in moral or physical escape, while her mother had lost all common sense. All Jeanne had was the memory of those who'd passed on: her grandmother, her father, Barnabé the sharecropper. Those people had cared deeply about Restanques. Sometimes Jeanne had the odd feeling that they were protecting her.

A faint noise made her turn around. It was Rosalie walking into the linen room, arms filled with a pile of towels. She was looking at Jeanne with a stunned expression.

"Ms. Jeanne! Do you need anything? Or . . . Oh, you're crying!"

"Don't worry, it's nothing."

Rosalie set the towels down on a table and walked over to Jeanne, who broke down crying and took refuge in the maid's arms. For a moment, they were close again, just like when they were little girls playing with dolls and making up stories.

Then something snapped inside Rosalie, and she could no longer hide the sadness she'd kept to herself since Laurent's departure. She, too, began crying.

"My God," Jeanne muttered when they both began to calm down. "What is wrong with us?"

"I don't know," Rosalie said, blowing her nose.

She and Jeanne looked at each other and then burst out laughing.

When they finally stopped, Jeanne said, "There's really nothing funny about it."

And they laughed some more.

"It does feel good," Rosalie managed to say.

When was the last time either one had laughed so hard?

"You know," Jeanne said, "things aren't so serious. Life gives, takes back, and gives again. In the blink of an eye, what you thought was going to be there forever disappears. We cry, and then we forgive and forget. Things get back to normal, and we wonder why we suffered so much."

13

RAYMOND DELESTANG TRIED TO reason with his sister. What was she thinking, marrying a man with less education than she had, someone who might only be in it for financial gain?

"Jeanne pitted you against me," Marthe said. "She's jealous because I'm getting married and she still hasn't found anyone."

Mother and daughter were trying to see as little of each other as possible. It wasn't very difficult, as their schedules had always been different.

"I never would have believed that Mrs. Marthe could do such a thing," Apolline said to Fanny. "To forget about her poor husband so quickly! I just can't believe it! What's going to become of us? Miss Jeanne won't be able to manage this place all by herself forever. . . . "

Refusing to be a prophet of doom, Jeanne continued to live up to her responsibilities without trying to guess the future. The olive trees had been trimmed, and soon it would be summertime. Since the sales of nougat proved successful, Jeanne planned on repeating her efforts. But what would happen when she lost her mother's olive groves after her wedding?

She'd written Laurent about their mother's decision, and she was hoping that he'd receive her letter before he left for the temples of Angkor in Cambodia.

"He absolutely has to come back," Jeanne told Rosalie, who couldn't agree more.

Jeanne would have loved to talk to Régis about her situation, but unfortunately, he'd never been more distant.

After he cancelled a date for the third time, Jeanne decided to write him: *If you don't feel like seeing me anymore, I'd appreciate you letting me know.*

When she didn't get a response, she asked Michel.

"I haven't seen Régis for more than a month," he said with a sheepish expression. "I've heard he often goes up to Paris on business."

"How often?"

"I don't know."

"What is it you don't want to tell me?"

"I don't like mingling in other people's business," Michel finally said, "but I wish you weren't attached to him. He's not the right man for you."

"You're probably right, but somehow I can't convince myself of that."

"Listen, Jeanne, it's best you should know. He's not free. Remember Henriette?"

"Yes."

"He's going to marry her."

"Marry her! How long have you known about this?"

"Two weeks or so. He didn't tell me himself, but people know about it. They talk about it."

Jeanne now had to believe in the law of cycles. For the past two years, bad luck had affected every facet of her life. She felt as though she were walking on quicksand. The sadness she felt to hear of Régis's betrayal quickly turned to anger. How could she have been so incredibly naive, so stupid! Memories came back to her, small things she hadn't paid attention to that now made it all so obvious. From the very start she'd been second fiddle. For a while she was tempted to go over to Régis's and smash everything in the house to pieces, but then she thought better of it. It would lend him too much importance.

"Are you mad at me for telling you the truth?" Michel whispered.

"No. It's better this way."

She now felt utterly empty, but at the same time, it was as though a thorn had been lodged in her heart.

"You need to have some fun," Sylvie told her later. "Come with me to Aix. The Guillaumins are having a ball for their daughter's, Nicole's, eighteenth birthday."

"But I hardly know her!"

"Don't worry! I'll ask them to send you an invitation, and they'll say yes. After all, your brother is on that trip with their son. . . ."

Jeanne, with her cousin's help, settled on black lace for the seamstress in Carcès to use for her new dress. She enjoyed nothing more than the fittings, during which she could pretend to be a fashion model.

"The sleeves are a bit too long," Ms. Lucie whispered as she plucked pins from the cushion on her arm.

Ms. Lucie had been dressing Jeanne since she was a little girl. Jeanne remembered the silky fabrics and wool that turned into magnificent clothing, which she exhibited with pride. Every visit ended with a glass of orange juice and hard candy. Jeanne felt at peace with herself in this doll's house where time stopped. She liked the smell of the place, a mixture of floor polish, vanilla, flowers, and the wicker mannequins that had belonged to the dressmaker for ages.

"A little bow below the breasts would be nice," the seamstress said. "Don't you think?"

With great precision, she adjusted, she corrected, and little by little, the fabric began to mold her client's body.

As Ms. Lucie worked her magic, Jeanne saw herself in the mirror and thought she looked worn and a bit gaunt. Was it because of her worries? Was she just tired?

"Your first ball," Ms. Lucie said. "You'll see, you're going to remember every detail for the rest of your life!"

The Guillaumin family lived in Aix. Their home's windows and balconies were decorated with a multitude of candles.

In the front yard, jugglers and mimes greeted the guests. They amused Jeanne and relieved her of some of the stress she was feeling.

The hosts waited for everyone in the vestibule. As a society woman, Suzanne Guillaumin was all smiles as her guests entered the house. Her husband, Bernard, was more reserved, but his dark eyes were kind. Nicole stood beside them, and her transformation surprised Jeanne. Wearing an embroidered gown and pearls, she looked like something out of a fairy tale.

"We received news from Jérôme yesterday morning," she told Jeanne. "They're in the Himalayas waiting for the rhododendrons to bloom, and then they're going to head for Angkor."

People filled the living room. Under the chandeliers and candelabras, the youth of Aix gathered, assessing each other, chatting, and laughing. Debutantes, young military men, future captains of industry, and politicians came to the Guillaumins', each dressed to the nines in search of a lifelong partner.

"A meat market," Jeanne muttered to herself as she observed some girls her age batting their eyelashes at dapper young men. In the background, mothers made plans and enjoyed the romance of the evening vicariously through their daughters.

Jeanne left Angélique and Sylvie Delestang, and began wandering from room to room until she wound up in the library. A photo of Jérôme on the desk next to an inkwell

DOMINIQUE MARNY

attracted her attention. Against her better judgment, she was
intrigued by the sight of the man she'd decided to hate. There
he was posing on the beach, and his expression exuded a self-
confidence that she envied. A memory came back to her: the
two of them in the Restanques library surrounded by books.
Jérôme had talked about birds, his attachment to Provence,
but also of his insatiable curiosity for the outside world.
Jeanne had realized then that Laurent could only thrive in the
presence of this unique, disconcerting man who had grown
up in this charming house.

As she leaned toward the picture, Jeanne heard a man's
voice.

"Oh, I'm sorry."

Turning around, she saw a man of thirty or so watching
her with an amused smile.

"My name is Antoine Laferrière," he said. "I'm a friend of
Jérôme's."

"Nice to meet you," Jeanne muttered.

"We were in the same squadron during the war. Since we
were both from the same region, we became friends quickly. I
live in Aix. What about you?"

"In Cotignac."

"It's known for good figs, isn't it?"

"And good olives," Jeanne said. "And good almonds, too."

Bursts of laughter came from the hallway, and then a
young woman opened the library's door and barged in, followed by her beau.

"We'll have privacy in here," he said, just before becoming
aware of Antoine and Jeanne's presence.

"This is actually a pretty popular spot," Antoine said. Seeing Jeanne head for the exit, he added, "But it's all yours for
now."

When dinner was served, Antoine managed to sit next
to Jeanne. Without understanding why, he found himself

attracted to her in a way he'd never experienced before. For him, love at first sight was something that happened in silly romance novels. But now . . . Jeanne's chestnut hair was held up by a rose garland headband that highlighted her pretty face and her bright, dreamy eyes. She seemed to be amused by what the man sitting on her other side was saying, some oaf wearing glasses. When Antoine saw Jeanne laugh and tap the man's wrist with her fan, he felt a pang of jealousy.

The temperature and volume both rose during the meal. Perfectly executed, it was a succession of dishes that honored Provence. Satisfied by the way the evening was unfolding, Nicole was looking forward to blowing out the eighteen candles on her birthday cake in complete serenity. She'd been looking forward to this evening since she was a little girl, and if things hadn't gone perfectly, she would have been terribly upset. In the candle's halo, she could see all the gathered guests—people who, for a variety of reasons, had links to her family. Some childhood friends and a few old classmates were there dressed like royalty, enjoying themselves, trying out their powers of seduction. On the sidelines, widows and women too old to marry tried consoling themselves with an abundance of sweets. They enjoyed the party's excitement, forgetting that once home they'd have to return to the heavy solitude that was theirs day in and day out.

As soon as the musicians resumed playing, couples headed for the main living room, where mirrors endlessly reflected bouquets of roses, lilies, and white tulips. The man who'd been sitting next to Jeanne led her to the dance floor. In a frenzy of sound and movement, she enjoyed her first cotillion. Breathless, she went along with the rhythm imposed by the dance, with its fun and complicated figures. Then there were waltzes, fox-trots, and some more waltzes, and time flew for everyone except Antoine Laferrière, who, sipping champagne, was waiting for a quiet moment to approach Jeanne.

He followed her to the greenhouse, where she'd taken refuge to rest for a minute. Sitting on a wrought-iron bench, she was fanning herself when he whispered, "I wanted to ask you to dance with me, but you're a very popular gal."

"What a beautiful spot," Jeanne answered, looking at the plants surrounding her.

"It's all Jérôme's work."

Against the murmur of a fountain and around basins in which golden carp slowly glided, foreign and tropical fragrances created an aromatic universe at once poetic and stimulating.

"He asked his parents' permission to build this greenhouse," Antoine said, "and every time he travels, he brings back rare plants."

"It's like being in a dream," Jeanne whispered.

Through every pore of her skin, she felt the intensity of this declaration of love to nature. She marveled at the exuberance of the trees, the plants, the cacti, the flowers, and the vines that mingled to form a personal and enchanting work of art.

As Antoine Laferrière set a chair beside the bench on which she sat, Jeanne noticed his beautiful hands. Elegant yet masculine, they contrasted with his stocky physique. He looked like most men in the South of France: thick brown hair, tanned complexion, and dark eyes. He vaguely resembled Régis, but with a more sophisticated demeanor.

"You look sad," he said.

"No, no . . . "

"You're not a very good liar."

After a brief pause, he added, "I'd love to see you again. Could I call on you in Cotignac?"

"Yes, maybe."

"Please, don't be so noncommittal. When could I come by?"

For a moment Jeanne was tempted to tell Antoine to forget about it, but his eager expression prevented her from doing so.

"I'll have more time after Easter."

Back in the living room, she ran into Sylvie.

"Where were you? I've been looking for you. Mother wants to leave."

In the hotel room they shared, the two cousins chatted until dawn. There was so much to talk about—what they'd seen that evening, how they'd felt, what they'd appreciated, what they'd disliked . . .

"Have you heard of a certain Mr. Laferrière?" Jeanne eventually asked.

"Of course! He came to the house last year. Nicole was also there that day. I actually thought she had a crush on him. Why are you asking me? Did he flirt with you?"

"Sort of."

"Tell me. . . . "

"Well, it's nothing much."

"You find him attractive?"

"No."

"Too bad! He's a catch."

"What do you mean?"

"His father was the head of one of the biggest law firms in the region. After he died, Antoine Laferrière took over."

Sylvie offered more details, but Jeanne heard none of them. Régis's face had replaced that of the young attorney in her mind. Why hadn't he been with her this evening? Why wasn't he there now? That was what she wanted more than anything in the world, to love Régis and to be loved by him just as much.

14

FOR SEVEN WEEKS, JEANNE worried she might be pregnant. Waking up each morning, she'd scan her bed sheets for the bloodstains that would have reassured her. Not being able to tell anyone about her fears, she spent sleepless nights wondering how she would handle this ordeal. Keeping the child was out of the question, so she wondered about Rémy's concoctions. There was also the abortionist that Augustine had seen, but Jeanne was scared for her life. Of course she hadn't heard anything from her lover, but even if she'd seen Régis, she wouldn't have told him about the situation. Blackmail was no way to keep a man, Jeanne believed. Doing such a thing was at odds with her concept of love.

Others, including Henriette, had no qualms about using such tactics. They were prepared to do anything to find husbands. Though never admitting it out loud, she'd long ago decided that one day she would bear Régis's name. To that end, she'd worked hard pretending that she was different from other women who dreamed of starting families, that she only wanted to have a good time. She was quite convincing, to the point where Régis believed her.

"It's the dream of dumb rich girls," she said every time Régis complained about women's fixation with marriage.

Finding the compact in his car had forced her to change her tactics and behavior. *JB*! She'd been right to be suspicious. Régis was seeing Jeanne Barthélemy, and the girl was a dangerous rival. Ready and willing to take any risk, Henriette went to bed with him as often as she could. She quickly became pregnant and wasted no time telling her mother about it. The woman cried and wailed and cursed her daughter but then took charge of things. If Régis Cuvelier wanted to avoid a huge scandal and public disgrace, he would do the right thing, and Henriette's mother was going to do everything in her power to make it happen. Hiding her glee, Henriette savored the victory but didn't feel so confident after talking to Régis about the situation.

"A kid?" he said, stunned. "Are you sure?"

"Positive."

"I hope you didn't tell anyone about this."

When Henriette didn't answer, he insisted: "Tell me!"

"My mother knows," Henriette said.

"Why the hell didn't you talk to me first?"

"I was confused. . . . I was scared to tell you. . . . "

"Listen, Henriette, you and I don't want that child. It'd be insane for you to give birth to it."

"You know how religious my parents are. They'd never go along with that."

Régis's face turned crimson, and he paced across his office. Nothing worse could have happened to him. Henriette, pregnant!

"You told me I didn't need to worry!" he shouted.

Aware that his fate had taken a drastic turn, he thought about his future. Stuck with a woman he didn't love, he'd soon be a father, a nightmarish scenario he'd always wished to avoid. He had no way out, though, except to break off all ties with his family. And that he couldn't do.

"I'm so sorry," Henriette kept saying.

Stunned, Régis looked at his future wife. What was he going to do? He imagined her fat from the pregnancy, breast-feeding a newborn—Henriette, who only cared about having a good time and flirting! It was like a bad joke! If only he'd stayed away from her!

"Régis," she whispered, "I promise that nothing is going to change. You're going to have the same freedom as always."

"How can you use that word while you're forcing me to do everything I despise?"

Over the course of the next few days, the two families met. The wedding had to take place soon. To their daughter's dowry, Henriette's parents added a house in Marseille. Not once did anyone ask Régis for his opinion. He had no say in anything. For a moment, he felt like storming out of the room, but at the sight of his father, so sick and weak, he changed his mind and decided to calm down. After all, it was a business transaction as much as anything else, and he figured that a forced marriage would save him from any union based on love.

The image of Jeanne came to his mind all of a sudden. Should he answer the letter she'd written him a few days before? He always preferred silence and flight over explanations.

In Cotignac, the church bells rang out to announce the widower's wedding. Wearing a carnation boutonniere, René Verdier stood at the altar as Marthe Barthélemy, led by her brother, walked toward him.

Sitting in the first row, Jeanne watched her mother who, in an off-white satin dress, was about to marry a man no one knew much about, if anything at all. From that day on, she'd be the only Barthélemy living at Restanques. She was relieved by the thought, as the atmosphere in the house had become downright oppressive. She tried to pray during the ceremony, but two words kept haunting her: *pregnancy* and *money*.

The mass came to an end, and the villagers crowded the church's square to watch the newlyweds. Verdier was puffing out his chest, while Marthe Barthélemy was all smiles. Most were puzzled by this second marriage, and they congratulated her with false enthusiasm.

A lunch was held at Bel Horizon. In Verdier's house, Jeanne saw some of the furniture that Marthe had brought over from Restanques, robbing it of some of its charm.

Just before they sat at the table, René Verdier came over to his stepdaughter and, before Jeanne could say anything, planted a kiss on her cheek. It felt like acid.

"Consider this house your home," he said in a sugary tone.

The meal went on and on. Under the disapproving gaze of Raymond Delestang, the master of the house kept placing his pudgy fingers on Marthe's hand, as if to draw attention to her new, shiny wedding ring. At the end of a lengthy discussion, Raymond had convinced his sister to keep her finances and property in her own name. Still, as long as she lived, her husband would have full access to all she possessed. Raymond's gaze fell upon Jeanne. She hadn't touched her food. Should he try to convince her to get rid of an estate she wouldn't be able to keep in the long run? That was, in any case, Angélique's opinion. She wished their niece would come live with them.

"At her age," she kept saying, "it's not right for Jeanne to be by herself in that house."

Right or not, Jeanne wasn't thinking about that now. She'd made an appointment with a doctor in Toulon to find out if she really was expecting. But three days before the appointment, she'd had her period. What a relief! The sky was blue again, and she no longer felt like she was carrying the weight of the world on her shoulders.

Easter weekend was fast approaching, and the world would be coming back to life. At Restanques, Apolline opened all the windows in the house to let in fresh air. Seeing her, Jeanne had the idea of going up to the attic to see what furniture and other things she could find among the items that had belonged to Marthe before her first marriage. In a cloud of dust, she discovered tall armoires, china cabinets, a desk, a flour grinder, and seven Regency chairs. She also found china from Apt and from Marseille, pottery from Anduze, and large baskets containing floral afghans that, once cleaned and ironed, looked awfully nice. With the help of the maids and some of the workers, she moved a number of the items downstairs, returning the house to its old atmosphere. Once spring cleaning was done, everything smelled of beeswax and lavender, and the living room and dining room were ready to welcome visitors. The first was Antoine Laferrière, who arrived in early April.

Jeanne had asked Sylvie and Michel to be there as well. She thought that the visit was going to be a chore, but it turned out to be quite pleasant. The attorney was bright, and he had a good sense of humor. But just the same, Jeanne wished he wouldn't look at her so intently, as she'd felt uncomfortable with men ever since her breakup with Régis. Sipping lemonade, she listened to Antoine as he told Michel about his passion for planes and his regret at not pursuing a career as a pilot for a commercial company at the end of the war.

"I miss flying terribly," he said. "It was such a thrill when we took off."

"You were heading for danger," Sylvie said.

"That's true, but the view from up there, the sound of the engines, the speed of the planes . . . I'll never forget the intensity of it all."

"People called you the Knights of the Sky . . . "

Without the war, there never would have been such a rapid development of aviation and, with that, the opportunity for young men to be trained as pilots. Antoine could recall the image of the countryside surrounding the Champagne castle that housed his squadron. The harsh winter of 1917 had enabled them to skate on the frozen pond, and he still kept a picture of the two dogs that had served as the squadron's mascots in his wallet. Never before or after had he experienced such brotherhood, such communion while carrying out a mission. . . .

"Twice, Jérôme saved my life," he said.

At the mere mention of his name, the room filled with Jérôme's presence, which annoyed Jeanne. War hero, expert botanist, loyal friend—the man seemed to possess every desirable quality.

"Without his intervention," Antoine continued, "I wouldn't be here right now chatting with you. He risked his life to shoot down the German planes that were chasing me."

"He never told us about that," Sylvie said.

"He's not the bragging type! For a man of his stature, he's very modest."

As the sun was about to set, Jeanne suggested they visit the garden. At that time of year, everything was starting to blossom with exuberance. Walking around an arbor covered with mauve Chinese wisteria, they headed for a basin lined with iris whose petals wavered between blue and violet. Jeanne loved such subtle tones. The pink of the Judas trees and the lilacs were like a hymn to spring. With eyes half-shut, Jeanne enjoyed the ambient fragrances and the coolness of the air. Antoine couldn't stop looking at her.

If he'd been attracted to her at the Guillaumins', he was now captivated by the combination of strength, femininity, and energy that the young woman exuded. The stylish yellow percale dress she wore gave her a modern look. Jeanne was a shining example of the new type of woman who'd held the country together as the men fought at the front. While some complained about the evolution, Antoine was all for it. He had no use for a relationship based on inequality. Jeanne had walked over to a honeysuckle bush to smell it, and when she turned back to face him, she smiled. It took everything for him to keep from taking one of her hands and kissing it.

"I have to leave," Michel said as they reached the rose garden.

Jeanne wondered if he was leaving to meet up with Régis and their group of friends. It seemed like it by the way he was dressed. She imagined them together in Hyères, in the gorgeous villa she'd visited, playing cards and listening to the gramophone. Régis would prepare everybody's favorite cocktail. After dinner, they'd no doubt dance. Henriette would wear her engagement ring and, with some of her girlfriends, discuss the wedding, which was not far off. Maybe Henriette would even tell them about their honeymoon destination. Venice? Naples? Feeling tears coming to her eyes, she turned around rapidly, and her dress got stuck to a rose bush.

"Here," Antoine said, "let me help you."

With calm and precision, he untangled the fabric from the thorns.

"There. . . ." he said. "And you didn't tear anything."

Yes I did, Jeanne wanted to say. *My heart. . . .*

15

FROM THE HOUSE'S WINDOWS, Jeanne could see the olive groves. Symbols of peace though they were, they were tearing her and her mother apart. Never would she forgive Marthe for depriving the estate of its means of survival and, in spite of the repeated invitations from the couple, she refused to go to Bel Horizon.

"Mother doesn't really want to see me," Jeanne confided in Apolline. "She's inviting me just so people won't say she abandoned me."

Rosalie's departure had been an additional blow she hadn't seen coming.

"I can give you a raise," Jeanne told Rosalie when she heard she wanted to go work at Bel Horizon, "but you'd be crazy to turn down the salary my mother is offering you."

A few days later, the maid gathered her belongings, wrapped the mirror François had given her in her nicest half-slip, and then walked the mile that separated Restanques from Bel Horizon.

She began by putting the house in order, as it had been neglected by the slovenly looking maid who greeted her.

Mado was her name, and for a long time she'd been in the habit of doing as little as possible around the house.

"Mrs. Verdier isn't happy with my ironing," Mado said. "That's why she wanted to hire you."

Marthe hadn't changed her habits very much. Locked in her room filled with too-flowery perfume, she read fashion magazines and romance novels, waiting for her husband to come home from work. Sometimes they went for short trips to Draguignan, Brignoles, and down to the coast.

"What about Paris?" Marthe said. "You promised!"

"We'll go in June. I told you that already."

But June came, and there was no preparation for a trip to the capital.

"I can't leave the estate. I've got too much work!"

"Ah, René, I heard that same excuse for years and years."

"Come on, don't be upset. You know I only want what's best for you."

Pouting, Marthe pretended like she was going to leave the room, but, contrary to his usual behavior, René didn't try to run after her and kiss her. She took a piece of hard candy from a crystal bowl and munched on it nervously. Things were going to be just as dreadfully boring here as they had been in Restanques, she told herself. How could it be any other way when you lived in the shadow of your husband? Her entire existence was based on idleness. Marthe was some sort of parasite that waited for someone to pay her some attention to come to life.

Not only did René Verdier realize this, he'd taken advantage of it to achieve his own ends. Crossing the olive groves that would soon maximize his earnings pleased him to no end. He would finally reach social recognition. Forget about the shoes that were either too small or too big and the worn-out clothes that the parish had given him when he was little. Forget all about the baiting and bullying from the other children who had scorned him for his clothes and his bald head, shaved for fear of lice. He knew nothing of his father. No doubt René's existence in the world was the result of some one-night stand. As for his mother, she'd been a traveling washerwoman. To ensure he wouldn't impede her freedom of movement, she'd put René in an orphanage and visited him every six months, and then once a year. He'd just turned fourteen when he learned of her death.

"You're not sad?" the nun asked René, surprised to see so little reaction at the news.

"Sad? Why should I be sad? I don't even know her."

After an apprenticeship with a blacksmith, he'd done his military service in Briançon. He was drawn to women, and every time he was able, he spent his meager pay in bordellos. But what he most enjoyed was observing the town's wealthy elite—how they behaved, what they wore. That was how he met Solange Fournier, an unattractive young woman, and the sole heiress to the rich owner of a large hardware store. The poor girl, who'd never been complimented by any man, put aside her pipe dreams of a Prince Charming to listen to the romantic declarations of an ordinary but eager man. Suspicious, Solange's parents warned her against him, but she wouldn't listen, and the young lady married René. A comfortable dowry enabled them to settle in a house downtown, and René began working in his father-in-law's store. The old man treated him harshly. René put up with the sarcastic remarks, while cursing Solange's infertility, which prevented them from appeasing Fournier with a grandchild. In spite of his lack of attraction to his wife, he continued to fulfill his conjugal duties and, in order to reward himself for it, enjoyed sultry affairs with women in the neighboring villages.

Years went by, and he continued playing the role of respectful son-in-law and devoted husband. In 1918, Solange died from the Spanish flu. René sold the house, as he wanted to get closer to the coast. In Cotignac, someone told him about Bel Horizon. He was ready to do anything to become the owner of an estate, including investing all his savings in buying land and restoring a farmhouse. The possibility of winning over Marthe presented itself just as he'd nearly run out of money. He used what little remained to charm her. He led her to believe that he was a wealthy man. He was also very considerate with her and managed to make her think that without him her life would be completely empty. But time was of the essence, as René was afraid that Laurent might come back. Influenced by that pain in the neck Jeanne, he might try to put an end to his plans. Once married, he felt much more at ease, though he still had to be careful thanks to that blasted separation of marital property that Raymond Delestang had demanded.

In order to iron things out after their argument, René went up to Marthe before dinner. He found her in their bed.

"I'm sorry," he said, walking over to her.

As Marthe remained silent, he knelt down beside her.

"I just want to see that smile of yours," he said.

Marthe turned to her husband.

"Please don't be mad at me," he whispered, his mouth against the side of her head. "The last thing I want is to upset you, but I feel responsible for Bel Horizon. And I have to do a good job managing what you have entrusted to me. When we do go to Paris—and we will, you know that—I'll devote all my time to you."

Marthe kissed René to make him stop talking.

It was now one year since Laurent had left. Still, there was nothing in his last letter about returning home anytime soon. He understood the difficult situation in which Jeanne found herself, he said, but as a prisoner of Angkor's beauty and mystery, he gave her carte blanche on decisions concerning Restanques.

"I'm going to give it one last try," Jeanne told Sylvie.

For a while now, she'd been thinking of making nougat

on a larger scale. The estate's almond trees were doing fine—much better than those at Bel Horizon, where they suffered from an infestation of green flies. Not only was Jeanne keeping all the almonds produced by Restanques, she'd also begun buying some from other producers and storing them. By September, she was ready to get to work in a larger and better equipped room.

In the meantime, with her presence, she encouraged the young women who split open the almonds as they sang:

> *Almond tree, you lovely thing,*
> *The first to bloom, you make hearts sing.*
> *A new year comes,*
> *Your white buds spring,*
> *My almond tree, you lovely thing . . .*

Though she still worked at the Verdiers, Rosalie went to Restanques as often as she could. Not only did she wish to show Jeanne that she wasn't abandoning her, she also hoped to get the latest news concerning Laurent. Would the day come when she'd think about him without feeling a pinch in her heart? There was nothing to hope for between them; she knew that. So why couldn't she turn her attention elsewhere?

On that early July evening, storm clouds were gathering, and she ran to Restanques to make sure she wouldn't get caught in the rain. On her right, a silhouette caught her attention. It was Augustine, who, arms filled with a heavy load of almonds, struggled to walk.

"Let me give you a hand," Rosalie said once she caught up with her.

"I'm okay."

"Come on. That's too heavy for you."

"Mind your own business, will you?"

"What's gotten into you?"

"What's gotten into me? Everything was fine when you

left to work for the neighbors. But that was too good to be true! You have to come back all the time to poke your nose into our lives. I'm sick of your little games with Joseph."

A large raindrop fell, then another.

"Come on," Rosalie insisted, "don't be silly. Give me that bag."

"Absolutely not!"

Stunned by the anger in Augustine's voice and eyes, Rosalie took a step back.

"I'd rather be struck by lightning than owe a favor to a whore like you," Augustine said.

"A whore? You're crazy!"

"I mean it. You've got your eyes on all the men, married or not!"

Lighting was now filling the sky above them, but as scared as she was, Rosalie refused to let it show to the woman who was insulting her.

"Joseph is never going to leave me," Augustine shouted. "Do you hear me? Never! So stop hitting on him."

"My poor Augustine, if you think that your Joseph needs any encouragement, you're terribly mistaken. He's the king of wandering hands."

The slap took Rosalie by surprise, stunning her for a second. But the slap she gave back was twice as hard. Scratching and biting each other, the two women rolled around on the ground, and anyone coming upon them at that moment would have seen a couple of hellcats with faces covered in mud. Younger and stronger, Rosalie soon had the upper hand.

Choking her adversary with both hands, she said, "Call me a whore again just to see what happens."

Then she let go of Augustine and staggered away from her. The storm was getting even worse, but she didn't dare join the workers in the dehusking room the way she looked. Deciding to hide in a barn and wait for the end of the deluge before heading back to Bel Horizon, she discreetly crossed the courtyard. As she was about to enter the barn, François came out of a room where he'd been sharpening his scythe.

"Rosalie?" he said. "What . . . "

Rosalie placed a finger on her lips so he'd keep quiet.

They took refuge in the barn, and looking at her, François whispered, "What happened to you?"

"I was in a fight with your sister. That bitch!"

"You're soaked, and you're shaking like a leaf!"

"No I'm not," Rosalie said, her teeth chattering.

"Come with me," he ordered, and guided her all the way to the back of the barn, to a small windowless room. There, he lit a candle.

Taking off his shirt, he said, "I'm turning around. Take off your blouse and put on this dry shirt."

As Rosalie did this, she had a hard time holding back her tears. Then, François took out the handkerchief he used to wipe his brow with during the day when the sun was strong.

"I'm sorry it's not too clean," he said, dabbing the young woman's cheeks.

Not used to such acts of kindness, Rosalie threw herself against François' chest and broke down crying. He didn't dare wrap his arms around her. He simply stood there, feeling Rosalie's soft hair against his chin. Little by little, she calmed down. He smelled of freshly cut grass and sweat, and his body was warm. He made her feel safe.

"Are you feeling better?" he asked.

She answered with a nod of her head. Outside, the rain was coming down with even more ferocity.

"I like to listen to the sound of rain hitting the roof," François said.

Rosalie smiled, turned around, and walked toward the wooden crate on which rested a pencil and a few sheets of paper. Letters had been written on the sheet she picked up.

"This is yours?" she asked.

"Yes. I come in here to teach myself to read and write. Nobody knows about it. Except you now. . . . "

"Is it hard?"

"It's not easy."

"Why do you do it?"

"Because I don't want to be ignorant my whole life. I'm interested in the sun, the stars . . . If one day I can manage to read, I'll be able to learn a lot more about them. What about you? Wouldn't you like to be able to read?"

"I don't think I could learn."

"I'd help you."

"Yes, maybe. We'll see. . . . "

16

WITHOUT HAVING SOUGHT IT out but because he proved himself an honest, conscientious worker, François was given an increasing number of responsibilities more important than picking fruit. Jeanne, who'd had the chance to assess his abilities over the past year, turned to him when anything unexpected came up. He worked long hours, slept little, and not only was he productive in the fields and groves, but he was good at calving and lambing.

"That boy," Apolline said, "is going to make a good foreman one day if he can keep it up."

"I agree," Jeanne said.

"You should hire him full time for the farm."

"Hire him! That'd be crazy!"

"What do you mean?"

"I've told you about our situation, Apolline. Who knows how long I'll be able to keep this place afloat. . . . "

"Exactly! By leaving the daily tasks to François, you'd be able to spend more time making your nougat business profitable."

It wasn't a bad idea. Jeanne thought it over and decided to give it a try. Stunned by the offer, François moved into a room

DOMINIQUE MARNY

that, though modest, was his very own, and his wages were the best he'd even earned.

Of course, the promotion made the people who didn't think much of François jealous. Not only did they stop speaking to him, they turned their backs on him when he showed up.

"Don't worry," Apolline told him. "They'll get over it."

The sadness François felt at being rejected by the others was tempered by the thought that Rosalie would now see him as a man of substance. Even though he didn't see her much, he couldn't wait for the opportunity to be alone with her again. Sometimes they just nodded when they passed each other, but he remembered every detail: the color of her skirt, a scratch on her forearm, a dent in her straw hat. He particularly remembered her expression, more or less pleasant from one encounter to another.

Rosalie, as a matter of fact, wasn't happy at Bel Horizon, and she cursed herself for accepting the Verdiers' offer so quickly.

In spite of her efforts, the house remained in disarray. Thrown here and there without care, the furniture she'd known at Restanques seemed to be waiting to be shipped somewhere else, and everywhere stood piles of folders and mail that hadn't been opened, as well as several items that the owners of the house seemed to simply refuse to put away.

When Mado found Rosalie washing the floors or dusting the furniture, she would say, "You shouldn't try so hard. They don't care."

"Maybe they don't, but I do!"

But Rosalie's hard work didn't influence Mado, who still did as little as she could. Nothing, actually, aroused any interest in her. All she ever did was stuff her face with food.

At the sight of Mado eating a particularly large amount of bread and cheese one evening, Rosalie asked, "Have you ever suffered from hunger?"

"Me? No. . . . "

Bit by bit, Rosalie had learned that Mado was from Martigues, where her father was a fisherman. The sixth of seven children, she'd grown like a weed. Her mother, more interested in her lovers than anything else, only thought of getting rid of her children. In the case of Mado, she planned on sending her to reform school. Aware of that fact and scared to death, the young girl escaped one summer afternoon, set on never coming back home. After wandering for a week, she wound up in Cotignac and ran into René Verdier. He was having a drink at the terrace of a café when he saw her get off a horse-drawn carriage. She had a dirty scarf around her head and wore a dress that was too short for her lanky, adolescent body. She looked around nervously. Verdier went over to her. What was she looking for? Work? Her timing was perfect!

What an odd decision it was to give the responsibility of keeping a farmhouse to a girl with no experience whatsoever, Rosalie thought. But then she discovered the true reason behind it.

Marthe Verdier was in town to get her hair done, and after her nap, Rosalie came down to the kitchen for a glass of water, when some noise coming from the office worried her. She'd assumed that Mr. Verdier was out and about, so there should have been no one in the house. Maybe there was a burglar in the office. Rosalie tiptoed toward the room and through the door's narrow opening saw René Verdier, his pants around his ankles, moving rhythmically against Mado as he clutched her exposed breast and said filthy things to her.

Rosalie was beside herself for the rest of the day. It was the violence of the scene that struck her, the things Verdier had been saying, and above all, Mado's submission to her boss. She was no saint herself, but Rosalie never would have considered her affair with Laurent to be anything like what she'd seen earlier that day. Never, until now! There were two ways for young men from wealthy families to lose their virginity: a bordello or one of the maids. Had she been a way for Laurent to become a man and nothing else? The memory she held in her heart of a real relationship between them began to disintegrate. It fragmented even more when, during dinner, she heard René Verdier tell his wife that he'd gone to the cooperative while she was at the hairdresser. Lies came out of his mouth with such ease. But weren't all men terribly good at inventing the reality that suited them?

On July 25, Rosalie made her way to Restanques to wish Jeanne a happy birthday.

"You're too late," Apolline told her. "She left."

"To Mr. and Mrs. Delestang's?"

"Yes, with that young man who's courting her."

Antoine Laferrière had arrived two hours earlier with a pile of books and a bouquet of red roses.

"You know my tastes well," Jeanne had said.

"I listen to everything you say with the utmost attention," Antoine said, laughing.

They'd seen each other many times since Antoine's first visit, and his feelings for Jeanne were just as strong, if not more so. He even thought of introducing Jeanne to his mother. But, for the time being, he simply enjoyed being with her. She was fanning herself gracefully, and the short sleeves of her lavender-blue dress exposed her tanned arms.

"Jeanne," he said in a low voice, "I don't know if I should ask you this, but I need to know. Is the idea of marrying me, one day, at all conceivable to you?"

"Marriage! We hardly know each other."

"Well, that could change if you would agree to see me more often."

"Look, Antoine . . . "

"It's okay, you don't have to explain yourself. . . . I get it."

Annoyed, Jeanne replied, "There's nothing to *get*."

Why was he ruining the day with a declaration she didn't

know what to do with? Peering into Antoine's brown eyes, she saw that happiness had fled from them.

"I'm sorry," she said, with a softer voice, "but this is all too fast. Give me some time."

"You're right," Antoine said. "But tell me one thing, just one. Is there a man in your life, someone you truly care about?"

"No," Jeanne answered, feeling like she was being dishonest.

But hearing about Régis's wedding had helped Jeanne get over the end of their relationship.

Three weeks earlier, an overexcited Sylvie had stopped at Restanques on her way back from Marseille.

As soon as she set foot in the house, she blurted out, "I ran into Henriette on the street. She's pregnant! At least six months!"

"That's impossible," Jeanne said. "They got married in April."

"Exactly! There must've been an emergency, if you know what I mean."

Stunned, Jeanne was unable to say another word.

"I can tell you one thing," Sylvie said, "she really caught him in her web. It explains Régis's silence, the way he disappeared on you."

Someone else hadn't hesitated to resort to the very blackmail that Jeanne had turned her back on. The worst of it was that the strong and mighty Régis had fallen for it, all in the name of morality and a sense of duty.

"Thank you," Jeanne finally muttered. "Hearing that will make it easier to get over him."

But even if today, as Antoine gazed at her longingly, she lacked any nostalgia for the past, she also didn't feel like she had the strength to be in a new relationship. Was it fear? A lack of attraction to the man sitting next to her in the car? In going to see the Delestangs with him, she'd tried to imagine

Antoine in the role of her beau, but she didn't feel anything inside. How much simpler everything would be if she had the same feelings for him as he did for her. She glanced at him. He had a pleasant face, and he inspired compassion and trust.

"I really like your region," he said as a golden light shone on the houses of the village of Entrecasteaux.

It was still hot when they arrived. Sitting under a lime tree, Michel was smoking his pipe. He got up to greet them.

"Happy birthday, dear cousin!" he said. Then he added, "Nicole Guillaumin just arrived."

"I didn't know you'd invited Nicole," Antoine said.

"She and Sylvie have become the best friends in the world," Michel said.

A table had been set on the terrace, next to a fountain. In honor of Jeanne, garlands of wild flowers surrounded the dishes containing her favorite desserts.

Jeanne kissed the woman she wished were her mother. "Aunt Angélique," she said, "you really are an angel."

The butler uncorked a magnum of champagne, and the dog, scared by the popping sound, barked until someone tossed a cookie its way. Sylvie arrived with a cake on which candles formed a crown of fire. Nicole was behind her, carrying presents for Jeanne.

"We're saving the best present for the end," she said.

Looking at everyone's expressions, Jeanne was intrigued and couldn't wait to see what it was.

"Laurent is on his way back," Nicole finally said.

"Laurent!"

"My parents received a telegram from Jérôme this morning. He got news that he was offered a position in Paris that he'd been dreaming about. Your brother, of course, is coming back with him. I had to tell you."

Jeanne felt as though she were in a dream. Laurent would be home! Like a little girl, she began to clap her hands with joy. The party became even more festive. The air smelled of freshly cut grass, and the sun bombarded the surrounding trees with its rays as it set. In treetops nearby, birds chirped away loudly. Laughing at something Michel said, Jeanne turned to Antoine and, furtively, touched his hand. The gesture didn't escape Nicole's attention, and it didn't please her one bit.

Through Sylvie, she knew about the young attorney's attraction to Jeanne, whom she considered a rival. Seeing their hands joined this way erased all hope she still had that Antoine would one day take an interest in her.

It was dusk when Antoine stopped the car at Restanques.

"I had too much champagne," Jeanne said, giggling.

They remained silent for a moment, Jeanne happy at the thought that Laurent was on his way home and Antoine gazing at her naked arm right next to his.

"Let's go up the alley," Jeanne said. "Walking a bit would do me some good."

After the stifling heat of the day, she enjoyed the cooler air of the evening. With her eyes shut, she took a deep breath and, listening to the rustling of the leaves, the birds in the trees, and the sounds coming from the buildings nearby, she felt in communion with this land of legends and fairy tales, of light and torrents, this Provence blessed by the gods.

Antoine walked over to Jeanne, and she rested her head against his shoulder. He put his lips on her cheek.

"I love you," he whispered.

Why did he have to complicate things? Everything was so pleasant, the two of them out there together, with the sensation of waking up from a long sleep. Why did he have to complicate everything?

17

SINCE SHE'D MADE THE decision to produce her nougat in greater quantities, Jeanne visited candy stores all over the region to take orders that, little by little, darkened the pages of the notebook she carried everywhere she went like some sort of talisman.

With pride, she walked around the work space she'd improved. Scrubbed vigorously by Apolline, the tools and utensils sparkled, and soon the smell of sugar and almonds would make everyone coming in salivate.

"That nougat is our only hope," Jeanne told Michel as they drove to Brignoles to run some errands.

Walking into the store of her first clients, the young couple that had taken a chance with her the year before, she realized how big of a challenge she'd taken on by starting a business she knew almost nothing about.

"Miss Barthélemy! My husband and I were talking about you just this morning, about your troubles."

"My troubles?" Jeanne said.

"Well, you know . . . your estate . . . "

"I don't understand."

"I'm sorry. I must be wrong then."

The woman seemed embarrassed.

"What have you heard?" Jeanne asked.

"That you've had some financial setbacks and that soon you're going to have to sell Restanques."

"Do you remember who told you that?"

"Yes. It was a man. He stopped in front of our window, and then he walked in to buy some pralines. We started to chat, and he asked me about our suppliers. When I mentioned your name, he told me to be careful because you were on the brink of bankruptcy."

Jeanne's heart was pounding. Who would try to harm her this way? Some competitor?

"What did he look like?" she asked. "Was he young?"

"He was in his fifties, I'd say. Not tall. Kind of fat. Not ugly, but not handsome, either. . . . "

"Did he have some gray hair?"

"You're asking too much of me, Miss Barthélemy! I can't remember!"

"It doesn't matter. I think I know who that charming individual is. And, I beg you, don't believe a word of that nonsense."

Verdier! No doubt he was the one trying to harm his stepdaughter. With her temples pounding and rage in her belly, Jeanne wondered what to do next. Should she go to Bel Horizon and confront Verdier directly? She decided to wait until she could gather more proof. Surely the candy shop in Brignoles wasn't the only place where he'd waged his insidious campaign of destruction. What was his goal? Was he trying to accelerate Restanques' downfall so he could buy it at the lowest price himself?

"If he thinks he can scare me or bring me down," Jeanne told Michel on their way back, "he's dead wrong. I'm even more determined now."

To that end, she doubled her efforts, and she displayed as much optimism as she could.

"I could've been an excellent actress," she said to Apolline.

The old maid nodded but remained worried. She said as much to Rosalie in secret.

"That snake in the grass . . . I'm not sure Jeanne can keep up with him. He's evil!"

"Since I'm over there," Rosalie said, "I can keep an eye on him. It'll be easy. He'd never suspect me."

She began to spy on Verdier, eavesdropping on his conversations. Twice a week he left Bel Horizon for business, and several times Rosalie found long hairs on his clothes after he returned. Marthe was unsuspecting, as her husband was always so kind and considerate. "Don't wear yourself out, honey," he'd say to her. "Let me handle things for you." All the while, his control over her estate increased daily.

As the important conversations between the Verdiers generally took place in their bedroom, Rosalie spent a lot of time putting away clothes in the adjacent linen room. For the past few days, René had looked tense. Things weren't going well at Bel Horizon, and instead of seeing his own inability to manage a farm operation, he blamed the others. How many workers had he fired only to replace them with even more incompetent ones? The olive harvest would soon begin, but the operation would pale in comparison to what Jeanne had established at Restanques. René took to locking himself in his office to drink while trying to find ways to become completely independent from his wife.

The maid cursed herself for not being able to read. What she could have uncovered in his desk drawers! It would have been so easy as he snored. A spy! That's what she had become. But in order to help out Jeanne and, even more so, Laurent, she was ready to do anything.

Since learning that Laurent was on his way back to Restanques, Rosalie was her old energetic self again. She sang along with the others as they husked almonds, and she laughed for no reason.

"You're awfully cheerful these days," Apolline told her.

"Summer is almost here!" Rosalie replied.

François also noticed Rosalie's mood change. But, unlike the others, he knew why. Rosalie was thrilled because Laurent would soon be back. Didn't she realize that such a long trip would almost certainly have made him a different man? François himself felt different, even though he'd never left Provence. Every single day, working at nature's behest reminded him that things should not be rushed and that what was meant to happen would always occur at just the right moment. If he and Rosalie were supposed to be together, their union would happen naturally. If not, there would be someone else, a young woman he knew nothing about who would cross his path. And it would be much more than just random chance. If someone had told him such a thing just a year ago, François would have dismissed it as foolishness. But his latest reading had also contributed to his changing views, as well as the lessons he was now taking on a regular basis with a teacher.

"Soon he's going to recite his own poetry to us," Joseph said, mocking François.

"Leave him alone, will you?" Augustine said. "He's not doing anything wrong."

The fig harvest had begun. As soon as the sun rose, François sent out the pickers, who worked until eight in the evening.

Augustine and Annie made sure to wear long-sleeved blouses, as fig leaves could wreak terror on the skin. With throngs of midges buzzing around them, they tried to forget about the tips of their fingers. In order to preserve the fruit's stem, each picker had to cut it with the nail of his or her thumb and index finger, and soon the pain became nearly unbearable. When their baskets were full, they emptied the contents into crates that a boy then hoisted onto a cart that took the figs to Cotignac. There, Mr. Broutin, the broker, weighed and stored them in a warehouse in huge wooden barrels until winter, when they'd be shipped out to jam producers.

Jeanne was counting on the profits from the fig crop to replace some of the farm equipment. The roofs on the barn and stables also needed fixing.

"Money goes out of our account as soon as it comes in," Jeanne said with a sigh.

Aware of the situation, Antoine tried to convince Jeanne that with him, she'd find protection and assistance. She listened to him and appreciated what he had to offer, but she couldn't help but forgot all about him as soon as he wasn't in her presence.

Tired of saying no, she finally agreed to meet Antoine's mother in Aix, in a spacious and comfortable house.

Dressed in black, Mrs. Laferrière greeted her in a living room that exuded old-fashioned charm. Her white hair was held up in a chignon, and she had bright, amber eyes.

"Good afternoon," she said to Jeanne, a bit coldly.

Antoine offered Jeanne a seat, and she felt that every movement she made might trigger some sort of derogatory comment after she left. An awkward conversation followed.

"My son tells me you live in Cotignac," the old lady said. "I often went there when I was young. It's a beautiful region."

As they traded banalities, Jeanne took in the stuffy and expensive environment that Antoine's mother seemed to enjoy. She noticed the heavy velour drapes in the windows, the busy wallpaper, and the knickknacks everywhere, as well as the many photos of a man who must have been Antoine's father.

"And this estate you're taking care of," Mrs. Laferrière said, "it must be a burden for someone your age."

"I don't have any choice."

"Are you optimistic about things?"

"I have to be."

"I understand you're living alone."

"My brother is going to return soon."

Jeanne was offered a cup of tea. More and more ill at ease, she wondered what she was doing in this house where, obviously, she wasn't welcome.

"It just seems odd to me that a proper young woman should live like this," Mrs. Laferrière said.

"Live like what?" Jeanne snapped back.

"Come now, young lady . . . Don't get angry."

"I am angry," Jeanne said, "and I'm leaving."

She grabbed her handbag and gloves.

Antoine rose to his feet.

"What is it, Jeanne?" he asked.

"It's your mother. She decided, even before meeting me, that I wasn't worthy."

"That's not true. You're wrong!"

"No, I'm not," Jeanne said. Turning to Clotilde Laferrière, she added, "Have a good day, madam. . . . "

Then she walked out of the room.

Antoine ran after her and blocked her way before she reached the front door.

"I beg you . . . It's a misunderstanding. . . . If you care about me just one bit, don't leave. . . . Not this way."

"Just so that things are clear between us, you should know that I'm never going to bow to any hypocritical bourgeois conventions. Your mother dreams of a docile young woman for you. That's not me."

"I don't care what my mother thinks."

"So why was it so important for me to meet her, then?"

Antoine looked so sad that Jeanne felt tenderness toward him for the first time, and she caressed his cheek. Still, the gap that had existed between them was now wider than ever.

Life's hardships had taught her to be independent, to refuse to play other people's games, and she insisted on being accepted for who she was.

"Let me go," she told Antoine.

"Antoine!" Mrs. Laferrière called out from the living room.

Antoine took Jeanne's hand and led her to the street.

"I'll walk you to the train station," he said.

"You don't have to. Besides, I feel like walking around town a bit."

"I'm going with you."

They wound up sitting on the terrace of an ice cream shop. Jeanne's face was still red from anger, and her eyes shone bright.

"Jeanne," Antoine said, "why are you always trying to hurt me? What's the point?" Without giving her the chance to answer, he added, "It's as though you were trying to punish me for something someone else did to you. Am I wrong?"

Caught off guard, Jeanne hesitated before saying, "I'm not trying to punish you, but I can't pretend to be someone I'm not. . . . "

She leaned toward him and spoke softly. "Antoine, open your eyes. I'm not the right woman for you. I need freedom, responsibilities."

"But you'd have responsibilities."

"Yes, whichever ones you chose to give me."

"You could have anything you wanted. I swear!"

She knew he was being sincere, but unfortunately he didn't trigger in her the sort of fervor and passion that Régis had. Antoine was a kind man, a nice man, someone without a fire inside. And Jeanne, full of contradictions herself, was scared that she'd be bored to death with him.

18

JEANNE WAS STILL UPSET from her encounter with Mrs. Laferrière when she arrived home. There, she found Sylvie leafing through a magazine.

"As soon as I learned the news," she said, "I came over to tell you about it. Régis . . . "

"What about Régis? What news?"

"Henriette had a miscarriage two days ago."

"No!"

Henriette began feeling the pain in the middle of the night.

"I told you not to eat so much of that chocolate cake," Régis mumbled, half-asleep. "But you wouldn't listen, and now you have indigestion. You asked for it."

Henriette woke him up again half an hour later.

"It's not indigestion," she said. "We have to get the doctor, and my mother."

The house turned into a hospital. Henriette's water broke. She was six-and-a-half months pregnant, and the child's chances of living were nonexistent. With the help of a midwife, the doctor delivered a baby that was taken away immediately.

When everything was over, the doctor went to Régis's office.

"It was a girl," he said.

What did the young man feel at that moment if not complete emptiness? His existence, which he already considered to have little meaning, now seemed even emptier.

"How's my wife?" he asked.

"She's resting," the doctor said. "But you can expect her to be very depressed when she fully appreciates what happened."

Régis drank brandy until dawn and then went over to Henriette's bedside, completely drunk. Weary, she opened her eyes and shut them immediately at the sight of her husband. His hair was sticking to his sweaty forehead, and his expression was the same as when he came home after a night out carousing. If only she could sleep for hours, months, years, to forget about her failed marriage and the loss of her child.

The midwife had tried to console Henriette, saying, "Please, don't cry. You're a young woman. Soon you're going to have me over for another baby."

Another baby! In order for that to happen, Régis would have to treat her as his wife, not some nuisance. As soon as they'd married, their relationship had become difficult, if not unbearable. Their honeymoon in Sicily had turned into a nightmare. Under a variety of pretexts, Régis would disappear, leaving Henriette alone and bitter. How long would he make her pay for the pregnancy and what followed? She could see in Régis's eyes that he resented her for having duped him. Now that she was no longer carrying their child, she thought of divorcing Régis. She wanted to be in a relationship with a man in love with her. But her parents would never accept a divorce! A victim of her own scheming, she was now the one feeling trapped.

From her bedroom window, she could see the bougainvilleas dancing in the breeze, and far out on the sea, a continuous flow of liners. How she wished she could leave this depressing room and set out to discover the world! Far from her hometown, her mingling family, and her horrible husband, maybe she'd regain her love for life.

"Régis," she said the first morning she came down to the dining room for breakfast. "I've had a lot of time to think. Things can't go on like this."

Régis didn't try to hide his surprise. He folded the newspaper he was reading and said, "What you're saying makes sense. What do you suggest?"

"I have an old friend from school who invited me to spend a month in Biarritz. I'm thinking of accepting her invitation."

"You don't have to ask me permission for anything."

"I'm not asking for your permission! I just wanted to let you know that from now on, I'll make sure we don't have to spend too much time under the same roof."

"That sounds reasonable to me," Régis said.

Henriette stared at her husband and fully realized that his rancor was such that he had no compassion for her whatsoever. Holding back her tears, she stepped out of the room without saying anything else.

Régis was relieved when Henriette left the house two weeks later. At last he'd be able to come and go without meeting his wife's sad gaze. Contrary to what she thought, he did care about Henriette's situation. Since he disliked living in the house that his in-laws had forced on him, he decided to spend a few days in Hyères.

It was early September, and the days were getting a bit cooler. He sat in the garden, in the shade of an umbrella pine. He tried to unwind, to forget about his demanding work and the tumultuous events of the past few months. Soon, he felt like seeing people. Many of his friends had taken Henriette's side. He thought of Michel Delestang, who'd remained neutral through everything. Why not visit him in Entrecasteaux and play some tennis?

"Mr. Delestang is on the terrace," the butler said when Régis showed up at the house.

"Is he by himself?"

"No, with members of his family. Mr. Barthélemy is back from his trip."

"My timing is bad, then."

Régis was about to leave when Sylvie came down the staircase, a camera in hand.

"Mr. Cuvelier!" she said.

Someone was behind her: Jeanne. At the sight of her, Régis's embarrassment gave way to a feeling of delight. Taken by surprise, he tried to make eye contact, but what he saw in her face was scorn, which put a damper on his enthusiasm.

Sylvie took pleasure in the awkward situation.

"You can't go, Régis," she said. "Please, join us."

Jeanne left them to meet up with Laurent.

Sitting on a bench next to Angélique, he was reacquainting himself with his roots. He'd arrived at Restanques in the late morning, as Jeanne emerged from the workshop where she made her nougat.

"Laurent!" she'd shouted when she saw him. "We weren't expecting you until the end of next week."

She'd laughed nervously and had hugged him a long time. Then she'd muttered, "My God! How you've changed!"

He'd gotten taller, bigger. His face had matured, his eyes shining with amusement at having taken Jeanne by surprise.

As she watched him now, Jeanne realized that her brother's transformation wasn't only physical. Laurent had become a man of action, someone who had a much broader view of the world than before.

However, he'd told his aunt, "I feel like I left only yesterday. Everything looks the same. Maybe my trip was just a dream?"

He rose to greet Régis Cuvelier. Though he knew nothing

about what Jeanne had lived through while he was away, Laurent did notice that his sister was purposely avoiding Régis.

Swept away by the traveler's stories, Régis was beginning to relax. He listened to Laurent talk about lands he'd never visited himself: Darjeeling in the heart of the Himalayas; the endless tea fields; the snow-capped peaks whose summits were in and out of the clouds according to the winds; the city of Kalimpong, where Tibetans came from the surrounding mountains to sell musk, gold, and gems; the roaring mountain streams; the orchids . . . The city of Angkor was particularly fabulous. There, stone and the jungle merged to honor gods whose centuries-old serene faces made men bow in silence. It was odd, under the darkening Mediterranean sky, to discover these faraway, exotic places by virtue of Laurent's words. He knew how to captivate an audience, and Jeanne was won over by the magic of her brother's recollections. He regularly mentioned Jérôme, praising his human qualities, as well as his knowledge.

"Jérôme taught me rigor and patience. He also showed me how to look beyond appearances and always double-check my assumptions."

Before leaving, Régis went over to Jeanne.

"I'd like to talk to you."

"What do we have to say to each other?"

"I was stupid and—"

"Come on, we're not going to go back to that old story. All that is dead and gone."

"Really?"

"Absolutely."

Even though her heart was beating rapidly as she uttered the words, Jeanne meant what she said. She'd felt a pinch in her stomach when Régis showed up, but now she found herself indifferent to the man whose attention she'd craved so desperately. No doubt she'd been in love with the qualities she'd bestowed upon him, creating an image that was deformed by her own desires. As for Régis, he seemed to have regrets. Now that Jeanne no longer wanted him, she was interesting.

She came back to Restanques before dinner, with Laurent a bit dizzy from drinking champagne.

The farm's courtyard was the scene of the usual end-of-day bustle: the milking of cows in the stable, the grooming of the horses, and many other tasks that the workers had to perform before mealtime. Spotting Laurent, François let go of his wheelbarrow, wiped his hands against his pants, and walked over to the young Barthélemy.

"Good evening, sir," he said.

"Good evening, François. I hear you've done well here since I've been away."

"Just doing my job, sir."

In the afternoon, Jeanne told her brother all about the difficulties the estate was facing, the choices she'd been presented with, and the decisions she'd made.

"Poor Jeanne. I had no idea you had so many worries."

In spite of his expression of concern, Laurent seemed distracted to Jeanne. No doubt he'd need some time to get used to being back home.

They were walking by the dehusking room as Rosalie came out.

"Rosalie!" Laurent said.

Saying nothing, she stared at him while Jeanne, in a hurry, headed for the house.

"I didn't think I'd see you," Laurent said. "Jeanne told me you're working for my mother now."

"That's right, but I come every night to help the girls dehusk the almonds."

"Good! That means we'll see each other again soon."

She'd waited all this time, had cried so much, just for this banal reunion? Watching him stride toward the house, she hated herself for having hoped for the impossible. Did he even remember losing his virginity to his maid? Walking like a robot, she returned to the dehusking room and, impervious to the passing time, liberated the fruits from their shells until her pain turned to numbness.

"You have to go say hello to Mother tomorrow morning," Jeanne told her brother after dinner.

"Don't worry, I'll be a good son. . . . " Then, to himself, he mumbled, "Funny not feeling anything for the woman who gave birth to you."

"I've told myself the same thing many times," Jeanne admitted. "Mother is like a stranger to me. I have a hard time believing that we're family. But let's talk about Verdier instead. He must be furious you're back."

"Jeanne, I have to tell you something. I'm not going to stay at Restanques."

"Are you telling me you're going on another trip?"

"Not exactly."

"Tell me what you have in mind! I don't understand!"

"I'm going to settle in Paris."

"You're going to work there?"

"I hope so."

"With Jérôme Guillaumin?"

"I wish, but he has nothing to offer me right now."

"So why do you have to be away from here?"

Laurent began pacing in the living room.

"I fell in love with someone on the boat," he blurted out, "and I want to be with her!"

"God!"

"She's an actress. She was coming back from a tour in Egypt."

Feeling as though she were in a bad dream, Jeanne uttered, "How old is she?"

"Twenty-five."

"And she's interested in you?"

"Thanks for the compliment."

"I didn't mean anything. . . . "

"At first she was more into Jérôme," Laurent said.

"What about him?"

"His mind was on other things."

"Laurent," Jeanne said, "please come back to earth and don't rush into anything. Maybe it's just a crush, you know?"

"Are you kidding me? She's the woman of my dreams! She's beautiful, she's nice, funny . . . and she loves me."

"That quickly!"

"We spent a lot of time together on the boat. It's a long trip, you know."

"Where is she right now?"

"In Marseille. I'd love for her to come up here so you can meet her."

Unable to sleep, Jeanne tossed and turned in bed, thinking about the day's events. Régis . . . Laurent . . . The two men for whom she would have given her own life had, for different reasons, betrayed her. The first by preferring another woman over her, the second by completely turning his back on the family estate she'd tried to keep afloat as much for him as for herself. Her bedroom window was open, so Jeanne could hear the wind caressing the lime tree's leaves and, once in a while, the hooting of an owl. Fleetingly, she thought about Antoine, who was ready to risk everything, including a falling out with his mother, in order to marry her. Wasn't he the ideal solution since he was willing to help her run Restanques? Maybe she should settle for a marriage of convenience. . . .

19

ROSALIE WAS SHAKING OUT a dust rag over the balcony's railing when Laurent arrived at Bel Horizon. From above, she watched him hand over his horse to the groom, straighten his tie, and head for the house's main door.

Mado opened it and showed Laurent to the living room, where he was met by René Verdier. After giving Laurent an overly enthusiastic hug, Verdier displayed a tremendous interest in his trip to Asia.

"Ah, travel! I envy you."

"I thought you were just attracted to our region."

"I mean when I was young. At your age, I dreamed of traveling the world. It must be thrilling."

"It is."

"You must've been disappointed when you learned you had to come back earlier than expected."

"No. I'm actually glad to be home."

Verdier's disappointment was obvious to Laurent.

"I missed Restanques," he added.

"Your poor sister has had to deal with an awful lot this past year. You have to admit that it was a very heavy responsibility for a young woman."

Marthe showed up, filling the room with the sweet perfume Laurent had hated ever since he was a little kid. He turned around, facing a woman with an overdone hairdo and a pink lace dressing gown that a woman half her age would wear.

"You lost some weight," was the first thing Marthe said.

And you look older, Laurent wanted to say, but he held his tongue.

Everything in the room seemed surreal to him: the tacky décor, Verdier's fake enthusiasm for everything, his mother's appearance.

She sat in an ugly armchair and told Mado to get some tea. Turning to her son, she said, "You could've brought me some from Darjeeling."

"I didn't think about it," Laurent said, realizing he'd left at Restanques the small statue of Shiva he'd meant to give his mother.

"It doesn't matter," René said. "I'll buy you some in Marseille, in that English shop you like so much."

Fifteen minutes or so had passed since Laurent's arrival when Rosalie came to tell Verdier that a wine merchant wanted to see him.

"Tell him to come back later."

"He's insisting."

"I don't care, girl. Just make sure he goes away."

So Laurent and his mother didn't have the chance to be alone together. With his bulging eyes, Verdier watched their every expression while trying to control the conversation. Laurent let him, just so he could gauge the man. A feeling of malaise overcame him, caused not only by the room's stifling atmosphere and the two unsavory characters, but also from something indefinable, the impression that misfortune had decided to settle in this house.

"What are you going to do these next few months?" Marthe asked.

"I haven't decided yet," Laurent said, lying.

"If you ever need my help," Verdier said, "please don't hesitate to come to me."

"And soon we're going to have to meet with your sister and make arrangements," Marthe said.

"Arrangements? What kinds of arrangements?"

"Well, you know, what we're going to do with Restanques. . . . "

"We? Restanques is no concern of yours since you took your shares and left."

"I'm thinking of Jeanne's future."

"I think Jeanne's future is going to be fine," Laurent said, turning to his stepfather, who remained silent. "We'll talk about all this later. I have to go back home now."

Not able to find the groom, Laurent went inside the stable to find his horse himself. He was holding it by the bridle when Rosalie walked in.

"I missed you," she said, out of breath.

Surprised by the declaration, Laurent fumbled for something to say when she touched his shoulder.

"What about you?" she said. "Did you think about me a little?"

"Yes, Rosalie. I never forgot about Provence."

"I'm not talking about Provence."

Firmly, Laurent prevented her from snuggling against him.

"Someone could see us," he said.

"Well, we could meet up somewhere else, like we used to do. By the river this afternoon?"

"I can't."

"How about this evening, before I go to the dehusking room?"

"Listen, Rosalie. Things have changed."

"You don't find me attractive anymore?"

"That's not it. I have other pursuits."

"That involve a woman?"

"Yes."

The world was crumbling around Rosalie. She now bitterly regretted having decided to face reality. How much more comfortable it would have been to prolong this period of doubt instead of looking for the truth. Now she had no more hope at all. A taste of nausea came to her mouth as she walked backward toward the exit. Another woman! Images tortured her imagination, her heart. Who was the other woman? What did she look like? Rosalie quickly found the answer, as all anyone talked about the following day was Suzie Delorme.

Laurent was waiting for her at the Brignoles train station. She gracefully set foot on the platform and opened a minuscule parasol. Wearing a smile that would have bewitched the most resolute misogynists, she raised a hand for Laurent to kiss.

"I'm so happy to welcome you to my home," Laurent said.

In the car, they talked about what they'd each done the last few days.

"What?" Laurent said. "You went to the theatre without me? Whom did you go with?"

"Are you going to be the jealous type?"

"You know that." Laurent leaned toward her, adding, "I just don't want someone else to show you a good time."

"Or fall in love with me."

"Certainly not!"

As they arrived at Restanques, the September light shone on the main house. Laurent, watching his lover's reaction, noticed that she seemed to like the place.

"It's beautiful," she said, as she evaluated the size of the buildings and the park.

Jeanne had been waiting for them on the lawn, reading a novel. Twenty-five years old my eye, she thought as Suzie came her way. She's at least five years older than that. No doubt she lied to Laurent about her age.

On the other hand, there was no denying that Suzie was stunning. On an oval-shaped face and under perfectly arched brows were two bright eyes flickering between gray and green. And when her full lips parted, they displayed sparkling front teeth.

"Welcome to Restanques," Jeanne said, as she observed Suzie's fragile shoulders, her gorgeous figure highlighted by a blue muslin dress.

She had to suppress a smile when she spotted Apolline and Fanny hiding behind a bush to get a glimpse of the young woman. She wished she could hear what the two had to say.

Over the next hour, Jeanne, Laurent, and Suzie chitchatted while walking around Restanques.

When they were done, Suzie said, "You must feel isolated around here."

"Toulon isn't too far," Jeanne replied.

"Still, there's not much to do in this part of the country, is there?"

"It's not exactly Paris," Laurent said, with a smile.

"You've got that right," Suzie said. "People must die of boredom around here."

Annoyed by her comments, Jeanne decided to leave the couple until dinner, at which time Suzie hardly touched her plate, to Apolline's dismay.

"It's too rich," Suzie said, making a face as she looked at the eggplant au gratin that the maid had just set on the table.

"Our cook is going to be disappointed," Jeanne said. "She prepared this dish especially for you."

"Suzie is an actress," Laurent said. "She has to watch what she eats."

Could it be that her brother was so smitten with this actress that he'd lost his own personality? The moon was full when Jeanne went up to bed and, through a hallway window, saw them both heading for an arbor out in the park.

Apolline showed up in the hallway with a carafe of fresh water.

"Dear God," she said, "that woman is going to lead him by the nose."

"I'm afraid so," Jeanne replied.

"I've never seen Mr. Laurent this way before. All gooey eyed . . . "

With her hair held by a white scarf, Jeanne was melting sugar when Suzie waltzed into her workshop.

Wrinkling her pretty little nose, she said, "Hmm, it smells good in here!"

"Your timing is perfect," Jeanne said. "Take this spoon and stir while I pour the almonds into the vat."

"Do you have an apron?"

"No."

"I didn't realize you were making the nougat yourself," Suzie said, grabbing the spoon.

"We can't afford to hire people to do it."

"That can't be! An estate this size!"

"Things aren't always what they seem. Our situation is precarious."

As she said that, Jeanne realized that Suzie's smile was drooping.

"Laurent hasn't told you about our problems?"

Jeanne never thought she would betray her brother, but the stakes were too high for her not to go all out. A woman like Suzie wouldn't stay with a man without wealth or connections, let alone one who lived in the country.

That evening, the actress complained of a migraine. The following day, she said her throat was hurting.

"Do you want me to call the doctor?" Laurent asked her.

"No . . . No . . . "

Miserable, the young man didn't know what to do as

Suzie lay on a chaise lounge, staring at the landscape with a morose expression.

"Jérôme has invited us to go to see him in Aix tomorrow," he said. "We'd better say no."

Suzie straightened in her chair and said, "We're going."

"But, honey, you're so tired . . . "

"Seeing people will cure me."

Back from their visit at the Guillaumin's, Suzie was cheerful. Nicole had sung a few songs, and then Suzie was asked to recite some poetry.

"I didn't expect it," she said, "but they were so insistent."

"You were terrific," Laurent kept saying.

"Oh, you know . . . In such charming company, it's easy to excel. . . . "

Jeanne, who paid the conversation little attention, was startled when Laurent said to her, "Jérôme is going to spend next weekend here."

"Why?"

"Because he's our friend," Laurent said, surprised by the question.

"Saturday and Sunday . . . That's really not good for me."

"Don't worry. We'll go over to Uncle Raymond's. Grape harvesting has begun there."

Suzie was bored, so she walked along the river until she reached the washhouse, where a few women were beating clothes on rocks while gossiping. At the sight of the young woman, they clammed up. Had they ever seen a creature so delicate, so beautiful? Though a bit haughty, Suzie still nodded at the washerwomen as she went by.

The sound of the water and the mud's acrid smell reminded Suzie of her childhood spent on the banks of the Ingre, a tributary of the Loire River. She'd grown up on the outskirts of a village, in a modest farm owned by her maternal grandparents. Each morning she watched her father leave the house for the pulp mill. When the wind was blowing east, the little girl could hear the bell that regulated the workday at the mill. Each day her father came home exhausted, eating his soup in silence while his wife berated him for not making more money. This obsession became little Suzanne's when she caught sight of the new chatelaine and her daughters, all wearing dresses trimmed with lace and hats overflowing with ostrich feathers and flowers. Suddenly her clogs weighed a ton, and she was ashamed of her old clothes.

After hearing her grandmother tell her over and over again that she was as pretty as a picture, she began to believe it, and as soon as she hit puberty, the village boys' attention convinced her that she was, in fact, beautiful. Still, she had waited until she was seventeen to be noticed, by a hatter from Tours at the town fair. He enjoyed Suzanne's favor as she took advantage of his money, but when after a few months she asked him to help her flee her house, he got scared. However, desperate at the thought that he might lose her, he put Suzanne up in Paris, where he visited her until she replaced him with a wealthier protector.

Suzanne became Suzie. She lived on Anjou Street, in an apartment with heavy drapes and lots of mirrors. But she hadn't reached her goal yet. In order to step onto the stage, she was prepared to do anything. For three years she lived with an older woman who helped her get into the business. Suzie's name wound up in small print on a few posters, but the war disrupted the beginnings of her career. Listening to her intuition, Suzie left France for Italy and then Turkey, before winding up in Cairo, where she found work as an actress on a regular basis. She was coming back to France when she met Laurent, whose youth was a nice change from the old fogeys she'd been sleeping with for years.

Some noise caught her attention. At one of the river's bends, someone was coming out of the water. Before the woman could grab her towel, Suzie had time to see her heavy breasts with the hard nipples, her large hips, and her round belly above her pubis. As the woman began to slowly dry herself, Suzie thought how the ritual resembled her own when she went swimming and cleansed herself of all that was unpleasant about her existence. The barking of a dog revealed her presence. Quickly, the swimmer wrapped herself in the towel.

"Can't you call off your dog?" Suzie said, scared.

"It's not mine!"

The dog was now growling at Suzie, exposing its long teeth. Suzie didn't dare make a move.

Rosalie came over with a small branch in her hand.

"Come on, dog!" she shouted. "Get away from here!"

The dog looked at her for a moment and then decided to leave.

"Thank you so much," Suzie said. "A dog bit me when I was a kid. I've been afraid of them since."

"You're new around here?" Rosalie asked her.

"I don't live here. I'm staying at Restanques for a little while."

In a flash, Rosalie realized that she was face to face with the one who'd stolen Laurent away from her. The wound was all the more cruel as the young woman symbolized everything Rosalie dreamed of becoming: sophisticated, elegant, modern, feminine.

There was no way she could imagine that at the same time, Suzie envied her freedom to be herself. By seeking to make herself into a character that everyone would like, the actress no longer knew who she really was, and her return to France made that even more obvious and difficult to handle. But she knew she could never go back. The smell of money clung to her, and, even more so, the desire not to ever be an anonymous person, a poor farm woman living in the shadow of a good husband devoid of any true ambition with a bunch of children to feed to boot.

"You should get dressed," she muttered to Rosalie. "You've got goose bumps."

Rosalie turned on her heels and, without a word, walked away quickly.

Why is she being so rude? Suzie wondered. *I didn't say anything unpleasant to her.*

20

APOLLINE KNOCKED THREE TIMES on the door, waking Jeanne from a chaotic dream. René Verdier was the first thing that came to her mind. For the past couple of days, she'd learned that he'd intensified his defamation campaign, telling candy-shop owners in the region that Jeanne was an amateur and that very soon Restanques was going to go under.

"He'll get tired of it soon enough," Laurent had said the day before, when Jeanne first told him about their stepfather's latest doings.

"Come on, Laurent. Think a little bit. This is the time when I take my orders!"

"So? Isn't your clientele growing every week? Look, the pages of your notebook are filled with delivery dates."

"Can't you understand that I'm sick and tired of being accused of incompetence, that I'm sick and tired of keeping this place afloat all by myself?"

"Don't get upset."

Jeanne didn't listen to what he started to say. She stormed out of the house and walked around the yard, kicking pebbles and clumps of earth out of frustration. Everything had lost its meaning, including her relationship with her brother, who'd become a stranger.

Her state of mind was the same this morning. Absent-mindedly, she got dressed and, after a quick breakfast, went to her workshop and stayed there until eleven thirty. Fanny was hardly ever helping her this year, and Jeanne's arm ached from stirring the nougat with a wooden spoon. After lunch, she allowed herself a nap under the lime trees, enjoying the sound of the leaves quivering above her head.

Once back in the house, Jeanne ran into Apolline.

"Mr. Guillaumin is in the living room," the maid said. "He's waiting for Laurent and that . . . lady friend of his."

"Goodness, I'd forgotten all about that!"

She tiptoed up the staircase. Gazing in her bedroom mirror, she saw a tired, drawn face. For a moment she thought of pretending to be sick and just relaxing in bed for the rest of the day. But she got a hold of herself and, after washing up with cold water and pinching her cheeks to redden them, she looked through her closet and selected a champagne-colored silk dress.

Jérôme stood up when she walked into the living room.

"Good afternoon, Jeanne," he said.

"Good afternoon," she said, blushing.

Avoiding eye contact with Jérôme, Jeanne turned to Suzie, who, cigarette holder in hand, was watching her closely. With the unpleasant feeling that Suzie had noticed her embarrassment, Jeanne sat in an armchair.

"Do you know where Laurent is?" she asked.

"At your uncle's," Suzie replied. "He's been forgetting all about me since harvest began over there. Thank God our friend is here to entertain me."

"I also enjoy the harvest," Jérôme said. "And I intend to meet up with Laurent to help out."

"Well, my dear," Suzie said, "those are very French concerns."

"I love our region, our traditions, our know-how! The more I travel, the more I'm attached to it all."

As he spoke, Jeanne looked at his sun-tanned face, his eyes that revealed an insatiable desire to learn, and his expression that betrayed his serenity. He didn't have to express his inner strength. It was there—obvious, reassuring. If Jeanne had always found Jérôme attractive, she now saw that his beauty was not merely physical.

"Nicole tells me you were offered a job in Paris," she said.

"That's right," Jérôme said. "At the Jardin des Plantes' museum. I've always dreamed of working there."

"I'll visit you," Suzie said.

While Jeanne rested, Laurent and Jérôme walked around the estate.

Standing in front of his medicinal garden, Laurent said, "My sister kept her promise. She took good care of my plants."

"Hasn't she done much more by devoting all her time and efforts to Restanques?" Jérôme said.

"Yes, of course."

"And you think it's a good idea for you to leave for Paris?"

"I have to!"

"Why?"

"If I'm not close to Suzie, she's going to forget about me."

"Is she really worth it?"

"Listen, Jérôme . . . she may not be your type, but that doesn't mean I have to agree with you."

"Still, you should think about it. It'd be a shame to sacrifice Restanques for a love that could end quickly."

"I don't feel like being reasonable."

At the Delestangs, harvest was in full swing. Spread out across the vineyards, laborers had been at work since early morning, cutting grape bunches from their stalks to put in pails that others poured into vats at the end of each row. Those were taken away by horse-drawn carts.

Wearing an old shirt and stained pants, Laurent was working with the others, while Jérôme gave orders.

"Careful," he told a boy trying to be faster than everybody else. "You're missing some bunches."

Everywhere in the fields, people broke out singing, as others joked and laughed. Wine was a symbol of life and an endless source of pleasure, and harvesting grapes was a thrill. Jérôme grabbed a pair of shears and joined in. The sun was high in the sky, but a slight wind made the heat bearable. As he worked, bent over the vines, Jérôme recalled a similar afternoon in Cassis when he had done the same work for his grandfather. He was twelve then and already fascinated by everything that had to do with nature. Right now, he was smelling the earth and loving it. Was there anything more intense than the sensation of belonging to a natural world abounding with wealth? To quench his thirst, he bit into a few grapes, which exploded in his mouth, inundating his tongue with a sweet, heady flavor. A few yards away, a woman was rubbing her aching wrist while her child tugged on her flowery skirt. Tired of the child's antics, the woman smacked him. Near the end of the day, the coming and going of the carts intensified. In spite of being tired and struggling endlessly with wasps, the harvesters kept on working. The fruits they were picking would soon transform into a beverage that people had enjoyed since antiquity. It would age in large barrels before filling bottles that would remind the world that in Entrecasteaux, Bacchus—the God of wine—was truly honored. At the end of the day, all the workers wiped their foreheads as water was distributed. At the far end of the field, two dogs began to fight and then stopped just as abruptly. Jérôme stretched his tired limbs, and then he and Laurent headed for the house. Angélique was waiting for them there, ready to leave for Restanques.

"My niece must be wondering if we've forgotten her invitation!" she said.

*   *   *

Jeanne hadn't had anyone over for dinner in weeks, and she spent the entire afternoon overseeing the preparations.

A table was set in the shade of a large oak tree. Jeanne put some heavy silver candelabras on the white organdy tablecloth along with colorful porcelain plates. Then she cut some dahlias and put the bouquet at the center of the table. She was both restless and gleeful as she made sure everything was just right. Was it because Restanques would be coming to life this evening? Or was it that she was going to reconnect with the atmosphere that had existed when she was a child, when her parents would invite dozens of friends and family members?

Jeanne could see herself as a little girl wearing her prettiest dress and following Apolline around to help her set the table. Her mother and father were up in their room getting dressed, and soon the first guests showed up. Hiding behind a plant, she watched them enter the vestibule. There was a friend of her parents she particularly liked. His name was Louis Berthoux, and Jeanne thought she would one day marry him. It didn't matter that he was already married and the father of three boys! She had eyes only for him as he chatted with Robert Barthélemy and, when he said hi to her, she turned beet red. Those memories now made Jeanne smile.

A bird landed by the breadbasket, then another. Jeanne shooed them away, and went to the kitchen, where Fanny was adding garlic to the leg of lamb that was marinating in a spicy wine sauce. A large blueberry pie was cooling on the table, and olive oil was heating on the stove. Soon Fanny would toss some sliced eggplant into it.

"Hmm," Jeanne said. "Even Aunt Angélique is going to be impressed."

Fanny simply shrugged. She didn't like for her cooking

skills to be compared to anyone else's, especially her cousin, who was the Delestangs' cook.

The meal was coming to an end, and everything had been just right. From his seat, Jérôme could see the house's lit windows reflected in the pond in which the frogs had begun their night-time symphony. He then looked at Jeanne's face, lit up by the candles. Radiant, she was chatting with Michel, who'd just taken a cigar out of its case. As she spoke with Angélique, Suzie grabbed Laurent's hand, in a gesture of ownership. With the way things were going, Jérôme rebuked himself for ignoring Suzie's advances during the crossing. Unlike Laurent, he would have resisted her charms and would have dumped her as soon as they arrived in Marseille. There was still time. The way she looked at him said a lot about her disappointment at not being able to seduce him, but his friendship with Laurent prevented him from taking such drastic steps. Even for the sake of saving him from a major bind, he felt unable to cause him pain. Down in the village, the church bells began to toll.

"Time to go to bed," Raymond Delestang said.

He was bushed at the end of a long day in the fields.

After accompanying the couple to their car, Jérôme walked to a stone arch that offered a view of the valley down below. There was Cotignac, all lit up. Then he saw Laurent, Suzie, and Michel head for the arbor. The actress and Laurent were arm in arm, and the three of them suddenly burst out laughing. The sky was filled with stars, which made Jérôme daydream. But then he heard some footsteps and turned around.

Jeanne was coming his way.

"Where are the others?" she asked.

"Under the pergola."

He didn't expect Jeanne to sit on the low wall next to him and, in silence, enjoy the peaceful September evening.

"Since I've returned to France," Jérôme finally said, "I can't fall asleep. I need to listen to the countryside, to hear familiar sounds . . . " After a short pause, he added, "I saw the work you've done around here, how you managed to keep your olive and almond trees in such great shape. Congratulations."

"In a way," Jeanne said, "I was lucky. There's been no freezing weather, no hail, no violent storms." More to herself, she added quietly, "There were plenty of storms in the family, though. . . . "

Jérôme didn't say anything, and Jeanne was grateful for it.

"Look," he said, "a shooting star."

"You have to make a wish," Jeanne said.

"A wish? I wouldn't know where to start."

"There's so much that you want?"

"Well, a few things."

"Like what?"

"You're so nosy!"

Jérôme liked Jeanne's laughter. He couldn't completely make out her face because of the darkness, but he felt some sort of connection between them. Spontaneously, he put a hand on her arm.

"You're cold," he said.

He took off his jacket and put it on her shoulders. They slowly walked back to the house. For the first time in a long time, Jeanne felt at peace with the world.

As they were going to leave each other, Jérôme whispered, "Laurent wants to show me the piece of land you own near La Ciotat tomorrow. Come with us."

"I haven't been there in a long time, but why not?"

Did he know that she'd follow him anywhere? In her room, Jeanne lay in bed and, her heart beating fast, admitted to herself that she was in love. What else could explain this strange sensation of both chill and fever, this impulse to laugh and cry at the same time? What else could explain this exhilaration she'd felt going up the stairs and walking down the hallway to her bedroom? As far back as she could remember,

Jérôme had never shown any interest in her. What was his life really like? Laurent had always been very discreet about it. Until dawn, she made up plans, hoping and doubting, praying that things would turn out amazingly but also fearing that absolutely nothing would come of it.

"I'm going crazy," she told herself when realizing she'd gone to bed without undressing. "But this is wonderful."

21

IGNORING THE TOWN OF La Ciotat, its resorts and naval shipyards, Jérôme took the road that ran along the coast.

After a while, Laurent said, "Slow down, we're almost there. . . . Okay, stop."

Stepping out of the car, Suzie said, "But it's too steep. . . . We're not going all the way to the bottom, are we?"

"Don't worry, honey," Laurent said. "I'll carry you."

Annoyed, Jérôme began walking down a path, followed by Jeanne, who wore the right clothes and shoes. The pine needles crunched under their feet, and they were careful not to trip over a stump or a rock as they made their way to the sea down below. Birds were flying above their heads: warblers, seagulls, and hobbies. Once in a while, Jérôme stopped to observe the flora.

"You're right, Laurent," he said. "This is a nice spot to build a garden."

Suzie was up on the young man's back.

"A garden?" she said. "Here? Away from everything?"

"You never told me about this," Jeanne told her brother.

"I had the idea when we were in India. Of course, you'd have to give me permission."

The property, which they'd inherited from their father, belonged to both of them. Jeanne had almost forgotten about it, but seeing the land right now, in the sun with the sea right there, she began imagining what it could become provided they gave themselves the proper resources.

"It would be the work of a lifetime," Laurent said.

"And a money pit," Suzie interrupted. "Why would any-one want to plant trees when there's so much else that can be done? I'm telling you, this is the last time you'll see me in this scrubland."

Laurent didn't respond, but Jeanne could sense that part of his dream had just crumbled. Unable to stand Suzie's chat-ter, Jeanne decided to walk all the way down the rocky beach. There, she took off her shoes and stepped into the sea.

Jérôme, for his part, continued his observation of the area, checking the quality of the soil, assessing the health of the oaks and the pine trees.

He then went over to Jeanne and said, "Clearing out this land is going to be a big job."

"You say that as if we were actually going to do it."

"You have to believe in projects for them to come to fruition."

"I don't think that Laurent is as determined now as when he first talked to you about his dream."

"This too shall pass."

"I'm not so sure."

"A few weeks in Paris are going to open his eyes. Then he's going to come back home, where he belongs."

Almost forgetting about Jeanne's presence, he added, "Is there anything more exhilarating than creating a space of light, poetry, and freedom that will remain long after we're dead and gone? Trees, flowers, and plants never betray us, and, if they don't live up to their promise, we are the ones responsible, either because of carelessness or some mistake. I love to examine them, understand them, tame them. I love to watch them come to life and grow. I then have the wonderful feeling that I'm communicating with nature, with life. Everything is contained in the plant world: birth, death, rebirth. To serve this world is a great lesson in patience and humility, as what we think we know is never certain."

"What are you going to do at the museum?" Jeanne asked him.

"I'm going to work with orchids. I've actually brought back many species from our trip. I'm going to plant some of them in the greenhouse at my parents'."

"I saw it."

"Really?"

Jeanne told Jérôme about the evening of Nicole's eighteenth birthday and how much the greenhouse had impressed her.

"Are you going to come back once in a while?" she asked.

"I hope so. Especially since I began to restore an old house not very far from here. Nobody wanted it when my grandfather passed. It was too isolated and in very bad shape. I was crazy enough to take on the project."

Jérôme laughed.

The sun was setting behind the cliffs, and the cove was now in the shade.

"They must've gone back to the car," Jérôme said when he couldn't see Laurent and Suzie.

"I promised Suzie that we'd go to Cassis," Laurent said when they all met up again. "She wants to see people."

"Excellent idea," Jérôme said as he slid behind the steering wheel.

Workers were picking up grapes in the fields all around the town of Cassis. How many glorious harvest seasons Jérôme had enjoyed as a child in this region, in a house surrounded with vineyards! With his sister, cousins, and a group of friends, he'd walked all over the coastline and sailed the sea, dreaming of one day becoming some sort of adventurer, preferably a pirate. Jérôme remembered the large slices of bread drizzled with olive oil he enjoyed so much and his visits to the garden with his grandfather, who taught him about vegetables and spices. The smell of mint made him dizzy. He loved basil and coriander, and the odor of a newly opened melon. He took great joy biting into tomatoes that needed no ingredients to be delicious. It was in this region that he'd first fooled around with girls, with one of his cousins, older and far less timid than he, and then with Anita, the sharecropper's daughter. She was pretty and, above all, she adored Jérôme. Leaving the others behind, they ran and hid in a shack, where they caressed each other, their curiosity insatiable. Anita's voice was a bit husky, and she had freckles and long, thin legs. Jérôme loved her round breasts, the taste of her skin, and the way she sighed when he kissed her. Even today he could hear the sound of her laughter.

In the harbor, people strolled by and watched the fishermen spreading their nets. The man selling marshmallows had aged, but Jérôme had no trouble recognizing him, still behind his stall, surrounded by the same sweet smells.

Jérôme pointed at the café where, after Mass, he used to sit with his parents to drink grenadine.

"This is a good spot," he said.

As they were settling on the café's terrace, Jeanne felt uneasy. It was where she'd had lunch with Régis many times the winter before. From her seat, she could see the hotel where they'd made love.

"Let's order some mussels and clams!" Laurent said.

The sky was turning pink, and children were playing blind man's bluff and leapfrog on the sidewalk. A sip of white wine filled Jeanne's mouth with an explosion of freshness. She met Jérôme's eyes and then looked at tourists getting off a cruise ship. As night was falling, the lights made the small harbor look more and more like a theater stage, where an operetta could have been performed. Jeanne imagined a young woman in love with a smuggler and arguing with her family, who wanted her to marry a nice winegrower. She could almost see and hear the choir of farm girls urging the young woman to be reasonable.

After the shellfish came the bouillabaisse. Anglers, redfish, rainbow wrasses, sea breams, and other fish had boiled in a sauce made of onions, tomatoes, and herbs. Its aroma filled everyone's nostrils, and Suzie, for once, didn't complain about her dish.

Her incessant chatter about this and that got on Jeanne's nerves. How could Laurent stand such prattling, such drivel? Every time she opened her mouth it was to toot her own horn.

But Jeanne's ears perked up when, after Jérôme left the table, the actress asked Laurent, "Do you think he's anxious to see that woman in Paris, the one you told me about?"

"No doubt."

"Even though she broke his heart?"

"I think he still loves her."

A dagger was piercing Jeanne's heart. Who was this woman? Until the end of the evening, she watched Jérôme, but he seemed relaxed, not perturbed in any way.

"Why don't you stay with us for another day or two?" Laurent asked him as they left the café.

"I promised my parents I'd spend a bit of time with them. They say they never see me. I also have to accompany Nicole to this awfully boring social event. So I really have to leave Restanques tomorrow morning, as planned."

Jeanne liked to get up early so she could enjoy her breakfast without rushing. Often, she brought her tray to the terrace, where she listened to the birds singing while she watched the morning mist dissipate. Early morning's fresh air was unlike any other. Today, she was sitting out there, the house cat snuggling against her, eyes half-shut, waiting for the few gulps of milk Jeanne usually gave her in a saucer.

"May I join you?"

Jérôme's voice startled Jeanne.

"I'm back from a long walk," he said.

"This early?"

"When I'm not too tired, I like to see the sunrise."

"Would you like some coffee?"

"Yes, that would be nice. I'll get a cup inside and be right back."

Everything seemed so natural with him, Jeanne thought. Unfortunately, in a few hours, he'd leave and would no doubt soon forget that they'd met at Restanques.

He came back to the terrace and soon began talking about his travels.

"Are you going to go on other trips?"

"Not anytime soon, I don't think. But I'll escape using my imagination. It's not a bad way to travel, you know."

"I don't doubt it, but I can't afford to do that. The way things are in my life, what I imagine might be too beautiful compared to reality."

"But this reality that surrounds you is beautiful."

"You think so?"

"I told you before. This estate is extremely well-kept."

"To what end, I wonder? Sometimes I ask myself why I devote the best years of my life living here, in the middle of nowhere."

"You're pursuing a dream—yours, which gives your life meaning. There are two ways of leading our lives, Jeanne. One, to be dependent on others and what they will or won't give you. Two, to live for yourself. What you're accomplishing here, right now, is going to be yours forever."

"I don't know about that. Restanques is in serious trouble."

"Maybe, but you're building your own fortitude. The difficulties you're facing every day are instilling in you a strength that's never going to betray you."

"I'd love to be able to believe you, but I feel like I'm at the bottom of the barrel."

Even as she was telling Jérôme about her frustrations, she regretted giving him this image of vulnerability. But she needed to talk about what was weighing on her. Forgetting all about the seduction game, she opened up to him—her nostalgia for a paradise lost, her broken dreams, her fears.

"Come with me," Jérôme said.

They got up and headed for the olive groves. The trees, which had bloomed in June, were now covered with fruit that was soon going to be harvested.

Jérôme stopped in front of one of the trees and said, "Do you know this Latin proverb? *'By plowing slightly around an olive tree, you request it to produce; by smoking it, you beg it; by cutting it, you force it.'*"

"I don't know that proverb," Jeanne said, "but I've lived by those rules. Unfortunately, you won't see our best specimens this year. They now belong to my neighbor."

Jeanne couldn't bring herself to say "stepfather."

"Laurent told me what happened," Jérôme said.

Silently, they continued walking among the trees, whose foliage was iridescent in the sun's rays. In the surrounding fields, some laborers were already at work. Spontaneously, Jeanne got close to Jérôme. She needed his strength and encouragement. Alongside him, she was inhabited by the fleeting sensation of no longer being alone in the world.

"Jérôme," she whispered, "I'm happy you came to Restanques."

"I'll come back."

"Really?"

"Absolutely," he said, sliding his arm under hers.

22

JÉRÔME'S DEPARTURE WAS QUICKLY followed by Suzie's. Laurent drove her to Marseille, where they spent the night together before going to the train station early the next morning.

"Hurry and come up to Paris with me!" she shouted from the train's window.

"I promise, but swear that you already miss me!"

As a response, she blew him a kiss.

Leaving Marseille, Laurent felt a terrible void, a kind of amputation. Nothing made sense to him, and the thought of going back to Restanques without his lover was unbearable.

"Mother wants to see us both tomorrow," Jeanne told him when he got home.

"What does she want?"

"She heard about Suzie."

"I swear, if she says one negative thing about her . . . "

Marthe was in the garden, drinking coffee with her husband. At the sight of her children, she said, "There you are!"

René Verdier greeted Jeanne and Laurent, before saying, "Well, I should go."

"No," Marthe said. "I want you to stay with us."

But Jeanne said, "I think you're right, sir. We need to speak with our mother. Alone."

Surprised by the young woman's cold and firm tone, the couple looked at each other.

"Okay, then," René muttered. "See you in a bit."

With an irritated gesture, Marthe tried to shoo away the wasp buzzing around her chair.

"The more you move," Laurent said, "the more it's going to pester you."

"I'm not going to let it sting me!"

They finally went inside the house and took refuge in the living room. It smelled of perfume and cold tobacco.

"I asked you to come over," Marthe began, "because I want to know what your intentions are. I was told, Laurent, that you invited a woman to Restanques."

"That's right."

"You think that's a proper thing to do?"

"I didn't ask myself that question."

"I imagine she doesn't mean a whole lot to you since you didn't bother introducing her to me."

"Maybe it's the opposite. . . . "

Remaining silent, Jeanne watched the effect this conversation had on her mother who, confused, fumbled for something to say. Her lack of intelligence made her resort to moralizing, the worse approach she could have taken.

"She can only be a tramp to settle with a boy the way she did," she said. "I was also told that she's much older than you are."

"Who's been telling you those lies?"

"I have my sources."

"Well, you need to find better ones."

"I disagree. . . . But let's talk about your future—yours and Jeanne's. It's time to make a decision before both of you are completely broke. What's more, Jeanne can't go on living

DOMINIQUE MARNY

alone. It's downright indecent, and it makes people talk. How are you going to find a husband that way?"

"That concerns me and only me!" Jeanne said.

"That's not true! If you and your brother are broke . . . who's going to take care of you? René?"

"Let's talk about your husband," Jeanne said, seething. "All he's waiting for is to buy Restanques for next to nothing. You're the only one that can't see his scheming. You really think he married you because he loves you? You really think he likes living with you?"

"How dare you speak to me this way? I forbid—"

"Do you even know what he's been plotting behind your back? Do you even know that for months now he's been going to my clients, trying to denigrate my work so he can drive me to bankruptcy as quickly as possible?"

"My poor dear, you're out of your mind. René only cares about your well-being."

"Sure he does!"

Jeanne saw that her mother's hands were shaking, and she herself had a hard time breathing. How could the three of them say such nasty things to one another?

"The truth is that you two can't stand to see me happy," Marthe said. "You would have preferred that I cried over your father's passing until I died myself, and you're inventing all kinds of horrible things just to punish me!"

Marthe broke down crying.

"I don't ever want to see you again, either of you! And don't you come crawling back for help when you need it."

Shaken by the entire scene, Laurent turned to Jeanne, who looked stunned.

"Mother," she whispered, "try to understand."

Jeanne put a hand on her mother's shoulder.

"Don't you touch me!" Marthe said. "Both of you get out of here, now!"

*　　*　　*

Once home, Laurent said, "Well, that went well. . . . "

"What did you expect?"

"The beginning of a dialogue. But you're right; I was naive. Stupid, even."

As Laurent spoke, he lit a cigarette and took a long drag.

"Still," he said, "she's right. We are going to have to make a decision. You can't continue living here alone, working for the two of us."

"I could do it if I had the hope that you'd eventually come back."

"Are you mad at me because I'm leaving?"

"Disappointed."

A pregnant pause followed, but nothing would have made Laurent change his mind.

"Suzie hates the country, and she has to live in Paris for her career as an actress."

"So you decided to sacrifice yourself!"

"*Sacrifice* . . . That's too strong a word."

"So I can do nothing but hope for a miracle. . . . "

"Jeanne, why are you being so stubborn? If we sold the estate, we'd have some money, a pleasant existence, no worries."

"What about the rest? The satisfaction of doing good work and giving work to others. Fanny, Apolline, what would become of them?"

"Are you kidding me? They're ready for retirement! They're old!"

"Exactly! Where would they go? They've always lived at Restanques."

"You're too much of a romantic for me."

Jeanne had the feeling that the ground was crumbling under her feet. And Laurent dealt the decisive blow when, hesitant, he added, "I have to tell you . . . I'm going to need my share."

"You know very well I can't buy it!"

"You're going to have to find a solution."

"What if I gave you regular payments?"

"That wouldn't work long-term. Of course, I'm not asking you to sell Restanques to Verdier, but I'm sure there would be other takers."

In spite of her desperation, Jeanne needed to do one and only one thing: buy time.

"Give me one year," she said.

"What good would that do?"

"My nougat sells more and more. It will add value to the property."

"I'm not sure about that."

"I'm really hopeful."

"Please, Jeanne, be realistic. You're never going to be able to buy me out."

"So many things can happen. All I'm asking for is one chance."

"I don't like it at all, but I just can't say no to you."

Though she should have been overwhelmed with worry, Jeanne felt imbued with a renewed enthusiasm. With great satisfaction, she realized that she could count on François, who was still doing wonderfully.

"You were right," Jeanne told Apolline. "He has all the qualities to become an excellent sharecropper."

"I wish Rosalie would think that, too."

"Rosalie?"

"Haven't you noticed the way he looks at her?"

If François had believed, if only for a short while, that he might have won over the young maid, he now had lost all hope. Since Laurent's return, she hadn't spoken to him. Worse, when they ran into each other, she looked right through him, as though he were invisible. The young man had been encouraged after their friendly encounters, and he'd been clinging to the idea that he might teach her how to read and write, but now he felt completely distraught. The hard work he put in day after day in order to become someone now seemed futile. He had better standing at Restanques and earned more than before, yet he was unhappy.

"You don't look well," Rémy told him.

François had been visiting the old shepherd regularly since the end of the wandering season.

A bit of time was needed for the two to talk freely, get to know each other, but eventually a trust between them set in. Rémy, who cherished solitude, began to enjoy teaching the young worker about the virtues of the foxglove plant, the marshmallow root, or the bryony, which he used to treat sick animals.

Sitting on the grass, the old man set his whip, walking stick, and the large leather bag he carried everywhere beside him. Living with nature, the stars, and his animals, he'd gained an acute awareness of time. Being in isolation and experiencing silence for so long had sharpened his concentration as well as his perception of his surroundings. It was said he could read people's souls, that he could predict the future. He was embarrassed about that, so he kept to himself the images that came to his mind when in contact with someone else. But in the case of François, the young man looked so distraught that Rémy decided to speak.

"Let winter go by and spring arrive," he said. "Then things are going to be easier."

"Easier?"

"Some things are going to happen that you're not expecting, things nobody can imagine. After that, everything is going to be clear."

"Terrible things?"

"In some instances, yes."

"Like what?"

"You don't need to know. But don't worry, nothing bad is going to happen to you."

"And the people I love?"

"Not really . . . "

Remy's attention turned to his dog, and François knew there was no use insisting.

In the next few weeks, the shepherd's words often came back to François' mind. What was going to happen? With great relief, he learned that Laurent was preparing for his departure to Paris.

"He's going to meet up with that horrible woman," Apolline kept saying to everyone who'd listen.

Rosalie didn't hear any of it, as she'd decided not to come to Restanques to dehusk almonds anymore.

"I have way too much to do at Bel Horizon," she told Jeanne.

And what she had to do was peculiar. Yet, nothing could have stopped her from carrying out the plan she'd come up with after she ran into Suzie. Just like the actress, she'd wanted to become rich, and to reach that goal, she had to use the means that were at her disposal. For a long time, René Verdier had been hitting on her. Forgetting that he was the Barthélemy's enemy or, rather, trying to get back at Laurent, she stopped resisting Verdier's advances. Nothing was easier than turning him on and then making him do what she wanted. They started by kissing, and he gave her presents—cheap knickknacks at first and then nicer things. Whenever he could, René went to Rosalie's door, which she didn't open.

"You little bitch. What is it that you want?"

"To make you crazy."

"You're such a tease!"

One evening, he pinned her against a wall and went for

her breasts. She let him until he slipped his hands under her blouse.

"Quit that!" she said.

Breathing hard, Verdier had a stunned expression.

"Not here," Rosalie said.

"Why not? There's nobody around."

"I want a nice room, in a nice hotel."

Their liaison began in Draguignan, in a hotel known for its discretion all over the region. A bottle of champagne was cooling in a bucket on the nightstand, and next to it was a plate filled with cookies.

That champagne will help me put up with him, Rosalie thought, as Verdier began caressing her.

"Not so fast," she said, heading for the cookies.

But Verdier had no intention of being patient. He grabbed Rosalie, lifted her skirt, and forced her to sit on his lap. At the end of that day, she knew that from then on, he wouldn't be able to do without her. As he was driving back to Bel Horizon, she watched the mediocre man who was so full of himself. She'd given him what she never was able to offer Laurent. To please Verdier, she'd had to squelch her pride and forget all about decency. But the worst of it all was that it hadn't been so difficult for her to do so. He put a hand on her knee. She forced herself to snuggle against him.

"When are we going to do this again?" she whispered.

The car swerved, and Rosalie stopped misbehaving.

In the next few days, she noticed with satisfaction that Verdier no longer paid any attention to Mado. As for poor Marthe Barthélemy, she'd become a laughing stock, a woman whose husband had slept with the two maids she was bossing around. And yet she and Verdier spent long moments chatting together. They even made love on occasion.

"You should talk to your daughter," René kept telling her.

"After what she said to me, I'd rather die!"

"But by burning bridges, you don't know what she might do!"

"So what?"

"Come now, Marthe, you can't lose interest in Restanques."

"I'm already fed up with it."

"Are you forgetting that we planned on buying it eventually?"

"What would we do with it? You have enough to worry about with your vines, and I want to have fun."

"Have fun! That's all you think about!"

Verdier felt hatred for the woman he'd never found attractive and that he'd spent so much time and energy winning over. She looked ridiculous with her frizzy hair, her pale complexion, and her young girl's dress. Why had he married such a pathetic women? At least his first wife had left him some money after she died. But Marthe! She brought with her a few nice olive groves, but the sacrifices he had to make living with her weren't worth it. He had to reassure her all the time about the supposed feelings he had for her. Images of Rosalie, gorgeous and naked, came to his mind as Marthe took him in her arms and kissed him. He wanted so much to free himself from her, but how could he do that without turning his back on what he'd planned all along?

23

JEANNE HAD TOO MUCH on her hands to miss Laurent's absence. To help her with the nougat, she hired two young women to take care of the packaging and shipping. She was on the road a lot to visit candy-shop owners and bring them the product. Sylvie often went along with her.

"Why don't you do some of the delivering by yourself?" Jeanne said. "I could pay you for it."

"Out of the question. I go on the road with you because I enjoy it, and I can make myself useful. I wouldn't want you to pay me for anything."

"I'm serious. Think about it. If you did the delivering for me, it would be a huge load off my shoulders."

Sylvie talked to her mother about it. What was unthinkable before the war was now acceptable. The tasks taken up while the men were off fighting the Germans were now ingrained. Just like the women who'd held the country together during the war, the new generation was allowed to work and get paid for it. Angélique gave her daughter her blessing, and Jeanne set up a work schedule. There were more and more orders, and the nougat continued to be delivered on time.

"We should open a shop," Sylvie said.

"You're forgetting that nougat only sells in the last months of the year."

"Well, think of something else you could produce. *Calissons*, for example. . . . "

"Let's not get carried away," Jeanne said.

The harvesting of olives was going well. Along with the other workers, Augustine and Annie were picking the violet fruits filled with oil. For two years now they'd given their time and energy to Restanques, and even though each still dreamed of going back home for good, they had grown attached to these fields. Augustine's main preoccupation remained not to lose Joseph. He now had his eyes on one of the girls who took care of packaging nougat for Jeanne. Even though she sometimes brought herself to admit that she'd never been truly happy with Joseph, Augustine kept trying to convince herself that, in spite of all his faults, he was the love of her life. The other men were no doubt not any better than him, and at least her husband had the benefit of being alive, when men were woefully missing in this postwar era.

One of the male visitors to Restanques, Antoine, had special status, as the employees thought he was Ms. Jeanne's fiancé.

"Apolline," Jeanne said, annoyed, "I told you a thousand times that I am not going to marry that man."

"Why not?"

"I'm not in love with him."

"You will be, with time."

"I won't!"

The emphatic way Jeanne had uttered that word surprised the old maid. How could she know that Jeanne fell asleep and woke up with the image of Jérôme in her mind? Jeanne simply couldn't forget about him.

Antoine had known Jérôme in Aix, so Jeanne tried to find

out more about his life, and more specifically that mysterious woman in Paris that Laurent and Suzie had mentioned.

"Who told you about that?" Antoine said.

"It doesn't matter."

"Jérôme hates when people talk about it."

Jeanne's heart was pounding.

"So?" she said. "He's not here right now to hear any of it."

"Well, it was toward the end of the war," Antoine said, reluctantly. "He met the wife of one of the men from our squadron just after the man had an amputation. They actually met at the man's bedside in the hospital. It was love at first sight for both of them, though they felt awful and guilty about it."

"What happened?"

"She obviously didn't leave her husband, but even after Jérôme left for Asia, they still had the same feelings for each other."

"You know her?"

"I've seen her many times."

"Is she pretty?"

"Pretty isn't the right word. She's charming and graceful. There's something very soothing and pleasant about her."

"Do you think you might have fallen in love with her yourself?"

"Maybe, if she'd been a free woman."

Jeanne couldn't help herself. In a low voice she asked, "What's her name?"

"Isabelle."

Jeanne thought it would be nearly impossible for her to compete with a woman Jérôme had been attached to for three years, especially one who had so many positive qualities. Jeanne, who was usually optimistic to a fault, felt helpless. Sentimentally speaking, was she doomed to be married to Antoine who, two days earlier, had again asked her to think about his marriage proposal. Why dream the impossible dream when he was there for her, at a time when everybody else was abandoning her?

"You seem to be very interested in our friend Jérôme," Antoine said, suspicious.

"I'm just curious."

"And would you like to know what he thinks about an eventual wedding between the two of us?"

"You talked to him about it!"

"Yes. . . . Anything wrong with that?"

"Anything wrong? I forbid you to spread false information about us."

"Jeanne, please calm down. I didn't mean to make you upset. Jérôme is a close friend of mine. I needed to talk to him about us."

"Stop saying 'us.'"

After what happened at his mother's, Antoine knew that Jeanne had a fiery temper. Still, he didn't understand why she was reacting so strongly to what he'd just said.

"Okay, then," he said, "I think I should probably leave now."

Jeanne felt great relief.

Yes, leave, she thought, *and go as far away as possible and forget all about my existence.*

Angry with him, as well as with herself, she listened to his footsteps as he walked out of the house.

Jeanne was stoking the embers in the fireplace when Apolline came into the living room.

"Dinner is ready," she said.

"Mr. Laferrière is not going to be with us after all. He left."

Laurent had rented a room in Paris not far from the Luxembourg Gardens.

He wrote his sister: *It's like a pigeon coop. From my bed, I can see the clouds in the Parisian sky.*

He'd just found a job in a bookstore nearby and, for a meager salary, was sorting and storing monographs in the back room. For the first two months, he maintained that he loved living in Paris, and then Jeanne started to sense some disenchantment between the lines.

"Maybe he's getting tired of Suzie?" she said to Apolline.

"Could be, but I'd be surprised."

Once he wrote about a visit at Jérôme's: *He's been extremely busy since a pharmaceutical company asked him to manage some studies.*

Just as busy herself, Jeanne didn't have time to try to figure out what really was going on in Paris, though Jérôme was still very much on her mind. Many deliveries left for Marseille and Toulon, where the Restanques' nougat was beginning to garner a very positive reputation. In every box of her nougat, Jeanne included a beautiful picture of Restanques. That was her way to counter the ones who were hoping for its downfall.

She hadn't heard from her mother since their bitter encounter. As for René, Jeanne often saw his car parked in front of the cooperative, but she never stopped to go talk to him.

The owner of Bel Horizon had no reason to complain about the gains he was making from his wife's olive groves. He had actually begun fudging the books to keep some of the money, which he then spent on Rosalie. Getting away with his maid had become an obsession, and each day he tried to find a way to avoid a conjugal life that he could no longer stand. Just looking at and listening to Marthe drove him crazy, and he began fantasizing about her dying of some illness.

Rosalie was fully conscious of the power she had over Verdier. She took full advantage of the situation. Not only did she accept the clothes and jewelry he offered her, she asked for money, which she horded in a box. Nothing pleased her more than the sound of coins hitting each other. In six months, she figured, she'd have enough to try her luck in Paris. There, just like Suzie, she'd find herself a rich man who'd make her forget all about Toulon, her alcoholic father, and that god-awful René Verdier. His sexual demands had no limits, and if at the beginning she had a very hard time satisfying him, she soon realized that she could get used to anything. For that she despised him, as well as herself.

"You're going to say that you have to go see your parents," Verdier told Rosalie as she was hanging some clothes to dry.

"Okay . . . "

"And I'll say that I have an appointment with my attorney in Briançon."

"You mean we're going to go away together."

He walked right up to her as she was hanging a white bed sheet, snuggled against her back, and began caressing her breasts.

"Does that sound good to you?" he whispered.

"Hands off, pal," Rosalie said, wriggling away from Verdier.

Resisting him was part of the ritual that he couldn't live without. René loved it when Rosalie stood up to him, when she treated him harshly. He loved it when they fought and then made up in bed.

"So," he said, "are you up for it?"

"We'll see. . . . If I feel like it. . . . "

Rosalie walked away from him without looking back.

When Marthe moved away from Restanques, she imagined that her existence would change altogether, but things were worse now than they were before. René no longer made any effort to be nice to her, withholding any kind of affection. He disappeared all day and spent his evenings reading the paper and drinking alcohol. At dinnertime, he mumbled a few words and as soon as he was done eating, went up to bed and fell asleep. Of course, going out or making love was out of the question. Distraught, Marthe's dreams were crumbling now that she could see what her husband really was: a bland, boring, uneducated, ordinary man. And she was stuck with him. On top of that, she no longer talked to her children, and almost all her friends were criticizing her for having married René Verdier.

"I have to go to Briançon," Verdier told Marthe one morning.

"What for?"

"I have an appointment with my attorney. Some documents to sign. It's about my first wife."

"I'm going with you."

"That's nice of you, Marthe, but I don't see the point."

"I need a change of scenery."

"Listen, honey, I don't think so. I'm going to deal with things from my past, and I don't want you to be involved in it. It'd be too awkward."

"I'll stay at the hotel while you're with your attorney."

"Frankly, I'd rather you stay here. When I get back, we'll go on a trip together."

"You've been promising that forever!"

"This time, I give you my word. We'll go to Menton."

Rosalie also lied. Looking distraught, she came into Marthe's room with a letter that René had written, modifying his handwriting.

"My mother has to go to the hospital," the maid said, "and my father can't take care of my brothers and sisters. She wants me to go home and help out for a few days."

"Well, since Mr. Verdier is also going to be gone, it should be okay. But tell Mado exactly what she needs to do while you're away."

Rosalie could then start thinking of Nice and its Promenade des Anglais, its ritzy cafés, and its expensive boutiques.

She'd dreamed of going there ever since she was a teenager. Cotignac, where she went in the late afternoon to buy sewing needles and thread, seemed ridiculous to her. Walking by the school, she ran into François.

"Well," he said, "we haven't seen you in while."

François was staring at her as though he knew all about her shady plans and secrets.

"I have a lot to do at Bel Horizon. . . . "

"Oh yeah?"

After a moment of silence, François added, "I liked it when you came over."

Rosalie started to walk again, but François kept up with her pace.

"Maybe we could see each other one of these Sundays."

"On Sundays, I'm resting. . . . "

As they were chatting, François realized there was something different about Rosalie. No one else would have noticed, but she looked sad and withdrawn to him. She'd also lost some of her vitality and radiance.

"Rosalie, you don't seem happy to me."

"Me? What are you talking about? And why don't you mind your own business anyway?"

"Don't be mad at me."

"Listen, François, you're nice and all that, but there's nothing between you and me. Get it?"

Not only were each of her words like blades piercing his flesh, the tone Rosalie used was unbearable. It was as though she was speaking to the world's biggest loser. But had he ever been anything else to her than some sort of pathetic fool? In the span of a few minutes, François had been robbed of his personality and had his dreams destroyed. Defeated, he turned around and slowly walked over to the presbytery, where he'd share a glass of sweet wine with the sacristan.

For the past few months, the old man had been lending

him Jules Verne novels. In spite of being tired, François read them until the middle of the night, traveling through space and time with the characters. Would reading such adventures ever counter the sadness that now filled him?

24

A STORM WAS RAGING, and Jeanne looked out the window at the drenched garden.

"I brought you the mail," Apolline said, leaving the envelopes on a table.

Jeanne went through them and, intrigued, opened the one that came from Paris.

Dear Jeanne,

I didn't want to worry you until now, but your brother is saying alarming things, and I am too busy with work to look after him as much as he needs. Suzie has left him. Between you and I, this would not be a bad thing if Laurent was not so distressed. I know how much work you have at Restanques, but if you could come up to Paris yourself, maybe Michel or Sylvie would be available to help. . . . What is important is for Laurent not to be alone. Of course, I offered to take him to Cotignac, but since he is hoping that he and Suzie will be together again eventually,

*he refuses to leave Paris. I think I might be able
to convince him to come down south with me
for Christmas, but no earlier. In any event, here
is my address: 36 Gobelins Street.*

Overwhelmed by the news, Jeanne tried to find a solution.
Stopping the nougat production was out of the question. Could
Apolline and Fanny take care of that while she was away? At
their age, that was asking a lot of them. Then there was Sylvie.
She knew the clientele, and she'd often helped Jeanne make it.

Her cousin agreed to take things over.

"I'm not going to be gone for more than a week," Jeanne
said. "I promise."

As she was giving François her last instructions, a worker
from Bel Horizon came running over.

Out of breath, he said, "Ms. Jeanne . . . something horrible
happened. . . . "

Jeanne frowned and said, "What's going on?"

"It's Mr. Verdier . . . The police came to tell us he's dead."

Dead! René Verdier!

"His car fell off a cliff, and Mr. Verdier died instantly. And
there's Rosalie . . . "

"What are you talking about!" François exclaimed.

"She was with him."

"Rosalie . . . " François muttered. "Rosalie . . . Is she also
dead?"

"To tell you the truth, I don't know."

"Where did it happen?" Jeanne asked, trying to understand the situation.

"Not far from Nice."

"That's impossible!" François said. "It has to be some
other woman."

"No. The police told Mrs. Verdier all about it, and she told
me to come over here."

"Let's go to Bel Horizon," Jeanne said.

As soon as they stepped out of the house, the stable boy came up to François.

"It's Brutus," he said. "We just brought him back from the field. It looks bad."

François went to the stable, while Jeanne grabbed her bicycle.

Not caring about the puddles that the rain had left, Jeanne pedaled as fast as she could to Bel Horizon, where no one was there to greet her.

"Mother," she shouted once in the house. "Mother!"

Feeling bad, she went up the stairs. Once on the landing, she saw Mado.

"Where's my mother?" Jeanne asked the maid.

"In her bedroom."

"By herself?"

"Yes."

Marthe was lying in bed, crying. Jeanne hesitated for a moment before going over to her mother. She had to forget about their past. She sat next to her and began caressing her hair, which made Marthe cry even more. Then she managed to calm down a bit and, her face covered with tears, told Jeanne how she'd been fooled.

"And like some poor idiot, I didn't suspect anything. They must've laughed at me all the time. . . . "

"Are you sure they were having an affair?"

"No doubt in my mind," Marthe said, and began pounding on the pillows with her fists.

She didn't seem to care that two people had died, Jeanne thought. She was too busy being angry. Jeanne herself had a hard time understanding Rosalie's betrayal. How could she have been romantically involved with the man who wanted to destroy Restanques? But this was not the time to questions things. It was time for action. Jeanne told the worker to go to the Delestangs' so that Raymond and Angélique could come over while she went to the police station.

"If only I'd listened to you," Marthe told her daughter. "But I was in love with him!"

What could she say to that? The roles were reversed, and twenty-year-old Jeanne found herself trying to calm down a woman of more than forty who was still, emotionally speaking, a teenager.

"No need to blame yourself this way. It's only going to make you feel worse."

Marthe threw herself into Jeanne's arms to cry over her feelings of guilt toward her children and her frustration at not being able to express her anger toward a husband who'd so humiliated her.

At the police station, Jeanne was relieved to learn that Rosalie had survived the accident.

"Mrs. Verdier must have misunderstood," the officer said. "She suffered leg and head injuries."

"How bad is it?"

"We don't know for now. But they'll know more at the hospital."

Jeanne would have to ask Michel to drive her to Nice, but in the meantime, she had to get back to Restanques.

As soon as Jeanne went through the gates, François came running to her.

"Rosalie is alive."

"Really? Is . . . Is that really . . . true?"

The tension accumulated over the past hours made him stammer. But Rosalie wasn't dead, thank God. And after hitting rock bottom, the news filled him to the brim with happiness.

"Does Apolline know about all this?" Jeanne asked him.

"Nobody at Restanques does."

This was a delicate situation, and Jeanne wondered how

to handle it. How was she going to tell people at Restanques that Rosalie and her boss were in the same car, miles away from Cotignac? She decided to tell everyone that Marthe had allowed her maid to travel with her husband, who was going to Nice on business so that Rosalie could spend some time with the young man she liked.

"A young man?" Apolline said. "She never said anything to me about that!"

"They met at the village a month ago," Jeanne said. "A nice boy from Nice, she told me. She also asked me to keep quiet about it."

"My God," the old woman said, wiping a tear. "To think that Rosalie could've died just because of some boy."

Jeanne, who had other things to do than console Apolline, left her with Fanny and went up the stairs to her room. There was the luggage she was supposed to take to Paris with her the following morning. Everything was happening at the same time! Laurent, her mother, Rosalie and Verdier, whose body would have to be claimed. The funeral would have to be organized, too. At that moment, it dawned on Jeanne that Verdier's death was taking a huge load off her shoulders. Her enemy was no longer alive! He'd gone into nothingness with his hate and Machiavellian plans. Jeanne felt no compassion whatsoever for the man who'd broken her family apart, had caused her so many sleepless nights, and, confirming his mediocrity once and for all, had had an affair with Rosalie.

Later in the day, Jeanne took Marthe to Entrecasteaux, where she was going to live for a while.

"She won't return to Restanques," Raymond told Jeanne, "and she wants out of Bel Horizon."

"That bodes well for the future!"

"I'm worried about the future, to tell you the truth! Your mother and Verdier were married under an arrangement of separate property. Do you know if he has any heirs?"

"I don't."

"If he does, Marthe is going to lose almost everything."

Accompanied by Michel, Jeanne walked into the hospital, where both the injured and the deceased had been sent. After taking care of the usual formalities, Jeanne left the painful task of going to the morgue to her cousin, while she headed for the floor where Rosalie was being taking care of.

"It was a close call," the doctor told Jeanne. "A piece of metal entered her skull right next to her temple."

"What about her legs?"

"Double fractures. A hip and a tibia. She might have a limp for the rest of her life."

"How long do you think you're going to keep her here?"

"We don't know yet. Does she have any family?"

"Her parents are in Toulon, but I'll take care of everything. She worked for me. . . . "

Jeanne didn't know why she felt like justifying herself.

Rosalie, who was sleeping, opened her eyes only at the end of the afternoon.

Surprised to see Jeanne at her bedside, she said, "You're here. . . . "

"Don't talk if it makes you tired," Jeanne said.

A long moment of silence followed during which Rosalie tried to make light of everything. Images were coming to her. The hotel in Nice where they had spend two nights. The beautiful room, the large bed . . .

"Where the car?" she asked.

"Shush," Jeanne said. "Don't get upset."

Snippets of a fight came back to Rosalie's mind. René made fun of her imitation-leather handbag. She got upset. He tried to make up with a kiss, but she pushed him away, hard. After that . . . she didn't remember. But a nurse had said something about an accident. Tears began streaming down her cheeks.

"Don't be scared," Jeanne told her.

"What about Mrs. Verdier?" Rosalie asked. "Does she know what happened? Apolline is going to tell my father about all this, and he's going to kill me."

"Stop thinking so much!"

Jeanne told Rosalie about the version of events she'd given her aunt, and that calmed her down.

"I can't say I'm sad that René Verdier is dead," Rosalie said. "Maybe you won't believe me, but I hated him, and I hated everything about us being together. I just didn't want to remain a maid until the day I die."

René Verdier's funeral was held in the church where he and Marthe had married. Marthe was a widow for the second time in three years. The feeling of her black veil sticking to her face disgusted her. To her right, in an oak coffin, lay the man she was never going to be able to scream at to express the hate and disgust she felt for him. Ignoring what the priest was saying, she began to think about what should have alerted her from the very beginning of her relationship with Verdier. She was also worried. What was going to become of her now? The attorney had informed her that Bel Horizon's house and some of its buildings were going to a distant cousin of the deceased living in Lyon, someone Marthe had never heard of. As for Restanques . . . For a number of reasons, there was no way she could return there. In reality, what she really wanted to do was move back to Marseille, the city of her childhood. But how could she do that? She could sell the olive groves that still belonged to her and buy an apartment with the profits. But then, how would Jeanne react? She glanced at her daughter. In spite of the efforts they both made to try to understand each other in these times of hardship, they remained strangers. Jeanne was always ready for a challenge and dreamed of success, while Marthe looked for ways of filling her empty days. Jeanne was earning money, while Marthe knew only how to spend it.

The ceremony was almost over, and the incense was making her nauseous. Then everyone filed out of the church, and a freezing wind accompanied the funeral procession to the cemetery. All the way there, Marthe shivered. Behind her was a crowd of people composed mostly of villagers who'd come more for convention's sake than sympathy for the deceased. Verdier had never been accepted in the village, but out of respect for Mrs. Barthélemy—she was still called that—people made an appearance.

Jeanne stood beside the freshly dug grave. From there she could see the vault where her ancestors and father rested. Dried up leaves littered the ground around it. Tightening her coat against the bitter cold, she thought about Laurent in need of help in the capital. The day before, Sylvie had hopped on a train for Paris. If only she could bring him back! Jeanne felt her strength failing her. Exhausted, she wished she could go to bed and lose herself in sleep. But she had to take care of her mother's situation, accelerate her nougat production, find someone to replace her cousin for the deliveries while she was away, and verify with François the contents of the barns and stables. Just thinking about it made her dizzy!

25

AS EXPECTED, MARTHE SANK into a deep depression once her anger dissipated.

"What are we going to do?" Angélique was saying. "We can't keep her here with us forever."

Having exchanged letters with Verdier's attorney as well as his heir, Jeanne knew that the latter wanted to sell the Bel Horizon house. Marthe would find herself without a place to stay and with little resources apart from her olive groves.

"She wants to sell those," Raymond said, "and you can't blame her. It's her right, especially since she renounced her claim on the house by not living at Restanques anymore. Hopefully the people buying Bel Horizon will also be interested in her land."

Jeanne didn't say anything, but the decision had been made. The following day, she left for Aix and went over to Antoine Laferrière's office. She spent thirty minutes in the waiting room until Laferrière walked in.

"Jeanne," he said. "Sorry to make you wait all that time. I was in a meeting and couldn't get out of it. What's going on?"

"I'd like to ask you for your advice."

Antoine turned to his secretary and said, "Make sure nobody disturbs us."

He then showed Jeanne to his office and sat next to her instead of behind his large desk piled with folders. In a few sentences, Jeanne told him about the latest events.

"If I want to save Restanques," she said, "I have to buy my mother's olive groves. The problem is that I don't have the money. I'd like you to help me get a loan. You know bankers. . . . They trust you."

"I should hope so. But, Jeanne, how are you going to repay such a large sum of money?"

"With my profits. Our olive oil is excellent!"

"I don't doubt it. But let me be honest with you. The bankers are going to argue that a bad frost or some sort of disease could wipe out your trees and your entire production."

"Well, I'll mortgage my part of the estate. Only mine, though. I don't want Laurent to be implicated in my decision."

"That's really dicey. You could lose everything."

"I have no other choice."

Antoine thought about the situation. Should he help Jeanne by risking his own capital? Their eyes met, and he understood that if he didn't support Jeanne, she was going to seek someone else's assistance. If badly advised, she might make costly mistakes.

"I'm thinking of one of my father's old friends," he said. "He might go for it."

"I knew you'd be able to come up with a solution!"

Antoine gave a sad smile and didn't express what he was thinking. Since their last meeting, he'd tried to tell himself Jeanne wasn't in love with him, and he'd almost convinced himself not to see her again. Yet there she was, barging into his office, to entrust him with what was most precious to her: Restanques's future, as well as hers.

She got up and took his hands.

"Antoine," she said. "I was harsh with you last time we saw each other, and I regret it. Please forgive me."

"You were harsh with me?" he said. "I don't remember that."

They both burst out laughing, and Antoine caught himself hoping again. Would it be like that every time she came to him?

Walking Jeanne out of his office, he said, "I'll let you know as soon as I have some news."

It was cold out, the wind nasty, but still the city's streets were animated, as they always were in the weeks leading up to Christmas. After experiencing so many conflicts and difficulties, Jeanne felt like having a good time. With great glee, she walked into boutiques, tried on hats and shoes, looked at handbags, and touched the fabric of a few dresses. She was won over by a green wool crepe dress and a couple of fluffy sweaters. She didn't care how much it all cost. As a matter of fact, the heaviness of her bags made her feel as light as a feather.

This sensation was short-lived. As soon as she was back on the road to Cotignac, she began feeling guilty when thinking about Laurent. Would Sylvie manage to bring him back home? In a laconic telegram, her cousin had said that she was trying to make him leave Paris with the help of Jérôme but that it was no easy task.

They arrived on December 20, and Jeanne's heart clenched at the sight of her brother. He looked drawn, lost. He was indifferent to everything.

"Our poor little Laurent," Apolline said. "That witch really did a number on him."

Trying to cheer up the young man, she and Fanny prepared his favorite foods, but Laurent barely touched anything.

He had nothing to say about Verdier's death and its ramifications, or about Rosalie's health.

"It was as though he didn't even see me," Marthe said after visiting him.

"He just can't get over that woman. It's an obsession."

"I knew this was going to end badly."

"We all did, Mother. The fact remains that he's deeply wounded."

"You're right, I'm sorry."

Marthe felt utterly uncomfortable in this house where she'd spent twenty years of her life. Everything about it had become foreign to her: the furnishings, the atmosphere. But she didn't feel at ease anywhere. What was she going to do?

"Wouldn't you like to live somewhere else?" she asked her daughter. "Away from Cotignac . . . "

The question took Jeanne by surprise, especially since she'd been on the verge of talking to her mother about buying her olive groves. She then made her an actual offer, all the while thinking how odd it was that she was forced to buy a heritage that should have been hers and Laurent's in the first place.

"I never thought of that," Marthe said. "It certainly would solve most of my problems."

She could picture herself in her own home in the Canebière neighborhood of Marseille, in an entertaining and well-to-do environment. She didn't think for a second about the risks that Jeanne was taking. But why worry since her daughter was always successful at what she did?

For a short while, Jeanne forgot about her troubles by caring for others, those who had nothing. She made some nougat for the orphanage, which would wind up—along with the presents she'd brought—under the Christmas tree there. Then she went down in the storeroom where Fanny kept salted meat and mason jars filled with tomatoes, kidney beans, pickles, and peas. On the floor were large earthenware jars containing olives. On the shelves were gooseberries, Mirabelle plums, apricots, and strawberry jam, as well as the famous "Cotignac," a quince jelly from a recipe dating back to the days of Louis XIV. The entire house smelled wonderful when Apolline melted the fruits in heavy copper pots. Ever since she'd been a child, Jeanne couldn't wait for them to cool down so she could have some on a piece of toasted bread. As she was carefully selecting items that a worker would take over on a cart to the orphanage the following day, she heard someone coming down the steps.

"Hello, Jeanne."

It was Jérôme, his hair dripping wet from the rain.

"Apolline told me I would find you here."

Unable to utter a word, Jeanne watched him walk toward her.

"You look like you've seen a ghost," Jérôme said with a smile.

He held her hands for a long time, and she felt that this was an emotional moment for him as well.

"What are you doing? I want to help you," he said, looking at the shelves around him. "This is a regular Ali Baba's cave. Hmm, cherries in liqueur . . . "

"Would you like some?"

"Absolutely."

They sat on wooden crates. Jeanne opened a jar, and they dug in and ate a few cherries.

"They're better than my grandmother's," Jérôme said.

"If you want to be in Apolline's good graces, make sure to tell her that."

Jeanne was now in good spirits. Outside, it was cold and gray, where conflicts and dramatic events unfolded. But here, in this dimly lit room, harmony prevailed.

"I wanted to see Laurent," Jérôme said, "but I was told he's sleeping."

"He has been sleeping an awful lot since he came back from Paris."

"Like all people who want to forget."

"Suzie leaving was that hard on him?"

"I didn't want to tell you in a letter, but he tried to commit suicide."

Jeanne was aghast.

"What happened?" she asked.

"Suzie called me one evening to say that she'd left your brother and that he'd threatened to kill himself. She was very worried. I immediately went over to his room. He'd slashed his wrists. . . . "

Stunned, Jeanne muttered, "My God, if not for you, he'd be dead right now. . . . "

"Don't make yourself sick over something that didn't happen. I hesitated for a long time to tell you about it. But we all need to be vigilant."

"Sylvie knows about it?"

"I asked her not to say a thing."

Overcome with sadness, Jeanne began to cry. She cried over Laurent, their lost childhood, and their hopes that seemed to vanish little by little. She cried over life's harshness, over how complicated and painful love was.

"I'm so sorry," she finally managed to say.

As a response, Jérôme took Jeanne in his arms, and she freed herself of all the pressure that had accumulated inside her the past many months—the grief, the struggles, the sacrifices. When she calmed down, Jérôme kissed her on the side of the head.

"I must look awful," Jeanne muttered.

Jérôme laughed and said, "Go get fixed up. But, before that, invite me to dinner."

Jérôme insisted until Laurent finally agreed to come down to the living room for dinner. Looking gloomy, he barely answered his friend's questions, merely mumbling. But Jérôme didn't let that discourage him, and he launched into memories of their trip to the Himalayas, notably their evenings at the Darjeeling Planters' Club and the money the young man had made at the hippodrome.

"Laurent had no clue how to bet," he said, "and yet his horses won all the time, and he made a pile of cash!"

That brought a smile to Laurent's face, his first since returning to Restanques. Jeanne could see how hard Jérôme was working to try to help his friend. Against her will, he'd taken Laurent to the end of the world, but since then he'd taken care of him. He'd never let him down.

"We can't play his game," Jérôme told Jeanne when Laurent stepped out of the room for a moment. "Having empathy for him is one thing, but feeling sorry for him is another."

Sipping a glass of brandy, he sat back and relaxed. Jeanne had lit a bunch of candles in the living room, the flames reflecting in the mirrors. Fire was crackling in the hearth, next to which the nativity scene would soon be set up. After being on the move so much and for so long, Jérôme enjoyed the harmony of this moment, all the more precious since it hadn't been planned. The attachment he felt for Jeanne was getting stronger and was moving at just the right pace for him. Wearing a garnet-colored velvet dress, she was caressing the cat that had just jumped into her lap. A ribbon held up her hair, giving her the appearance of a little girl.

Jérôme often wondered about her love life. In Paris, Sylvie had mentioned an old relationship of hers, in Marseille, a thing of the past supposedly. . . . But what about Antoine Laferrière? Was she going to marry him? He was dying to know.

"When are you going back to Paris?" Laurent suddenly asked Jérôme.

"January tenth. Something like that."

"I might go with you."

Jeanne shuddered, but Jérôme's expression reassured her.

"What do you two have planned for New Year's Eve?" he asked.

"Nothing yet," Jeanne said.

"Well," Laurent said, "I'm going to bed."

"Nicole is having a party," Jérôme said. "You know how she loves to have fun. Sylvie and Michel are going to be there. You should come too."

"Jeanne can go if she wants," Laurent said. "I'm staying here."

Jérôme didn't insist. He glanced at his watch and said, "It's late. I have to head back to Entrecasteaux."

"You can sleep over here if you want," Laurent said.

"No, I'm staying at your uncle's for two days. But I'm going to come back tomorrow to pick you up. I want to show you my house in Cassis. The renovations are progressing very nicely."

"That's nice of you . . . but I don't really feel like going anywhere."

Once again, Jérôme didn't argue with Laurent.

"Good night, Jeanne," he said.

Jeanne walked him to the front steps. After the heat in the living room, the cold air felt like a slap.

"Go back inside," Jérôme said. "It's freezing out here."

And he ran to his car.

Laurent was in his pajamas, smoking a cigarette, staring off into the distance, when Jérôme walked into his room.

"You have ten minutes to get dressed."

"What are you talking about? I told you last night I didn't want to go."

Jérôme tossed a sweater and some pants at his friend.

"Come on, we're wasting time. I'm waiting for you down in the library."

An hour or so later, Laurent and Jérôme crossed a vineyard under a hazy sun and wound up in the hollow of a small valley where a winegrower's house stood. The renovations were almost complete.

"The perfect spot for a hermit," Jérôme said with a smile.

The house was made up of a single room on the ground floor, which contained a large fireplace. A ladder led to the attic that was going to be used as a bedroom.

"The workers are almost done digging the well," Jérôme said.

Laurent paid little attention to his friend's detailed description of what he was going to plant around his refuge. Why had he agreed to come here? He was tired and cold, and getting antsy. He couldn't wait to get out of the house. He preferred Restanques' gloom over the projects Jérôme was going on and on about.

Alas, the day was only beginning. On their way back, Jérôme decided to go to the piece of land that Suzie had hated so much.

"I've been thinking about this spot," Jérôme said. "I'd love to help you out if you did decide to create a garden here."

"You know I can't afford to do such a thing."

"Come on, Laurent, wake up! When I first met you, your head was filled with dreams and nothing seemed impossible to you. You were talking about parks, tropical greenhouses . . . Don't tell me all that vanished because of a woman who wasn't able to recognize your qualities!"

"Don't talk to me about Suzie, please."

"As a matter of fact, I do want to talk about her! Look at what she did to you! And if I hadn't shown up at your place that night, you'd be six feet under right now."

"Shut up!"

"No. I'm not going to coddle you anymore."

"If you think you can make me change my mind about her, you're wrong."

"Listen, Laurent. You're not the first one to be heartbroken because of a woman, and you won't be the last. . . . "

"You know about that firsthand?"

"It's no secret. I was in love with someone who wasn't free."

"So?"

"We had the choice to keep on betraying a man who was her husband and my best friend or stop doing just that. We decided to put some distance between us."

"You're not seeing her anymore?"

"I haven't in two months."

"And you're not sad?"

"Much less so than if we'd decided to stay together."

"That all sounds crazy to me!"

They were heading down the hill toward the sea. In spite of the gray winter sky, the site had lost none of its charm.

"Just imagine . . . " Jérôme said. "Terraces right over there overflowing with plants and trees. And here, we could have a harbor for people to sit and gaze at the sea. And there, picture a bandstand where an orchestra would play nice music for visitors on Sundays."

Jérôme's descriptions were so evocative that Laurent began to picture some sort of Garden of Eden filled with rosemary, Aleppo pines, cork oaks, rhododendrons, and azaleas—all for the pleasure of people coming here. Still, the woman he was in love with had turned her back on him, and the void felt like an amputation. Everything was colorless, joyless. What he experienced was a succession of days during which he had to pretend he was alive while his heart was in tatters.

That same day, Jeanne accompanied her mother to see the attorney. There, they met René Verdier's cousin, a decent-looking man who still seemed surprised to find himself the owner of an estate that, once sold, would enable him to buy a nice house in Lyon.

"One of my clients is interested in purchasing Bel Horizon," the attorney said. "He's ready to make an offer."

Turning to Marthe, he asked, "Are you reading to sell your olive groves as well?"

"Not for now."

A date was agreed upon for Marthe's move. At the beginning of January, she would live with a friend in Marseille until she found a place of her own. In the meantime, she would have to celebrate Christmas and New Year's, two holidays that would be a painful reminder of her two deceased husbands, as well as her uncertain future.

Jeanne tried her hardest to ensure that Christmas Eve would be like those they enjoyed at Restanques until the war, and the results were positive. Laurent was in slightly better spirits, and Marthe didn't fight with her brother, Raymond. Throughout the evening, Jeanne had the inescapable feeling that her destiny and Restanques' were intertwined. That very morning, she'd received a letter from Antoine, informing her of the banker's conditions for the loan.

Let me say it again, Antoine wrote, *you're playing for all or nothing*. He'd underlined the sentence and then added: *And remember that if you and I were married, you'd free yourself from most of your worries.*

After she told Raymond Delestang of her plans, he also warned her.

"Are you sure Laurent won't let you down?" he asked.

"He gave me his word not to do anything for a year."

"His word! In the state he's in, I'm not sure it's worth a whole lot. . . . "

"I'm taking that risk, just as I'm taking the risk of not listening to you. I've often heard that in difficult times, you have to trust your intuition."

1921

26

TWO DAYS AFTER CHRISTMAS, Jeanne's bedroom turned into a fitting room. Stepping over half-slips and evening gowns left on the carpet to form colorful piles, the young woman looked at herself in the long mirror.

"I don't know if I should dress in green or in blue," she told Apolline, who was helping her try things on.

"I like you in blue," the maid said.

"Let's put them both in the suitcase," Jeanne said.

How could she have guessed that strep throat would prevent her from going to Aix? Until the very last moment, she'd hoped that the suction cups and potions administered by the doctor would make her feel good enough to attend the New Year's Eve party, but her fever wouldn't go away. She was too exhausted to truly be disappointed, and she was half-asleep when her cousins came to pick up Laurent. He'd had no choice in going, as the Guillaumins had been so insistent.

But at ten o'clock, Jeanne began thinking about this special evening she'd been so looking forward to attending. She could picture the house decorated with holly and mistletoe, and she could almost smell the oranges studded with cloves, as well as the punch. Imagining Jérôme surrounded by his guests made her pulse race. Sometimes hot, other times cold, she tossed and turned in bed, unable to fall asleep. Her mouth dry, she drank a few sips of water. Her nightgown was drenched in sweat. With unsteady steps, she walked over to her chest of drawers to get another one. Her weakness worried her. How much longer would she feel so awful? On a chair, the suitcase that contained what she'd planned on taking to Aix seemed to mock her. Annoyed, Jeanne went back to bed for what would be one of the worse nights of her entire life. Everywhere on this very night people were dancing, laughing, eating, while she was all by herself feeling miserable. Several times, Apolline came up to see how she was doing. If Jeanne hadn't told the old lady to go to bed and get some sleep, she would have stayed up all night to watch over her, just like when she was a child.

"What would I do without you?" Jeanne said, holding Apolline's hand.

She'd never said anything of the sort to her own mother, but she was too tired to think about that. Also, she didn't know that Apolline knew her secret, the love she was feeling for Jérôme.

Jeanne got better more quickly than she expected but was depressed when she looked at herself in the mirror. She appeared drawn, her skin gray, with circles under her eyes.

Jérôme found her in that frame of mind when he showed up unexpectedly.

"Hi Jeanne," he said, trying to meet her gaze. "I didn't see you on New Year's Eve, and I heard you were doing better, so I decided to come for a visit."

"Jérôme . . . " Jeanne muttered. "I thought you'd left for Paris."

"I wasn't going to do that without seeing you!"

"But Laurent told me—"

"Laurent is always confused. How he is doing, by the way?"

"A bit better. Thanks to you."

"Kudos to him! He's finally beginning to get a grip on reality."

"Michel invited him to spend a couple of days in Entrecasteaux. We could go there."

"That's exactly what I had in mind."

Silence set in between them, until Jérôme said, "You don't believe me? I'm not in the habit of lying. You know that."

He walked over to Jeanne. She felt his breath on her cheek, then his lips on hers. And then everything became very natural, both losing themselves in the desire they had for each other. Jeanne wrapped her arms around Jérôme's neck, and they kissed. She shut her eyes, abandoning herself to the pleasure she'd fantasized about for such a long time. She felt dizzy as he kissed her and whispered in her ear words that stroked her heart and soul. He took her face in the palm of his hands, kissed her again, and then looked her in the eyes. Neither one of them was trying to hide any emotions.

All day long in Entrecasteaux, Jérôme was thrilled by Jeanne's presence. He drove her back to Restanques, and they both knew he wasn't going to leave after dinner. They couldn't wait for the meal to be over so they could be alone.

"Please prepare the red room for Mr. Guillaumin," Jeanne told Apolline.

And that was where she joined him once all the lights in the house were turned off and silence had set in. Only the bedside lamp was lit, giving the room a romantic glow.

"Jérôme . . . " she whispered.

He gave her a long kiss. Then, drinking in her scent of jasmine, he caressed her neck. The skin was as soft as he'd imagined.

Jérôme freed Jeanne's breasts from the lace that held them.

Soon she was standing naked before him, enjoying the way Jérôme admired her and then how he began caressing her body. He guided her to the bed. A clock chimed in the next room, but they didn't hear it, as they were so absorbed in their desire for each other. In the arms of the man she loved, Jeanne was learning about true complicity, this subtle and inexplicable bond that united them beyond the senses, something she knew she was already addicted to.

"You are so beautiful," Jérôme said.

The words added to Jeanne's excitement. She locked her legs around Jérôme's waist, and both abandoned themselves to the ecstasy of the moment.

Later, curled up in bed with her lover, Jeanne experienced a wonderful feeling of well-being—a mixture of gratefulness, trust, and inner peace. Outside, the wind was blowing softly, and in this bed, against Jérôme's warm body, she felt as though she were on an island, protected from any intrusion. Words came to her lips, but it was too early to utter them, she thought, so she chose to keep quiet and simply enjoy every second of this extraordinary night.

"Are you okay?" Jérôme asked her, worrying about Jeanne's silence.

"More than okay. What about you?"

"I feel in total harmony with the world. It's such a rare feeling, so precious."

The following day, Jérôme decided not to leave Restanques.

"Unless you're kicking me out!" he said.

In front of the staff, they decided to adopt a friendly attitude toward each other, speaking formally. But no one was fooled.

"She thinks we're blind," Apolline said, chuckling. "Like we never had flings when we were young!"

"This morning," Fanny said, "she was singing in her office."

"She must've been happy paying bills!"

The two women burst out laughing.

Jeanne was a million miles away from thinking about such comments. She was simply focusing on enjoying every moment of Jérôme's presence until his departure for Paris in three days. Many times she caught him gazing at her. What was in his mind? He expressed none of his thoughts until the evening.

"I'm going to miss you, you know," he said.

Without him realizing it, Jeanne had begun to occupy a large chunk of his life—even though it went against his plans. After he and Isabelle broke up, Jérôme had decided to have only short-lived affairs. No way was he going to fall in love anytime soon. It was too complicated and, ultimately, heartbreaking. As he'd tried to console Laurent, Jérôme himself was striving to get over the void caused by not seeing Isabelle anymore. He missed her laughter, the sound of the bracelets clanging together on her pretty wrists, her joyful voice, and her penetrating eyes.

"Jeanne," he asked. "The man who was in your life a while back, I suppose that you were in love with him."

"I thought I was."

"It wasn't Antoine?"

"No."

As Jérôme reached for his cigarette case, his arm hit a carafe, and it crashed onto the floor. Was it a warning against pursuing a conversation that might soon take the form of a confession on their part?

"This is good luck!" Jeanne said, before picking up the shards of glass.

Then it was their last night together, and Jeanne wanted to be the most gifted, sexual woman in the world for her lover. Taking charge, she melded their bodies and souls, integrating everything that surrounded them: the dark sky outside, the hooting of an owl, the slamming of a shutter by the wind, and the very house that protected them. When Jérôme brought her to an incredible orgasm, it took everything for her not to say, "I love you."

Jérôme also wanted to express his bliss in being with her.

"Tell me that you're going to remember this evening forever," he said, as he penetrated her.

Everything must come to an end, and Jeanne was struggling not to display the unbearable sadness she felt as her lover was about to leave.

"When am I going to see you again?" she asked, as Jérôme put on his coat.

"Apolline promised to look after you," he said, taking Jeanne in his arms.

"Well, I see that you guys have been scheming behind my back."

She smiled, but she really was cursing Paris as well as Jérôme's profession, which monopolized most of his time. But how could she blame him for wanting to care for his fellow man by trying to find cures for different ailments? Many times Jérôme had passionately talked to her about his work, the research he did in his lab.

"It's such an exciting and yet humbling experience," he'd said.

Jérôme tied a scarf around his neck and hugged Jeanne tenderly.

"My darling," he whispered in her ear.

Then he quickly turned around and, crossing the threshold, said in a sad voice, "See you soon."

Torn between exaltation from the visit and grief after Jérôme's departure, Jeanne decided to lose herself in work. Raymond had taken Marthe to her friend's in Marseille, and now the Bel Horizon house needed to be emptied out. With the help of Sylvie, Jeanne organized the move. Some of the furniture would go back to Restanques, while other items were going to be stored until Marthe found a permanent home. As for the rest, René Verdier's heir could do whatever he wanted with it.

Before leaving the house, Jeanne went into each room one last time to make sure she hadn't forgotten anything.

In a closet she found the letters René Verdier had sent Marthe during their courtship. Jeanne tossed them in the fireplace. For fear that some of the letters her mother wrote might fall into the hands of strangers, she rifled through the drawers of the imposing desk that had belonged to Verdier. Among some bills, she found a few francs, some agricultural medals, many photographs of naked women, a garter belt, and lists. The first list contained the names of the women Verdier had slept with, along with his misspelled comments about them. The second list detailed his possessions. As for the third one, Jeanne had to read it a couple of times to be certain she wasn't dreaming. All of her clients were itemized: the candy-store owners in Aix, Brignoles, Draguignan, Toulon, Marseille, and Salon—every single one of them. Next to their names were the dates when Verdier visited them. He'd watched her every move! This discovery left her shaken with disbelief. She knew Verdier had tried to harm her, but she'd never imagined that he'd be able to come up with such an elaborate smear campaign. But there was more. In a notebook, she found a detailed account of Restanques' plots of land. Next to each plot was the ridiculous amount of money he planned on offering after he was able to take down the estate financially! One more thing attracted Jeanne's attention: the purchase order for a medallion. On it was a drawing of the jewel—a rose surrounded by a garland spelling out Rosalie's name.

At that moment, Sylvie showed up in the room and said, "Are you okay? You look pale."

"It's nothing," Jeanne said. "I'm a bit tired, I guess. . . . "

*   *   *

Jeanne was handing the attorney the keys to the Bel Horizon house when he said, "The new owner told me that he's interested in buying Ms. Verdier's olive groves. He's making a good offer. I wrote your mother about it."

"You wrote her in Marseilles?"

"Yes, at the address she gave me."

"You could've talked to me about it first."

"I'm sorry, I didn't think it concerned you."

Jeanne remained angry until evening. Verdier's cousin had made an offer that she could never match, and her mother might be tempted by a quick and lucrative transaction.

"You have to help me," she told Laurent.

"How?"

"You could talk to Mother."

"Are you kidding? She'll do just the opposite of what I ask her!" Laurent put out his cigarette in an ashtray. "Why are you so hard-headed about this, Jeanne? I've told you a hundred times: let's get rid of Restanques. We'd have fewer worries, more freedom of movement, and we wouldn't have to struggle to find money all the time."

"Are you going back on your word?"

"No! I'm just trying to make you see straight."

27

ROSALIE NO LONGER NEEDED medical care. She was about to leave the hospital room where François had visited her when he was able to take two days off for the New Year.

Without telling anyone, he'd taken a train for Nice. How could he have guessed that he was showing up at the very worst of moments? Rosalie barely glimpsed at him when he walked into her room. His enthusiasm dampened by this reaction, François staggered over to the bed. Scowling, Rosalie pulled her blankets up to her chin.

"Rosalie," François said, "how are you doing?"

"Not good."

"Are you in a lot of pain?"

"Yes."

"I brought you a few cookies and some dates," he muttered, setting the bag on the nightstand. "Some chocolate, too. . . . "

"That's nice of you," Rosalie said, not looking at her presents.

"Are you mad I came?"

"No, I don't care one way or the other."

Stunned and hurt, François wondered what had made him decide to come. He looked at Rosalie. Her hair was a matted mess, and she was pale. She displayed none of the charm she once had, but he was still attracted to her. The silence in the room went on forever. François thought about the long train ride, all the money he'd spent on such a pitiful moment.

"I'm tired," Rosalie finally said.

"You want to sleep?"

She nodded.

"Okay, then, I'll leave you alone."

"Yes, thanks."

In the hallway, François ran into a nurse. Her pleasant face gave him some comfort.

"I was just with Rosalie Pervenche," he said.

"Yes," the nurse said. "She's not doing so well. But you can't blame her, poor thing . . . Did she tell you?"

"Tell me what?"

"She learned this morning that she'd have a limp."

"A limp . . . You mean for the rest of her life?"

"Yes. The doctors are certain of that."

François shivered. Rosalie and her vitality . . . Rosalie always light on her feet . . . He wanted to run back to the room, take Rosalie in his arms, and tell her that, for him, she'd always be the most beautiful, the most graceful of women. The nurse kept on talking, but all he could hear was the pounding of his own heart.

Distraught, François left the hospital. What was he going to do in this town while waiting for the next train to Cotignac? Without knowing it, he made his way to the Promenade des Anglais, virtually deserted on this winter's day. Walking pass the mansions and restaurants, he was overwhelmed by so much luxury. As he approached the casino, François imagined himself walking along the promenade with Rosalie on a gorgeous summer afternoon, surrounded by a festive crowd. Children in bathing suits would splash in the sea. Young couples would buy sweets from street vendors. It would be hot, maybe too hot . . . Rosalie would wear a white wide-brimmed hat and, in the evening, they'd go to a ball, and she wouldn't be ashamed to dance since he'd make her forget about her limp.

He snapped out of his reverie and wondered how he'd get over the one he was so much in love with. Up ahead on the walkway was an old lady sitting on a bench. A black wool scarf covered her hair. François watched her as she took a sandwich out of a paper bag, tossed a few crumbs to the seagulls surrounding her, and began to take small bites. François went over to her. After all he'd gone through today, he needed to talk to someone.

"Hello," he said. "Do you often come here?"

"Yes," the old lady said. "I don't like eating by myself, all alone in my kitchen."

He sat next to her, and they began chatting. The woman told François that she'd lost both her husband and her son in the war.

"After that," she added, "I started to hate our house, so I get out as much as I can, and I often have the chance to run into someone, like you today, and chat for a while. But what about you, son? What are you doing here? You're not from the area . . . "

"That's right. I'm just in town for the day."

"Ah, how I'd like to be young again, just like you, and think about the future. You work on a farm?"

Surprised, François said, "Yes."

"I could tell because of your hands."

As their conversation continued, François began to feel better. The old lady had spoken about the future, something that didn't mean much to her. What could she now expect from life? None of the two beings she'd cherished would ever come back to her. But what about him? He felt like he had no right giving up. In spite of what it looked like, there was still hope. Rosalie was alive, and so was he. If she came back to Cotignac, he'd eventually manage to sway her.

With newfound determination, François approached his boss.

"Miss Jeanne," he said, "I went to see Rosalie."

"In Nice?"

"Yes."

"I heard she will remain handicapped. It's so sad."

"I'm worried about her."

"So am I. I've been thinking about it. Having her come back here after everything that happened might not make sense. At the same time, I don't want to abandon her."

"Take her back, Miss Jeanne. Please."

François had uttered those words with such fervor that Jeanne stared at her employee.

Moved, she said, "I'll see what I can do."

Who would have thought that Rosalie would be the one resisting the idea?

"I don't want to go back to Restanques," she told the doctor when he said that she would soon be able to leave the hospital.

"But Ms. Barthélemy is ready to take you back! Don't you realize how fortunate you are?"

Did he mean that her limp would prevent her from getting work anywhere else? Tears were stinging her eyes.

"It's my decision."

Where was she going to go? The thought of living in Toulon horrified her, but she preferred that to the idea of limping in front of Laurent. That was the problem going back to Restanques. Appearing before him crippled after he'd complimented her so much on her beauty prevented her from making the sensible decision.

It took Michel Delestang's best arguments to overcome

the maid's stubbornness. She agreed to come to Restanques for the night. Jeanne was the one who suggested Michel pick up Rosalie. After taking care of the paperwork, he waited for the young woman in the hospital's entrance hall, where she showed up walking with a cane.

"Oh!" she said at the sight of Michel. "Nobody told me you were here!"

"Did you think I was going to let you take the train?"

As they were talking, Michel guided Rosalie to his car.

"I have to tell you," she said, "I do not want to set foot in Cotignac."

"Don't worry. We're going straight to Restanques."

After all that time in the hospital—the bleak corridors, the sick people, the nurses and doctors in uniform, the smell of ether—walking on a city street felt wonderful to Rosalie. As they crossed Nice in Michel's automobile, she took in the colorful crowds of people, the bustling traffic, the constant movement, and it made her enjoy life again. But soon she felt exhausted and fell asleep as soon as the car reached the countryside.

When she woke up, Michel said, "Don't be too proud at Restanques, okay?"

"What do you mean?"

"If you refuse what people offer you, Rosalie, you're only going to punish yourself. Do you hear me?"

As they passed through Restanques' gates, Rosalie had only agreed to spend the night there and to speak with Jeanne the following day.

Apolline greeted her with tears of joy, and Fanny gave her a long hug. Rosalie was surprised at how happy she was to see them again.

"God," the cook said, "we were so worried about you!"

Sitting at the kitchen table, Rosalie rediscovered the familiar smells that brought back happy memories. She also couldn't remain indifferent to the comforting aspects of this place she'd known since early childhood.

Her aunt set a plate of pork and rice on the table.

"Eat," the woman simply said.

Slowly, in a subtle manner, Rosalie's reticence began to falter. After so many disillusions, so much pain, so much sadness, where else would she find such a friendly environment? The heat given off by the oven felt wonderful. Fanny was at work making a potato cake. The cat was meowing in front of its empty dish. Everything was in its place, and everything Rosalie had wanted to escape so badly now seemed precious to her.

Rosalie was heading for the room she'd shared with Apolline when Laurent stepped out of his bedroom down the hall. There was no way she could avoid him, so she kept on walking until they were face-to-face.

"How are you doing, Rosalie?" he asked.

"I've been better," she said.

"I'm so sorry. . . . "

If he seemed genuinely sad, she understood that he would have felt the same for anyone else in her position. She'd loved him, and out of jealousy, she'd tried to punish him, which had led to a mess of gigantic proportions. She also saw that Laurent no longer looked like the happy, intrepid young man she'd known. What had happened for him to be so out of sorts? Suzie, no doubt. . . . Funny, it didn't matter to her. Rosalie realized then that she didn't care about Laurent anymore, so she decided not to fight against her destiny: to remain at Restanques.

"What happened has to remain a secret between us," Jeanne told Rosalie the following morning.

"No one knows? Really?"

"No one except my mother."

"Dear God, if she ever saw me here!"

"It's not going to happen. She swore she'd never come back to Cotignac."

"Are you going to tell her I'm working here?"

"Why would I want to do that?"

"What about Mr. Laurent? Does he know the truth?"

"How many times do I have to tell you, Rosalie? Nobody here knows about your relationship with René Verdier."

"If you only knew how ashamed I am of it!"

"Forget about your shame, and concentrate on the present."

"The present," the maid said, looking at her damaged leg.

"I know what you're thinking, but life goes on. Besides, no matter what you think, you're still beautiful."

"Beautiful! No man will ever say that to me again!"

"Just keep your eyes and ears open."

Rosalie produced a skeptical pout and tied an apron around her waist before heading for the back of the house, where there were boots and shoes to shine.

Jeanne sat at her desk and began going through the pile of bills. The season had been successful, but the income she'd made with the nougat wasn't enough to cover all the estate's expenses. Only the olive groves belonging to Marthe would give her the financial security she'd been striving for since her father's death. With the help of Antoine, she'd managed to obtain an appointment the following week with the banker who was willing to give her a loan.

Rosalie walked into her office.

"There's someone here for you," she said.

"I'm not expecting anyone," Jeanne said.

"A Mr. Coursange would like to talk to you. He's with a young woman."

Coursange! Bel Horizon's new owner. Jeanne figured he wouldn't be much different from René Verdier.

"Show him to the living room," she told Rosalie.

*   *   *

Wearing a jacket and riding breeches, Jacques Coursange looked to be fifty years old. He had a pleasant face and a firm handshake.

"Good morning, Miss Barthélemy," he said. "I'm your new neighbor. Let me introduce you to my daughter, Marianne."

The tall young woman took a step forward to shake Jeanne's hand. She had mischievous eyes, milk-white skin, and a wild mane of brown hair.

In the course of the conversation, Jeanne learned that Jacques Coursange was a wine merchant and that his daughter was starting a teaching career in Brignoles.

"For a long time, my wife and I had been looking for a house in the countryside. Mr. Rouvel, the notary, told us about Bel Horizon just when we were getting discouraged. The house needs fixing, but the land is fertile. As for the view, the name of the estate couldn't be more appropriate!"

As the meeting continued, Jeanne found her guests more and more pleasant. Why did they have to be interested in the olive groves?

"I understand that Mr. Rouvel has sent my mother your offer, but she's already negotiating with another possible buyer."

"I'm very sorry to hear that. Maybe you could talk to your mother on our behalf?"

"I don't know about that."

Jeanne was playing with fire. She'd learned only a couple of days earlier that her mother had her eyes on an apartment in Marseille. If Jeanne didn't come up with the money Marthe needed soon, her mother would accept Jacques Coursange's offer.

"I hope that you're going to come over to our house for dinner," Marianne told Jeanne as she and her father were leaving. "My mother would be so happy to welcome you there."

"I would love to," Jeanne said, shivering in the cold.

For the past few days, the temperature had dropped abnormally, and Jeanne was beginning to fear for her trees. Both almond and olive trees could be killed by the frost. Everybody in the region still had in mind the horrible winters of 1837 and 1870, when ice storms wiped out the harvests.

"Imagine if I take out that loan on a year when the olive trees don't produce anything?" Jeanne said to Sylvie.

"Jeanne," her cousin said, "you're scaring us all. You're making my father sick with worry."

"Don't say any more, or I'm the one who's going to be sick. . . . "

28

THE WEATHER HADN'T CHANGED for the better when Jeanne went to her appointment with the Marseille banker, Mr. Salmon.

Looking preoccupied, Antoine was waiting for her in the banker's office. The two men had just finished going over the contract. The young woman committed to repay the loan within five years. If she didn't manage to do so, part of Restanques would no longer be hers. Antoine had insisted the mortgaged fields be those on the estate's outskirts.

"That way, you'd get to keep the house," he told Jeanne.

Jeanne's heart was pounding as she signed the documents, but she told herself that this was the best thing to do, as she was confident she'd be able to make Restanques a success.

When they were done, Mr. Salmon walked her to the exit.

"Well, Ms. Barthélemy," he said, "I wish you the very best of luck."

Once out on the sidewalk, she thanked Antoine.

"Without you," she said, "I never would've gotten this loan."

"I'm still not convinced that this was a good idea, but let's go for a hot chocolate."

They walked into a café where other folks had taken refuge from the cold, drinking rum or hot wine. Through the fogged-up windows, the city seemed lifeless, and a stranger never would have imagined the usual commotion on the street. Was it because of the low, gray sky and the cold temperature that no one in the café seemed to enjoy themselves, not even the card players at the back of the room?

"When are you going back to Cotignac?" Antoine asked.

"This evening. I'm going to spend the afternoon with my mother, and then we'll have dinner together." Out of the blue, she asked, "Have you heard from our friend Guillaumin lately?"

"Nothing! I only know that Nicole is going up to Paris soon to spend a week with him."

How many times had Jeanne hoped that a letter from Jérôme would be in the morning mail? Had he already forgotten about her? Was he back with the woman he'd talked to her about? She had a hard time imagining that he'd used her, but Régis had shown her how deceitful men could be, and she couldn't dismiss the hypothesis altogether. She watched Antoine put a sugar cube into his hot chocolate. His attitude indicated that he'd understood that she would never love him, and this realization relieved her.

"Antoine," she whispered.

He looked at her straight in the eyes and said, "I know . . . but let's not use the word *friend* yet. It's too early for me."

Marthe had asked her daughter to meet her at the apartment she wanted to buy, four rooms on the second floor of a bourgeois building with a spotless staircase smelling of beeswax. As soon as she walked into the apartment, Jeanne felt suffocated. How could anyone live in a place like this, far from flowers and trees and wide-open spaces?

Showing Jeanne a living room with a black marble fireplace, she said, "In here, I'll be able to have friends over to play bridge. Let me show you my future bedroom."

She'd already figured out where she was going to put her furniture. Jeanne had never seen her mother so enthusiastic about anything before.

"I'm finally living the life I always wanted," Marthe said. "Nobody here knows I'm a widow, so I can go for walks, to the movies. The owner of this building even invited me to dinner. . . . "

Jeanne looked at her mother. Marthe simply couldn't help herself. She had already probably concocted in her mind some sort of romantic saga around that invitation. *Let's just hope*, Jeanne thought, *that this man isn't another René Verdier. . . .*

"Have you talked about a price yet?"

"No, that wouldn't be proper!"

"Mother, I beg you, hire someone competent to take care of this."

As she uttered the words, Jeanne had the feeling she was wasting her time. Her mother had launched herself into a new adventure, and no one would be able to prevent her from doing things her way. Jeanne decided to talk to her about the olive groves instead.

"I don't know," Marthe said. "What are people going to say if I sell the groves to you? Of course, according to tradition, I should give them to you and your brother, but times are so difficult for a woman on her own. . . . This Mr. Coursange seems very serious."

"You're not going to change your mind on me, are you? I have the money!"

"Yes, I know. . . . "

"Mother, if you sell that land to Mr. Coursange, you're never going to see me again."

"Jeanne, calm down."

"Only after we finalize our transaction. I understand your worries, I appreciate your situation, but there's a limit to my patience! Let's get this done!"

She hated raising her voice at her mother, but that was the only way to impress her.

"I'm also tired of all this," Marthe said. "At my age and in my situation, I should have peace and quiet."

"Exactly."

They had to talk some more before Jeanne finally got what she wanted. Marthe agreed to sell the olive groves to her.

They left the apartment building. Marthe was going back to her friend's.

"I'll meet you there before dinner," Jeanne said. "I need to go for a walk."

"But it's freezing out!"

Protected from the cold by her fur-trimmed coat, Jeanne quickly walked down the street, taking big gulps of air. As she neared the center of town, more and more streetcars went by her, and the crowds on the sidewalk grew denser. Most people were bundled up. She arrived in the Old Port and, in spite of the cold, stood and looked at some of the docked ships. She felt energized. Finally things were settled. Of course she didn't know what the future held for her, but at least the die was cast. She glanced at a public clock and decided to buy a present for Ms. Pascale's grandson and then headed for the candy store.

"What a nice surprise!" Ms. Pascale said. "I didn't know you were in Marseille!"

Jeanne gave her the box that contained a metal tumbler.

"You shouldn't have!" Ms. Pascale said.

"How's the baby?"

"Great. He's only three months old, but he looks twice that age. At night, he turns into a little demon. He's waking up and crying all the time. My poor daughter is exhausted. . . . But let's change the subject. We sold all your nougat."

"That's wonderful. I can't believe it."

"Our clients were fighting over it! And believe me, they're

connoisseurs. They're used to quality products here. . . . Oh, there's Henriette! Everybody is coming for a visit today."

Turning around, Jeanne stood face-to-face with Régis's wife.

"Good evening, Jeanne," her old rival said, holding out a hand.

"Good evening."

Both embarrassed and a bit stunned, they found nothing else to say to each other.

"And how's our Régis?" Ms. Pascale said. "We never see him anymore."

"Don't be mad at him," Henriette said. "He's been working awfully hard lately."

"He still hasn't met our little Sylvain."

Jeanne stepped aside but looked at Henriette in a mirror and found that she'd lost some of her old sparkle.

"We're having dinner at my mother-in-law's," Henriette said, "and she adores your fruit bars. I'm here to buy some."

"Well," Jeanne said, "I should go."

"No," Ms. Pascale said. "Stay a while."

"You're busy. I'll be back."

"Okay then, see you soon. And thanks again for the present."

Jeanne left the store.

"A very courageous young woman," Ms. Pascale said. "But wait a minute, you know Jeanne, don't you?"

"A little."

On her way back home, Henriette was deep in thought. She opened the door and was greeted by the dog. She walked into the living room, where Régis was reading the paper, drinking some whiskey.

"It's late," he said. "I was worried. Where were you?"

"My history class finished later than usual, and then I went over to your godmother's store."

"Yes . . . "

"Know who I saw there?"

"Who?"

"Jeanne Barthélemy."

"Really."

"You're not going to ask how she's doing?"

"Sure. How is she?"

"As pretty as ever."

"Besides that?"

"She seemed to be in a hurry."

"What do I care about that? What I want to know is how you are doing. How's your cold?"

Henriette poured herself a glass of Porto.

"I'm okay," she said.

Régis got up. Henriette heard him come her way.

"You didn't kiss me just now," he said.

"Germs."

Régis wrapped his arms around Henriette and pressed his lips against hers.

"You know I'm never sick. What is it you're trying to do? It's been going on for months! You're trying to get back at me?"

"What are you talking about?"

"You're so distant. You used to love me."

"Yes."

"But not anymore?"

"Listen, Régis, your parents are waiting for us, and I'd like to freshen up before we head out."

"You're staying right here."

"What do you mean? What's gotten into you?"

"I'm getting tired of your little game. It's as though you want to leave me out of everything that's important in your life."

"You're right."

"Why are you doing this?"

"I'm protecting myself."

"Stop clinging to the past! I've changed."

"Great! Because you've changed, you want everything to go exactly your way? You may have a short memory, but not me. Because I was in love with you, I made the biggest mistake I could. It was not only stupid on my part but dishonest to impose a child on you. I was ready to do anything to keep you."

"You never did anything to show me you wanted me so much before you became pregnant!"

"That's because I thought that would make you go away."

"You might have a point there. . . . "

"So, what was I supposed to do to make you leave Jeanne?"

"You knew about that?"

"Of course I did. But what's the point of living in the past? I don't want to talk about Jeanne, or the god-awful way you talked to me after our wedding, the sleepless nights when I waited for you to come back home from some bar or a bordello, or the way I felt when I was pregnant, like some sort of criminal."

"Stop that!" Overwhelmed, Régis grabbed his wife by the arms. "What do I have to do, Henriette? Tell me what I need to do for you to forgive me."

"I'd tell you if I knew. But I don't think there's anything."

"You really don't love me anymore?"

"Something broke inside me."

"Give me one last chance. You've also changed a lot, and I'm beginning to love you the way you are today, more resolute, more independent, deeper. Let's try not to hurt each other anymore. Thanks to you, I've come to realize a lot of things, and I think I've overcome a lot of my fears, including becoming attached to someone."

For a long time Henriette had hoped to hear these words, yet now they left her almost indifferent. But why give up all hope? In matters of the heart, things sometimes took wild, unexpected turns.

Her nose began to run, and she looked for a handkerchief. Régis, in a magician's gesture, produced his.

"Tada!" he said. "And it's clean. I swear!"

Henriette smiled as she accepted the hanky.

29

BACK HOME FROM MARSEILLE, Jeanne saw that she'd received a letter from Jérôme: *I know it's been a long time since I wrote you. Please forgive me. One of my colleagues has been on sick leave, and I've had to cover for him on top of my own work. Every night I wanted to write you, but I was too exhausted. Jeanne, how I hate all those miles that prevent me from holding you in my arms. Do you think about your botanist at times? I'm kissing the dimple in the small of your back . . .*

Jeanne read and reread the letter, and then, her heart bursting with joy, went up to her bedroom. Rosalie was there, lighting a fire.

"Thank you," Jeanne said. "It's so cold!"

"Tonight, I'll warm up your bed before you go to sleep."

"Good idea," Jeanne said. "What about you, Rosalie. Not too tired?"

"No, I'm fine."

"You know, you can have the small room next to the kitchen if you'd like. You'd be more comfortable there. Unless you prefer Apolline's company."

Her own room! Nothing could have made Rosalie happier, as she yearned for silence and solitude. Once in her new quarters, she unpacked her things. She didn't have very much—her clothes, a few seashells, and a doll she'd won at a fair. All the presents that Verdier had given her wound up in the river. She hung above her bed the religious images she'd received from the hospital chaplain. She set on her nightstand the mirror that François had given her. They'd run into each other twice since her return to Restanques, and he hadn't said much. No doubt he was upset with her because of the way she'd behaved when he visited her in the hospital.

As a matter of fact, François had decided not to press things anymore. If and when she was ready, Rosalie would come to him. For now, he was happy to know that she was protected from the cold, unemployment, and hunger—especially now, with this awful weather. . . . How cold would it actually get? What would the trees tolerate? Many days passed, during which he feared the worst could happen, that years and years of work might be annihilated overnight by the frost. Jeanne did all she could to hide her worry but kept going to see her employee to ask how things were out in the fields.

Jeanne found no solace from Laurent. His behavior surprised everyone, including Rosalie, who saw nothing in this taciturn and idle man that matched the person she'd fallen in love with. Shutting himself in his bedroom, he spent his days doing nothing but dwelling on memories, good and bad. He'd also received a letter from Jérôme, who was living his dream in Paris. This made Laurent even more depressed. On the shelves all around him were the books on geography, science, and botany on which he'd spent all his savings when he was a student. On his desk were the notebooks he'd filled with his observations, as well as albums of photos he'd taken during his travels in Asia.

"I'm never going to have the strength to travel again," he said to Michel, who came to visit him on a regular basis.

"I bet you will," Michel said.

"You're going to lose your bet."

"What are you doing to yourself, Laurent? Why are you turning your back on your talent and your wonderful knowledge? I used to envy your passion so much! I would've sold my soul to the devil to be like you, to have aspirations that were so out of the ordinary."

The person his cousin was talking about was some sort of stranger whom Laurent had no desire to meet. Hiding in an environment where he didn't have to prove himself, he lived with his pain and almost regretted that Jérôme had saved his life. Nobody could understand the despair that was gnawing at him, the anguish that left him paralyzed, his dreadful feeling of emptiness.

He felt even worse when Sylvie came to kiss him goodbye before leaving for Paris.

"I didn't know you were going back," Laurent said.

"Nicole asked me to go with her."

Images of the days when he first settled in Paris, when Suzie completely monopolized his time, came to Laurent's mind. He'd had to accompany her everywhere—the theater for rehearsals, the dressmaker for fittings, the restaurant to eat and drink with friends. All that remained of that glorious time were ashes, and this depression that cut him off from the others.

Rosalie often came in to clean his room or bring him some clothes, but he paid no attention to her. As for Jeanne, he wished he could help her, but she was working toward a future that he was unable to even fathom. He didn't care one way or the other about Restanques being sold.

"Thank God the temperature is finally rising," she told him one morning. "I can't tell you how scared I was."

Work began out in the fields. Little by little, nature woke up again, and before long, it would be bursting with color. It would soon be Mardi Gras, and the residents of Cotignac began planning for it. In keeping with tradition, many days of festivities would take place. A make-believe marriage would be orchestrated, with the participants dressed as their ancestors. There would also be masquerade balls, so people went to the milliner to rent out masks and costumes.

The preparations were in full swing when Laurent, who left Restanques only to buy cigarettes, stepped out of the tobacco shop. All around him people carrying baskets of food were coming and going and children chased each other, shouting and laughing. All that commotion made Laurent dizzy. He climbed into his car.

He'd just left the village when a young woman waved for him to stop.

"You wouldn't happen to be going in the direction of Bel Horizon?" she asked.

"Hop in," Laurent said.

The woman put her easel and a box of paints in the back seat.

"Thank you so much," she said.

"You're a painter?"

"Well, I paint. Once in a while. . . . Cotignac's fountains inspire me. I've done a series of pictures of them."

The woman had a pleasant voice, and Laurent turned to her. She wore a gray felt hat on top of her copper-colored mane of hair. Her eyes were dark and bright, and she had a dazzling smile.

Pretty, Laurent thought.

"Do you live around here?" she asked, once settled in the front seat.

"At Restanques."

"Really? That means we're neighbors!"

"You must be the one and only Marianne that my sister has told me about."

Many times Jeanne had gone over to the Coursanges, with Laurent always declining to go along with her.

"I don't have anything to say to them," he said every time.

But now, sitting next to Marianne, he perked up.

"I'm slowly getting to know the region," she said. "We used to live in Valence, but my father wanted to move to the countryside."

"And you like the change?"

"I like everything that's new."

"Really?"

"And, just as you did, I want to travel. For now, I teach in Brignoles, but I hope that one day I'll work abroad. Egypt, for example."

The thought of Suzie, who'd gone on a tour of Egypt, broke the spell.

"Have you been there?" Marianne asked.

"Just a quick stopover in Port Said."

Laurent's car passed by a cart pulled by a donkey and then stopped in front of Bel Horizon's gates.

"Thanks for the lift," Marianne said, grabbing her things. "This is heavy!" Then she added, "I hope to see you at the house soon, with your sister."

"Don't count on it," Laurent said. "I hate chitchat."

"What chitchat? Do you think I spend my days sitting around chitchatting, as you say, and eating bonbons?"

"Whatever," Laurent said. "I just don't like leaving the house."

Confounded by his attitude, she stared at Laurent for a while before muttering, "It's odd . . . We're both young, and yet I feel like I'm talking to an old man. There's nothing vibrant about you."

Refusing to hear anything else Marianne had to say, Laurent put the car in gear and stepped on the gas pedal. Who did she think she was, judging him that way?

"That Marianne Coursange is one serious pain in the neck," he told Jeanne later that day.

"Marianne? She's a wonderful person! How do you know her?"

Laurent quickly described their encounter.

"You should keep your distance from her," he concluded.

Tired of her brother's behavior, Jeanne didn't even try to reason with him.

"I've run out of patience with him," she told Rosalie later. "And I don't think I'm the only one. How can you stand someone who's always complaining and moaning? Especially since he had everything going for him!"

"He can't see that."

"You're right."

"And he has all the time in the world to wallow in his sadness. If he was as busy as I am, maybe his attitude would be different."

Rosalie never complained. On the contrary, she did everything to overcome her disability. Her leg often hurt, in the evening mainly, at the end of her workday. By herself in her little room, she tried not to opine about her lost dreams. She had yearned for so long about achieving social status and wealth, but fate had punished her for her greed and duplicity. . . . The hardest part was to control her pride, particularly when Augustine and the other workers gave her looks of pity.

"Are you going to the ball?" Annie asked her.

Rosalie wondered if Annie was being mean to her, or if she was simply oblivious.

"No, I'm not," she said.

Jeanne had given her staff the day off so they could go to Cotignac and enjoy the festivities. In spite of their age, Fanny and Apolline got all dressed up and were ready to go. They laughed like little girls as they climbed onto the carriage that was going to take them to the village along with the other workers.

Rosalie waved at them and then decided to go for a short walk. Soon the almond trees would blossom, her favorite time of the year. Deep in her thoughts, she walked until she reached the farm. She went by the dehusking room, where she'd spent so much time, and remembered all the plans and schemes she had in mind then. She never could have imagined that she would one day have no feelings whatsoever for Laurent.

A few yards ahead of her, she spotted François, who was tending to a dog's wounded leg.

She stopped next to him and asked, "You're not going to town with the rest of them?"

"No."

Making sure the bandage was nice and tight, he didn't raise his head.

"There," he said to the dog. "You'll be good as new in no time."

The dog licked François' hand and then hopped away.

"François . . . " Rosalie said.

"Yes?"

"I haven't always been nice to you."

"Forget about it."

"Are you angry with me?"

"Of course not. . . . "

"You're different with me."

"I simply got that you don't want anything to do with me."

"Not anymore."

"Ah . . . "

Rosalie wondered how he could remain so calm, and François himself was surprised that his heart wasn't beating in his throat. Something had just happened. Slowly, Rosalie was coming to him. That's what he thought, though he couldn't be sure.

"Have you eaten?" she asked him.

"Not yet. I have to feed the horses now, but if you want to wait a bit, I cooked a stew. We could share it."

"Okay. In the meantime, I'll make some vanilla pudding."

They sat together at the kitchen table. Rosalie noticed that François had changed his shirt and combed his hair.

"I brought a bottle of wine," he said. "A present from Ms. Jeanne that I was keeping for a special occasion."

"It's very nice of you, but . . . "

François handed her the glass he'd just filled.

"Come on," he said, "let's drink to your return to Restanques."

At the beginning of the meal, François and Rosalie talked about this and that, but then, as they grew a bit tipsy, they tackled more personal topics.

"Do you think you're going to spend all your life at Restanques?" François asked.

"I'll stay as long as I'm wanted."

"You don't want anything else out of life?"

"That's just for me to know!"

She said it with a harsh voice, so François kept quiet.

"Well," Rosalie said. "It's getting late. I better turn in."

She got up and headed for her bedroom.

The following evening, everyone was stunned to see Rosalie walk out into the yard wearing an old dress and a hat found in the attic.

"Well, well!" Fanny said. "You finally decided to have some fun!"

"Where's François?" the young maid asked.

"In the shed over there."

Rosalie found François putting away some tools.

"I didn't want to go to the village without telling you," she said.

"I'm going with you," he replied.

In the stifling heat, the villagers were dancing and laughing in the streets on this Mardi Gras evening, every single one of them wearing their best costumes, as prizes would be awarded later on. At the sight of the crowd, Rosalie recoiled. How was she going to be able to participate in the wild dancing? Here and there she spotted young men who, before her accident, had courted her. She'd turned them down with disdain. It was now their turn to laugh at the cripple! Suddenly Rosalie felt François' arm under hers, and he guided her to a quieter area. They gazed at the crowd.

"Look at that pirate," François said. "Pretty impressive. . . . "

But Rosalie was looking for Jeanne. She'd helped her with her costume. She finally saw her chatting with a Roman senator wearing a toga.

Rosalie started to relax a little.

Sensing that, François said, "Let's dance."

And before Rosalie had time to say anything, he grabbed her by the waist.

"Close your eyes, listen to the music, and forget about everything," he said.

She didn't want to dance; she wanted to resist, but she let herself go. Soon she felt exhilarated, and she and François turned and turned to the sound of the music under the paper lanterns hanging across the street. She felt François' body against hers, and that gave her strength. Until now, how had he been so kind to her, so protective?

30

FRANÇOIS WANTED ROSALIE TO be proud of him, so he worked twice as hard as before. After the cold snap, the trees had been trimmed and mended, and a good harvest of almonds and olives was expected.

Relieved, Jeanne concentrated on the house's renovations. She hired painters, and soon the living room, dining room, and bedroom walls were covered in pastel colors. The armchairs and sofas retrieved from Bel Horizon were sent to be upholstered, and the lampshades were replaced to dispense a softer light.

"Why all the changes?" Laurent grumbled.

"There's nothing better for morale than a new décor!" Jeanne said. "Besides, you know the saying: 'People lend only to the rich.' If we want to succeed, we have to project an image of success, starting with the house."

Recalling the idea Sylvie had had a few months ago, Jeanne set up a room with large windows displaying information, tools, and samples concerning the production of nougat and olive oil.

"You should create a detailed catalogue of your products," her cousin said.

"That's an excellent idea," Jeanne said. Then she sighed. "What I am going to do without your advice?" Sylvie had decided to move to Paris.

"I found a job in a perfumery," Sylvie had told her parents when she came back from the capital.

Nothing could have displeased Raymond and Angélique Delestang more than this news. For their daughter, they'd imagined a proper marriage with a respectable man from the region. But nothing they said could make Sylvie change her mind.

"We thought you were happy working with Jeanne," Raymond said.

"It wasn't enough," she said. She went on describing how wonderful Paris was. "There's nothing going on around here! It's always the same, day after day!"

Marianne's presence made Sylvie's departure less painful for Jeanne. Contrary to the past two years, she didn't try to avoid Bel Horizon. Elisabeth had fixed up the house with taste. Get-togethers there were happy events, with excellent food and bottles of good wine. The lady of the house played the piano, with Marianne singing along. Soon, the Delestangs were also invited over, and a small social circle was created.

Impervious to all this, Laurent remained isolated in his room. Split between exasperation and worry, Jeanne tried every day to make him snap out of his state.

"Marianne Coursange is throwing a party for her students," Jeanne told him. "She needs help."

"So?"

"Michel and I are going to be there to organize games for the kids. You should join us."

"So Michel got sucked in?"

Jeanne became very angry.

"Sucked in?" she said. "You're the one who's been trying to suck us in all these months with your woe-is-me behavior.

If you want to know the truth, everybody has had it up to here with your moods. How much longer are you going to moan over a breakup that, in reality, was the best thing that could've happened to you?"

"I won't let you talk to me this way!"

"I don't care. Look at yourself! You've become some sort of wet blanket, all because of a mediocre woman."

Insulted and furious, Laurent threw Jeanne out of his room and, hands shaking, lit a cigarette. He caught sight of himself in the mirror: a bleak face and a stooped silhouette. He remembered what Marianne Coursange had called him, an old man. His hair was a mess, he had a three-day beard, he wore rumpled pajamas, and his nails were dirty. Suddenly, he was horrified by his own negligence. He was ashamed. He walked over to the bathroom, cleaned himself, washed his hair, and shaved. He then opened his closet and selected a tussor suit. Once dressed, he wondered what he was going to do next.

He didn't feel like he could face Jeanne, so he went out to the garden, where the strong scent of mimosa in bloom made him dizzy. Squinting from the sun, Laurent took hesitant steps among the pepper plants and the eucalyptus trees. Nature, his old and dear friend, was exerting its attraction on him once again. He walked for quite a while, experiencing sensations that had been foreign to him for a long time. He made his way to the medicinal plants that had captivated him when he was a teen and that Jeanne had cared for while he was abroad. Even now the entire garden was in very good shape. A few times, he bent down to pull a weed out of the ground. A beetle landed on his hand. Laurent stood still as the insect scurried to the tip of his index finger before taking off. Was this a sign of good luck? He remembered Jérôme's advice. Nothing was more satisfying than completing a project on which we'd worked long and hard. Losing the notion of time, Laurent continued his walk for hours, having to stop once in a while, as he was in bad physical shape after being idle in his room all that time. Around the property, everything was in its place. Down the by river, the washerwomen sang as they worked the way they always did, the fields were bustling with laborers, and the grass gave off its usual wonderful odor. The sun's rays energized him, and it was with a lighter heart that Laurent returned to Restanques.

During dinner that evening, Jeanne didn't mention a thing about their confrontation. He was grateful for that. Did she notice that he was more talkative than he'd been for a long time? She didn't mention anything about it.

The next few days, Laurent went out of the house more and more. He was seen taking care of the garden, and he went to Hyères where there was a plant nursery.

"He bought new books on trees," Rosalie told Jeanne, "and he fixed up his herbarium."

"Well, well, I didn't expect that much at this point!"

Laurent continued to do better. He even began playing tennis with Michel. He sometimes ate at the Delestangs', and took interest in agricultural work once again.

One afternoon he was on his way to inspect the harvesting of almonds when a group of children came out of the pine forest.

"Mister," one of them said to Laurent, "could you help us?"

The child was holding a map, and he and his friends, boys and girls all aged ten or so, were trying to solve a series of clues.

After pointing them in the right direction, Laurent asked where they were coming from.

"Bel Horizon," one of the kids said. "Our teacher organized a treasure hunt."

There were other clues on the map.

"Come with me," Laurent said, guiding the children to the bridge that crossed the river. Then they headed for a cave.

"I don't want to go in there," one of the little girls said. "I'm scared."

"Okay then," the boy with the map said. "Wait for us here. We'll be right back."

At five o'clock, they'd solved all the clues and headed back to Bel Horizon filled with pride.

The boy with the map turned to Laurent and said, "We're going to tell the others that we ran into you just a little while ago. Otherwise they're going to think we cheated."

"I have an idea," said Pauline, one of the girls. "You can carry me on your shoulders, and I'll pretend I hurt my ankle. That will explain why you're with us."

Once in the house's yard, Laurent carefully set Pauline down on a rattan chair. At the same time, Marianne was walking out of the house. She ran to the girl.

"Pauline," she said. "What happened?"

"Nothing major," Laurent told her.

The children began talking at the same time, telling their teacher about their day.

Standing aside, Laurent gazed at Marianne. The cotton dress and white flat shoes she wore gave her a modern, sporty look. Her students were gathered around her, showing her their map and explaining how they'd solved the clues. She listened and then told them to have a snack while waiting for the other groups to arrive. Under large parasols, tables had been set, covered with a wide variety of pastries.

Marianne turned to Laurent and said, "My mother baked all that."

Jeanne and Elisabeth Coursange came out of the house carrying carafes filled with lemonade.

"Laurent!" Jeanne said, surprised to see him there.

Turning to her hostess, she said, "Let me introduce you to my brother."

Giving Laurent the head-to-toe, Mrs. Coursange said, "I was very much looking forward to meeting you."

The arrival of another group of children interrupted them. Soon the yard was bustling with excited kids talking about their treasure hunts.

Laurent stood next to one of the tables, eating a cream puff and enjoying the moment. The house had changed quite a bit since his last visit. The façade's stones had been cleaned, and the shutters were given a coat of green paint. Recently planted wisteria was now climbing up the sides of an arbor, and large earthenware jars were filled with wallflowers. A big dog was running from one table to the other looking for food, barking. Tired of its antics, Marianne took the dog inside. Then she announced the winners of the treasure hunt, and of course Laurent's protégés had the best score. Pauline—who'd forgotten that she was supposed to limp—received her prize from Marianne, who was looking at Laurent with a grin.

"I didn't know you guys were so resourceful," she told the winning group in a mocking tone. "You answered all the questions perfectly, and so quickly. It's almost a miracle."

Laurent gave Marianne a complicit smile and said, "Cotignac kids are very smart, you know."

Tireless, the children wanted to play more games. Wickets and mallets were brought outside, as well as skipping ropes and a ball. Laurent watched Marianne play dodgeball with some of the kids. She threw the ball right at Laurent, who caught it and hurled it back at her. Trying to avoid the ball, Marianne slipped on the grass and wound up flat on her back, to the great pleasure of the children. Laughing, Laurent went over to her.

"Aren't you ashamed to attack a defenseless creature such as me?" Marianne said, a wide smile illuminating her face. "And in front of my students on top of that!"

Laurent helped Marianne to her feet. Her hair was disheveled, and her dress had a grass stain on it, but she didn't seem to care one bit.

She's a free spirit, Laurent thought.

Parents began to arrive to pick up their children and drive them home. Laurent was about to leave himself when Mrs. Coursange suggested he stay for dinner with Jeanne.

"My husband will be happy to meet you," she said.

"I don't know . . . " Laurent said.

He glanced at Marianne and was annoyed that she was paying no attention to him. She didn't seem to care whether he'd accept her mother's invitation or not. This indifference made him decide to stay.

Right away Laurent thought that Jacques Coursange was friendly.

"Every morning when I wake up," he said, "I feel privileged to live in Bel Horizon. I was told that you're also passionate about this region. . . . "

The two men were talking as Marianne was getting changed. Taller than most women, she had delicate shoulders, narrow hips, and long legs. Since his breakup with Suzie, Laurent had found no women attractive. This evening, however, he wasn't immune to his neighbor's charm.

Dinner was a very pleasant affair. Elisabeth Coursange had a knack for making her guests comfortable, and Laurent was chatty. Seeing him in such a good mood, Jeanne hoped that he was finally over his depression. He was even making long-term plans, she noticed, listening to him talk about a hedge maze he was thinking of creating at Restanques.

"I have a book on that topic," Marianne said. "I can lend it to you if you'd like."

"You're interested in plants?"

"I'm interested in a bunch of things."

It was late when Laurent and Jeanne left.

"You were right," Laurent said on their way back home. "They're very nice people."

31

JUNE WAS COMING TO an end, and the olive trees' flowers had turned into little bunches that would transform into fruits in a few months. The air was filled with freshly cut hay, and Jeanne basked in the sun's heat. In her heart she believed that this would be an exceptional summer. The house's atmosphere was upbeat. In the kitchen, Fanny prepared meals for Jeanne and Laurent and their frequent guests. Apolline made the silverware shine, and Rosalie washed the organdy tablecloths.

Holding them up, she told her aunt, "They look like bridal veils."

"How come you're always referring to marriage? Something going on?"

"Of course not!"

"What about that François? I'm sure he'd love to take you to the altar."

"That is wishful thinking, dear auntie."

Apolline had to bite her tongue not to continue this conversation, and Rosalie kept on working quietly. That evening, however, Rosalie thought about what her aunt had said. If François asked her to marry him, would she say yes? Putting away some glasses in a cupboard, she recalled her dreams of grandeur. How it all seemed far away! She thought she was so much in love with Laurent that nothing else in the world mattered. Now he meant absolutely nothing to her. How could such strong feelings simply dissipate that way? She felt the same about her obsession with money. It was all gone.

Someone knocked on the door, and François walked in.

"It might rain," he said, "so I'm bringing you the clothes that were hanging."

"You just had to tell me!"

François was like no man she'd known, and little by little she was won over by the kindness that was contained in everything he did.

"I'm going to be done a bit earlier today," he said. "You want to go for a walk or something?"

"As soon as my shift is over."

Night was falling when they met up behind the barn.

"You want to go to the village?" François asked.

"I don't know."

"What would you like to do?"

"Things are nice here."

They headed for a grassy hill and sat down. Looking up at the sky, François pointed at the stars.

"That's the Big Dipper," he said. And he went on talking about other constellations, the planets, and the Milky Way.

Rosalie listened with the fascination of a child.

"You know so many things!" she said.

"When I was a kid, I was so jealous of everyone who went to school. I would've liked to become a teacher."

"Any regrets you never were able to do that?"

"Regrets are a waste of time," François said.

"I agree with you."

"What about you? What were you dreaming about when you were a kid?"

"I envied the rich, but I eventually learned that they're no happier than we are. Take Mr. Laurent for example."

"Apparently he's doing better."

François was dying to ask Rosalie about Laurent. Was she still in love with him? He shut his eyes to better soak up her presence. He was grateful she kept quiet. Around them, the countryside was peaceful.

"Rosalie . . . " François finally whispered.

She snuck her hand into his and said, "This is so nice."

Never before had she experienced such a sensation of calm. What she felt for François was unlike anything she'd ever known. It wasn't passion, but the discovery that, with him, life could be pleasant. For the first time, she imagined a future with him. He'd be there for her, and she for him. Always. She was suddenly filled with the desire to make him happy, a just reward after everything she'd put him through.

"François," she said. "There are things about my life that I'm not proud of."

"Do you feel like talking about them?"

"No."

"Let's forget about it all, then."

"Why aren't you judging me?"

"When you love someone, you try to understand them, to accept them for what they are."

"But the other men I knew, they cared only about themselves!"

François smiled and, inhaling deeply, took Rosalie in his arms.

"I'm never going to be a rich man," he said, "but if you want me in your life, I'll always take good care of you."

"You really want us to be together?"

"Yes. What about you?"

"Yes, but there's one thing you need to know. . . . "

"What's that?"

"It's not because I have a limp that I'm marrying you."

The very next day, everyone at Restanques got the news. Apolline shed a tear of happiness, and Fanny thought about the wedding cake she was going to bake.

Worried, Rosalie asked François, "What is your sister going to say?"

"I don't care."

But Augustine was gracious.

"Poor Rosalie has had enough hardships," she told Annie. "I even told Joseph to shut up when he said that my brother was an idiot for marrying a cripple."

Oblivious from the gossip, Rosalie was feverishly planning the big day. Jeanne offered her not only a wedding dress, but a trousseau as well.

"That's too much!" Rosalie said.

"Who's the boss around here?" Jeanne said, laughing.

Jeanne took great joy in the positive atmosphere that now prevailed in her home. During her daily stroll, she stopped to contemplate the almond trees, which, when things were at their darkest, had enabled Restanques to survive. More than the olive trees, they'd become the estate's emblem. Weren't those almonds allowing her to produce the nougat everyone thought was excellent? Little by little, things were getting back to normal. Settled in her apartment in Marseille, Marthe played the role of happy widower, sending her children a letter once in a while.

"I just hope she doesn't blow all her savings," Laurent kept saying.

"Don't say those things!" Jeanne replied. "We'd have to take her back here!"

The two siblings were close once again, not only on a personal basis, but as it pertained to Restanques as well. Not only was Laurent taking some of the daily duties away from Jeanne, he was also bristling with projects.

"I think we should start a tree nursery," he told his uncle Raymond.

"That's a great idea!"

To that end, the young man drew up plans for a greenhouse and showed them to an architect. Just like his sister, he decided to borrow money.

"If we don't want to wind up in the ditch," he said, "one of us has to be successful."

"One of us?" his sister said. "I don't like pessimistic talk. We're both going to be successful, and that is that!"

"And later," Laurent said, "we're going to build that garden on our plot of land by the sea."

As he said the words, Jeanne recalled the time they'd gone there, with Jérôme and Suzie. It was such a long time ago, or so it seemed to her.

"I thought you didn't care for that spot anymore," she said.

"Well, I went back and I changed my mind."

He didn't add that he'd gone there with Marianne, who, unlike Suzie, had loved the site. After a swim in the sea, they'd discussed how the land could be cleared and how it could then be transformed into a beautiful garden. Marianne's knowledge of plants and flowers had pleasantly surprised him.

"I've always been interested in flora," she said. "And don't forget, my dear, that I teach science."

The summer vacation gave the young woman a lot of free time, and Laurent spent more and more time at Bel Horizon. Was Marianne attracted to him, or did she only see him as a friend? He couldn't tell, since she treated him nicely while keeping some distance between them, an attitude that irked Laurent. But Marianne's strong personality prevented him from showing that he was attracted to her.

Laurent got more annoyed when realizing that Michel was also interested in the young teacher. He even caught himself hating his cousin the day Marianne chose Michel as her tennis partner. They were playing doubles with Sylvie, who was home in Entrecasteaux for the summertime. Most of the balls whizzed by Laurent's racket and, humiliated, he went back to Restanques as soon as the game was over.

He remained there for a few days. When he finally decided to go to Bel Horizon, he was told that the Coursanges, including Marianne, had left for Menton. Having just gotten over Suzie and the trauma of the separation, Laurent's mental equilibrium was threatened. In his mind's eye he saw Marianne having fun at regattas, dancing and laughing with men at balls, and forgetting all about Cotignac. That night, he dreamt about both Suzie and Marianne—odd and confusing dreams. He woke up in a sweat in the middle of the sweltering Provence night.

A week went by before Laurent saw his neighbor again. She was chatting with Jeanne and Sylvie in front of the house, the three of them sitting on lawn chairs. Marianne's face lit up when she spotted Laurent.

"Hi! Great to see you again. I brought you some plants."

Marianne got up and took Laurent to the courtyard. There were many pots containing rare, delicate, and fragrant species.

"My parents went nuts when they saw me turn the car into a garden," she said.

"You thought about me while you were gone."

"You doubted it?"

"Frankly? Yes."

"What about trust?"

"Someone betrayed me before. I got burned."

"Maybe so. But not everyone is the same, you know."

"Marianne," Laurent said in a low voice. "You completely shook me up. I thought I didn't want anything out of life anymore. I wasn't expecting anything good out of my existence, and then I met you. But I'm scared."

"Of me?"

"You're such a free spirit. You're so independent."

Not caring whether someone might see them, Marianne caressed Laurent's cheek.

"I'm also a bit afraid of you."

Laurent grabbed Marianne's fingers and brought them to his lips.

"Why?" he asked.

"You're secretive, dark. You can be curt at times . . . "

"You've already helped me change a lot. Don't stop now. . . . "

"That's a nice challenge," Marianne said, before going back to her friends.

32

JÉRÔME HAD PROMISED TO visit in early August. *A well-deserved break*, he'd written Jeanne. Both excited and apprehensive, she prepared for his arrival. Had he changed? Thanks to Sylvie, she knew that he spent virtually all his time between the museum and a pharmaceutical research lab.

"He works too hard," Sylvie said.

"Does he talk to you about me?"

"Rarely."

What did "rarely" mean? Was it that Jérôme was being discreet about his feelings? Was it that Jeanne wasn't on his mind much? What about that old lover of his? Had he seen her again?

Jérôme arrived at Restanques just before Jeanne returned home from Cotignac. Getting off her bicycle, she realized that her clothes were wrinkled because of the heat.

"Are you happy to see me?" Jérôme said.

"I didn't expect you until the weekend."

"I wanted to surprise you."

As they were walking inside the house, he added, "I came to take you away."

"Like some knight in shining armor?" Jeanne said, smiling.

"I want to show you my house in Cassis. The work is complete. Besides, I'd love for us to be alone."

They left before lunch. *Our first escapade*, Jeanne thought as Jérôme's car was leaving Restanques. The countryside was flooded with the sun's rays. People kept their shutters closed, trying to keep their houses as cool as possible.

Jérôme stopped the car in front of an inn with a terrace overlooking the river.

"So many times I wanted to jump on a train to come down and see you," Jérôme said, "but things at work were so insane."

After a brief moment of silence, he said, "I thought you might accompany Nicole when she came to visit me."

"I had too many problems to solve at Restanques," Jeanne said, keeping to herself that she was afraid of Paris.

Jérôme bought the food they'd need for their refuge, and then they took a road that snaked through vineyards. Out in the distance, they could see the sparkling sea.

"You know," Jérôme said, "I've traveled a lot. But nowhere else have I seen such diversity, such beauty as here. Everything is there, the Mediterranean Sea, the gorgeous countryside. It's so colorful, so poetic—it never ceases to amaze me."

Admiring her surroundings, Jeanne kept silent until they reached her lover's house.

Turning the front door's key, Jérôme said, "This is the first time I've been inside since the renovations were completed."

The living room was white, immaculate, with straw-bottomed chairs around a walnut table and bookshelves covering an entire wall. On one of the windows' ledges stood a large vase of red roses.

"I told the keeper we were going to be here today," Jérôme said.

"You were that certain you'd be able to lure me here?" Jeanne said with a smile.

"I was hoping I would. . . . "

Jérôme took their luggage upstairs, and then set up candles in the bedroom. It had a large bed with a mosquito net and linen sheets that gave off a scent of lavender. Jeanne had followed Jérôme, and she gazed at the colorful enamel jug on the floor, the quilt folded on an armchair, and the old-fashioned pictures of the Provence countryside on the walls. Delighted by the place, Jeanne and Jérôme smiled at each other.

Back outside, Jérôme took a hammock out of a shed and set it up between two trees. He then put some cushions on a long bench.

"Make yourself comfortable," he said, before walking over to retrieve a bottle that was chilling in a bucket down the well.

He opened it, took a sip of the wine, and, satisfied, poured Jeanne a glass.

"To us."

As they did every evening, birds were flying up above, and from afar came the clanging of bells—a herd of goats. Jeanne soaked up the sounds and sights, as well as Jérôme's presence. He was sitting next to her, his arm around her shoulders.

"I don't know how many times I've thought about the moment we'd be together again," Jeanne said. "I couldn't wait for it to happen, and yet it scared me. So many days have passed since you left for Paris! I was afraid you'd be different."

"Maybe I am, a little. . . . "

"What about me? Do you think I've changed?"

"You look more serene than the last time I saw you, more at peace with yourself."

His fingers rested on the nape of Jeanne's neck. She smiled and leaned back against his hand. Jérôme leaned on her, and they tasted each other's mouths. Her skin smelled of sunrays and freedom. Soon both were naked, and in the setting sun, they forgot about everything except the passion they had for each other.

When it was dark out, Jérôme lit some oil lamps and candles, and he and Jeanne prepared a meal composed of cold ham and potatoes cooked under the ashes.

"It's like being on a real vacation," Jeanne said, with a happy laugh.

Over the course of the next few days, they continued to live in isolation. Leaving his lover in their warm bed, Jérôme got up at dawn and came back from his long walks with baskets of fruit and bread, which they ate under a tree. In the mornings they went to the sea, where Jérôme would take Jeanne to the coves he swam in as a child.

"Back then," he said, "I dreamed of living in foreign countries."

"What about now?"

"Traveling once in a while will be enough."

Jeanne smiled and remained quiet.

"What are you thinking about?" Jérôme asked her.

"Does it matter to you what I'm thinking?" she said.

"More and more. . . . "

Jeanne snuggled against him. She didn't feel like asking him or herself too many questions. She simply wanted to enjoy their time together. What did she know about him, really? Did she know that he liked to sing while getting dressed, that his favorite color was green, that his nose was often yellow from smelling flowers, that he could swim for hours, that he hated losing at cards?

Spending hours having conversations with Jeanne or just sitting next to her as they both read, Jérôme discovered the pleasure of simply sharing time with another person. He hadn't experienced this state of well-being with anyone else.

It was wiping away his fear of losing his freedom if he got involved with someone seriously.

"Jeanne," he whispered as they were lying in bed listening to the sounds of the night, "I've never been happier in my life. With you, I have everything I want and need."

"I feel the same way."

"The words scare me . . . but I think I love you." With his mouth against Jeanne's shoulder, he added, "But you live in Cotignac, and I'm in Paris . . . "

"Hush," she said. "Let's not talk about tomorrow."

"But what about you? What are your feelings for me? Do you have some affection for me or . . . are you going to marry Antoine Laferrière?"

"Please don't tell me you believed that gossip."

"Well, to some extent. And it made me very upset."

"Jérôme," Jeanne said, "you may be a great scientist, but when it comes to feelings, you lack intuition. I love you too. I've been in love with you longer than you can imagine. As a matter of fact, I think I've been in love with you since the first day we met."

"In spite of all the bad things you said about me when I took Laurent on our trip?"

"Don't make fun of me."

In the middle of the night, they were still confiding in each other, opening themselves freely and completely, creating the bonds of trust necessary to build and sustain an intimate relationship. As they experienced those hours that would forever remain in their memories, Jeanne discovered the bliss of shared love, a feeling that made her want to move mountains. Invested with a new strength, she felt ready to face any challenge, including that of keeping the man who'd captured her heart.

Unfortunately, their escapade came to an end. As Jérôme was locking the house's door, Jeanne felt her throat constrict.

He'd promised to stay with her at Restanques for three days before spending some time with his parents.

The Cotignac village square was bustling with activity when they arrived there to buy a newspaper. Some men were playing *boules*, surrounded by people commenting on their every move. A bit farther, women were filling jugs with water at the fountain, chatting and laughing, while their children were noisily chasing one another. The church bells rang, but no one paid them much attention. People were sitting at the cafés' terraces, drinking coffee or wine, just shooting the breeze.

It had been eight days since Jeanne left Restanques, and going through its gates she hoped that nothing bad had happened during her absence.

The cat was sprawled on the grass, watching the gardener watering the flower beds around the house. On the second floor, Apolline was opening the shutters.

"Is my brother around?" Jeanne asked her.

"You'll find him out back, behind the orchards," Apolline said. "He went there with Miss Marianne. And he invited some people over to celebrate your return, you and Mr. Guillaumin."

Knowing Apolline's taste for love stories, Jeanne could easily imagine the questions the old maid must have now seeing her with Jérôme. The way she looked at him said a lot about her hope that he would become part of the family.

Jeanne shut her eyes and took a deep breath, enjoying the odors given off by the vegetation surrounding her. Then, arm in arm, she and her lover headed for the other side of the orchard, where cherry and plum trees were crammed with fruit. Unable to resist the cherries, Jeanne grabbed a few and shared them with Jérôme. They joined Laurent and Marianne, who were measuring a plot of land covered with wild grass.

"What do you think of this spot for a greenhouse?" Laurent asked the botanist.

The two men launched into a discussion on the topic.

"They've completely forgotten about our existence," Marianne said, and both women burst out laughing.

The heat was letting up when they all walked back toward the house. Looking at its façade through the trees, Jeanne thought about the past two years. Her decisions and all her hard work were finding their meaning amid this summer evening, with the past and the present merging. People were gathered in the yard behind the house. The Delestangs and the Coursanges were waiting for them, chatting and enjoying the drinks Rosalie had poured them. Jeanne's refusal to capitulate was rewarded by this perfect moment. Next to her, Laurent was holding Marianne's hand. Turning around, she saw Jérôme walk her way. He'd left for a minute to pick a rose for her. Later, much later, she would recall the sky streaked with purple, the song of the birds, the cat still sprawled out on the lawn, and the elation she felt at that very moment. Jérôme smiled at Jeanne, handing her the rose. New stories were going to unfold, ones that future generations would tell each other, stories with characters named Jeanne and Jérôme, as well as Laurent, the man who built greenhouses and created a wonderful garden overlooking the Mediterranean Sea. Marianne would also be a main character in those stories. Life was coming back to Restanques, thus reconnecting with the golden era when its founders and their descendants watched over its well-being. . . .

ABOUT THE AUTHOR

Dominique Marny was raised in a family that loved art, literature, adventure, and travel. In addition to being a novelist, she is a playwright and screenwriter, and is a regular contributor to the French literary magazine *Plume*. She has also written five books about her great-uncle Jean Cocteau. Marny lives in Paris.

EBOOKS BY DOMINIQUE MARNY

FROM PUBLISHERS SQUARE
AND OPEN ROAD MEDIA

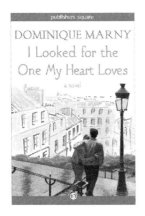
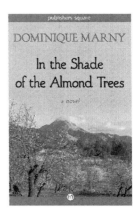

Available wherever ebooks are sold

publishers
square

Publishers Square, a subsidiary of Place des éditeurs, a publishing group based in Paris, is dedicated to bringing commercially successful French authors to American readers. Its list covers a wide range of genres, with an emphasis on women's fiction, thrillers, and historical fiction, and includes authors such as Françoise Bourdin, who regularly hits the French bestseller lists. Publishers Square believes that the best stories have a universal appeal, and hopes to break down the barriers between American and French readers in the digital age.

FIND OUT MORE AT

WWW.PUBLISHERS-SQUARE.COM

Publishers Square is one of a select group of publishing partners of Open Road Integrated Media, Inc.

OPEN ROAD

INTEGRATED MEDIA

Open Road Integrated Media is a digital publisher and multimedia content company. Open Road creates connections between authors and their audiences by marketing its ebooks through a new proprietary online platform, which uses premium video content and social media.

Printed in Poland
by Amazon Fulfillment
Poland Sp. z o.o., Wrocław